Why Ann Arbor?

A novel by
Jerry Prescott

© 2006 by Jerry Prescott - 1st Edition

Published in the USA by
JCarp Publication, LLC
P.O. Box 234
Milan, Michigan, USA

All rights reserved. No part of this book may be reproduced in any form or by any means, except in the context of reviews, without the written permission of the author.

Publisher's Cataloging-in-Publication
(Provided by Quality Books, Inc.)

Prescott, Jerry.
   Why Ann Arbor? : a novel / by Jerry Prescott. -- 1st ed.
   p. cm.
LCCN 2006926742
ISBN 0-9758805-4-3

   1. Religious pluralism--Fiction. 2. Jesus Christ--Fiction. 3. Second advent--Fiction. 4. Pluralism (Social sciences)--Michigan--Ann Arbor--Fiction. 5. Ann Arbor (Mich.)--Fiction. 6. Religious fiction. I. Title.

PS3566.R374W55 2006   813'.6
                      QBI06-600267

Acknowledgments

Foremost, I wish to thank Hazel Proctor for her unwavering enthusiastic encouragement and wise council in bringing this book into being. Once again, she has been a delight to work with in this process.

I'm appreciative of the work of Kathryn Zumberg who was the first one to preview this novel as she deciphered my handwriting and entered it into her computer. In addition to her positive feedback, she suggested several ways in which the story could be enhanced. Thank you, Kat!

I also wish to express my gratitude to those of you who read initial drafts and provided me with valuable feedback. Your insights, observations, suggestions and words of encouragement spurred me on. These family members and friends include my loving and supportive wife, Lorna, who keeps me humble; my enthusiastic sister and brother-in-law, Joan and Kit, who boost my ego; my daughter, Dorie, with her keen sensitivity; my son, Tom, with his no nonsense critical eye; my sister-in-law, Martha, who ably helped with the editing; the George family who warmed my heart with their enthusiasm; my supportive pastor, Doug Brouwer; my publisher, Jay Carp, whose suggestions were very perceptive; and many others. You'll see I've incorporated many of your suggestions in this novel. My sincere thanks to all of you.

Why
Ann Arbor?

Chapter I

The first time I saw Him was on a Saturday morning in mid-July at the Farmers Market in downtown Ann Arbor. My wife, Beth, had sent me out with a short list of honey-dos, one of which was to stop at the market to pick up some items for the small dinner party we were hosting that evening.

As I was paying for some tomatoes and a quart of blueberries, I noticed some commotion in a nearby aisle. Several dozen people were clustered around a man, intently listening to what He was saying. The appearance of the man nearly took my breath away. He was wearing a gleaming white robe with a cord sash. Even from a distance, I could see the kindly smile on His face and a sparkle in His eyes. I glanced around to see if someone was filming the scene. With His long hair and beard, he looked similar to one of the actors in Mel Gibson's movie about Jesus Christ. The morning sun glistening off His hair created a halo effect.

Along with several others who had also noticed the commotion, I moved up the aisle in the direction of the group. The man had just finished saying something that brought smiles to the faces of those surrounding Him. There were several children of varying ages standing in front of Him and His hands were resting on the shoulders of two of them.

Continuing to smile, He held up His hands as He said they were creating a problem by clogging up the aisle. He said He'd been informed that individuals or organizations passing out literature or talking to patrons about some issue or cause were to station themselves in a separate section of the market. Suggesting the size of the crowd gathered around Him could create a problem there as well, He informed everyone He'd be going over to the parking structure on the other side of Main Street, a couple blocks away. He encouraged all who wished to accompany Him, to follow Him to the parking structure.

The woman standing next to me turned her head in my direction. She had a wide-eyed expression on her face as she asked me whether I'd noticed the scars on the palms of the man when He'd held them up. Before I could answer, she asked me if I thought the man was truly Jesus Christ.

I smiled in response, as I was shaking my head no. I told her that He really looked the part though as I watched Him in His sandals strolling off with several dozen people in pursuit.

I looked at my watch. I hadn't had the opportunity to hear what He'd been saying earlier. I was tempted to follow the group so that I could listen to what He had to say. But I was already running a little late with a few more stops to make. After another purchase, I headed back to my car.

Chapter II

Beth heard me as I drove in the garage and opened the back door to greet me.

"Need any help carrying things in?" she asked.

"No, I'm fine. I'll just make a couple trips," I replied.

"You made good time. I forgot to have you help me put a leaf in the table before you left. I'm glad you didn't get held up. You can help me now. Was there a crowd at the market?"

I nodded my head yes as I placed several bags on the center counter.

"And as a matter of fact I nearly did get waylaid. I'll tell you about it after I get the rest of the stuff out of the car."

As I returned with the second batch of purchases, Beth was taking the tomatoes out of one of the bags.

"Good job, Mike! These are beautiful! Hope they'll taste as good as they look. So where did you nearly get waylaid?"

"At the Farmer's Market. There was a young man there attracting a crowd in one of the aisles. He was dressed in biblical garb with long hair and wearing sandals. My first thought was that He was costumed and made up to be filmed in a movie or ad of some sort, but I didn't notice any cameras. He had a wonderful smile and there were dozens of people, including several children, clustered around Him. They seemed to be mesmerized by Him and what He was saying."

Beth stopped unpacking my purchases, taking interest in what I was saying. She smiled as I continued.

"I didn't actually have a chance to hear what He'd been saying. I just heard Him explain that the crowd He'd attracted was creating a problem. He said He'd be going over to the parking structure on Ashley and invited all who wanted to come join Him. I came close to taking Him up on His offer."

Beth smiled again with a questioning expression of her face; I smiled back with a little laugh.

"You really had to have been there." I continued. "There was almost a glow about Him, His pure white robe, the look on His face. There was a magnetism about Him. Nearly fifty people trooped off after Him."

"I'm sorry you weren't one of them, even though I'm glad you got back to help me," Beth replied.

I started to tell her about the comments the woman standing next to me had made about seeing the scars on the palms of the man's hands. But the phone rang and I stepped over to answer it. The viewer showed it was the Strattons calling, two of our dinner guests. I told Beth who was calling as I handed her the phone. Beth conversed with Mary Stratton for about five minutes as I busied myself putting away the remainder of my purchases. After hanging up, Beth explained that Mary was just calling to see if she could bring anything and to check on the dress code. Then she asked me if I would help her with the leaf for the table and also get out the wine glasses. With our involvement in preparations for the evening, we didn't get back to further discussion of the incident at the Farmers Market.

Chapter III

The Strattons were the first guests to arrive, shortly before 6:30pm. Rob is an attorney in general practice in Ann Arbor. Mary is employed in the Admissions Office at the University of Michigan. Their daughter, Whitney, graduated from the University of Wisconsin and is currently working on her Masters in language studies in Ann Arbor. Our other guests were Dr. Jerry Hanson and his wife, Joy. Jerry is an internist and practices at St. Joe's. Joy works part time as a consultant for government medical grants. They're neighbors of ours. Tom and Kristi Cloverdale were neighbors in Ann Arbor Hills where we'd lived before moving to a condo in Travis Pointe three years ago. Tom is an English professor at the University of Michigan. Kristi is a former elementary school teacher. Brad and Tory Babcock are fairly new friends and frequent golf partners. Brad is a stockbroker and Tory's a busy mom, raising five kids.

Though everyone in the group is fairly well acquainted with one another, the only time this specific grouping of friends seems to get together is when Beth and I have orchestrated it. It was a nice evening and we were able to enjoy our cocktails out on the screened porch.

One of the main topics of conversation was the pending announcement by the President of his choice to fill the latest vacancy on the Supreme Court. It never ceased to amaze me how otherwise generally compatible people could be so diverse in their opinions when it came to politics. Though there were only five couples present, all ends of the political spectrum seemed to be represented as each of us aired our beliefs. Tom and Kristi Cloverdale were involved liberals whose views were widely shared in the University community. Because of the dominance of the University, like many other college towns, Ann Arbor is a liberal stronghold, heavily favoring Democratic candidates in every election I can remember. Brad and Tory Babcock are at the opposite end in their views, staunch Republicans and Catholics. Rob and Mary Stratton often joked they always cancelled each other's votes. The Hansons and ourselves could probably be classified as middle of the roaders or moderate Republicans. We were very liberal in our thinking compared to the Babcocks, probably backward thinkers in the opinion of the Cloverdales.

During dinner, there were several compliments about the tasty tomatoes. Beth said they could thank me for them, that I'd picked them up at the Farmers Market that morning. Mary Stratton said her daughter, Whitney, had also been at the Farmers Market then.

"She had a very unusual experience. There was a young preacher there. Maybe you noticed Him too, Mike?"

"As a matter of fact I did. Although I didn't have an opportunity to hear much of what He had to say. When I saw Him He was about to head over to the parking structure on Ashley with a crowd of people in tow."

"Whitney was among that group," Mary explained. "She said by the time she got there nearly two hundred people were present."

"What did she think of Him?" I asked.

"Oh, she was very impressed. She was gushing over Him. You know she's a language major. One of the things that she was most impressed with was the fact He was fluent in over half a dozen languages as He addressed the crowd. She said He'd glance at someone in the audience and begin addressing them in their native language. Just briefly. The vast majority of time He spoke English."

"What did He have to say?" Joy asked. "Did she elaborate on that?"

Mary nodded. "She said it was basically a simple message. That there is a God, a loving caring God. A forgiving God. That we should love God. And that we should also love our fellow man."

"I told you I saw Him," I said. "But you might want to tell the others how Whitney described Him to you."

Mary nodded and smiled as she explained what her daughter had told her about the young man's dress and appearance. "She said He was very impressive, very charismatic. He used a couple of modern day parables and seemingly had everyone enraptured, listening to every word."

"What's the man's name?" Tom asked. "Did He indicate what church He's affiliated with or religious order?"

"She didn't say. I don't know if He said. She did mention that He'd referred at one point to God as His Father, but He'd later said God was the Father of everyone."

"Did He take up a collection?" Brad asked.

"Not that Whitney mentioned, I don't think so."

I was debating whether I should tell them what the woman standing next to me had said about noticing scars on the man's palms and asking me if I thought He was Jesus.

"How long did He speak?" Kristi asked. "Did Whitney stay there until the end?"

"She did. It was less than an hour. She said that it seemed like only a few minutes and was surprised when she glanced at her watch to check the time. She was there as He thanked the crowd for taking time to listen to what He had to say. He concluded with a brief prayer. Some had called out asking when they could see or hear Him again. He'd smiled, saying He really didn't have a set schedule, but He was heading over to the Robert Delonis Center to chat with someone. I think you all know that's the name of the downtown homeless shelter."

"Mary, did Whitney comment on whether this man appeared to be acting on His own?" Tory asked. "Or did it appear He had an entourage of people with Him?"

"She didn't say one way or another," Mary replied. "I had the impression she thought that He was flying solo."

"Sorry I have to interrupt," Beth said. "I want to let you know what I've planned for dessert. You have a few choices to make."

Chapter IV

I pitched in to help Beth with the clean up. I also was full of compliments for the excellent dinner. "I think everyone truly had a good time, and between discussing the possible Supreme Court nominee and hearing more about the young man I'd seen at the market, we didn't lack for conversation."

Beth had nodded her head in agreement and then asked if I had any more thoughts about the young preacher. I then told her about the conversation I had with the woman who had been standing next to me at the market. Beth was a little annoyed that I hadn't shared the information with her earlier. She also questioned why I'd been hesitant to share that information with our guests. My only explanation and somewhat lame excuse was to say seeing the man had left me a little confused and searching for a simple explanation for His appearance.

"You mean you think there's a possibility this man is really Jesus?" Beth asked. I replied that I realized how crazy that seemed and that it was the reason I hadn't confided in her earlier and our guests this evening. Beth smiled and suggested we should both sleep on it.

After a restless night, I was up early the next morning. Following a trip out to the curb to get the *Ann Arbor News*, I microwaved a cup of last night's left over coffee. I took it out on the porch along with the newspaper and settled in one of the chairs. I savored moments such as that.

One of the headlines on the front page of the local section caught my eye. "A New Ernie." There was also a photo alongside the article. Ernie was a name and a person familiar to nearly everyone in Ann Arbor. He is a middle aged homeless man who has roamed the streets in downtown Ann Arbor for over five years. He is very gregarious and often speaks with an Irish twang, frequently mumbling and seemingly carrying on a conversation with himself. He is very friendly and non-threatening, often cheerfully greeting people and engaging them in conversation, suggesting that they lighten up and enjoy life. One of the many things he has become famous for is putting a couple of quarters in expired parking meters, doing his good deed about half a block ahead of the meter reader. Similar to the old "Kilroy Was Here" stickers, Ernie leaves his card on the windshield of the car next to the meter he's just fed. The driver realizes that Ernie has probably saved him or her a parking fine.

There is a box on the wall near the entrance to the homeless shelter with Ernie's name on it where people can put money through a slot, to thank him for his efforts and also provide him with funds to keep recycling quarters into expired meters.

Ernie has also made a name for himself by his practice of passing out cards to smokers with his five-step program to quit smoking. Smokers have been known to cross the street to avoid a confrontation with Ernie.

But most of all, Ernie is famous for cheering people up, sharing his smiles and zeroing in on people who looked particularly stressed or saddened with a message to count their blessings and enjoy them a little more. Perhaps it is the "There but for the Grace of God go I" message that Ernie's appearance communicated that is most effective. Ernie shuffles along with a stooped back and people, perhaps rightly so, surmised maybe all of Ernie's brain cells aren't properly functioning, possibly the result of drug use at an earlier age. Though he always seemed to have a twinkle in his eye, sometimes it is accompanied by a vague stare. Ernie is nearly as famous as Ann Arbor's Shakey Jake, a street musician who resembles Ray Charles and even sold T-shirts with his own photo on them.

The article began by identifying Ernie Smith. It was the first time I'd seen or heard Ernie's last name. Like Michigan's famous football coach, Bo Schembechler, he is one of those handful of unique individuals readily identified by a single name.

My eyes widened as the article went on to tell of Ernie's meeting with a religious preacher at the downtown homeless shelter Saturday morning. A staffer who witnessed the meeting with Ernie was quoted in the article, saying that after speaking individually with a handful of residents who were at the shelter, the young preacher had engaged in a brief conversation with Ernie. They'd then joined hands and touched foreheads as they appeared to close their eyes in prayer. Suddenly, the staffer was quoted as saying, "Ernie's body began to shake and he began to grow two, three, four inches taller. I quickly realized he was simply standing totally erect. I also noticed as Ernie stepped away from the man, he was walking confidently with no sign of the shuffle I'd always associated with him. He was beaming as he expressed his thanks to the man. It was an amazing transformation. Ernie's stature, speech, facial appearance and eyes had all changed. I'd never recalled seeing him looking so alert, so with it."

The article went on to say Ernie had accompanied the young

preacher over to the new Y.M.C.A., a few blocks from the shelter. After some initial confusion, the man had addressed over a hundred, mainly teenagers, in the top floor gymnasium. Cathi Phillips, the President of the "Y", was quoted as saying, "He held those kids nearly spellbound for over half an hour. It was amazing."

As I finished the article I was reminded of my own reluctance to tell Beth or our friends about my experience at the market. The reporter had focused the article on Ernie. There was no mention of the name of the preacher, where He was from or what His message to the youngsters had focused on.

"Anything in the paper that I should be aware of?" Beth asked as she came out onto the porch to join me.

"As a matter of fact, yes," I told her. "I'll get you a coffee while you read this article. I think you'll find it of interest."

After church, Beth and I met friends for a round of golf at Barton Hills. Chip and Ruth Pollard were frequent golfing partners. Chip is a recently retired engineer from Ford. Ruth is active in the community and has served on several boards in the non-profit agency field. She'd also served a couple terms as a Trustee on the Ann Arbor Board of Education.

During a snack break at the halfway house, Ruth asked us if we'd seen the article in the *Ann Arbor News* about Ernie. We replied that we had and Beth encouraged me to tell them about my seeing the young preacher at the Farmers Market. I briefly filled them in and also told them about my conversation with the woman asking me if I'd noticed the scars on the palms of the man's hands and whether I'd thought the man was Jesus.

Rather than prompting questions or additional conversation

on the subject, I found that I'd inadvertently closed the dialogue. Chip and Ruth had glanced at one another and simply nodded as I'd spoken.

Chapter V

Beth and I talked about the *Ann Arbor News* article again later that evening. We shared a chuckle over how people were generally reluctant to get into conversation where religion was involved and the Pollards' reaction to my comments.

A short time later, Beth had been on the phone with a friend discussing Ann Arbor Thrift Shop business. The woman had brought up the subject of the *Ann Arbor News* article. She said she'd heard the young preacher had recruited a few followers. She'd heard that He and a few of them were staying at the Campus Inn, an upscale hotel which borders on the University of Michigan campus. Beth's friend had said that in her opinion, those were pretty pricey accommodations and raised the question of how this preacher's ministry was being funded and by whom. Beth had replied she was wondering about that herself.

There was another article about the preacher in the *Ann Arbor News* on Monday. This one made the front page and was a rather lengthy one. Headlined "Abortion Dialogue On the Diag," the article stated the mysterious preacher, who had first appeared on the scene at the Farmers Market on Saturday morning, had spoken to a crowd of several hundred students on the Diag Sunday afternoon. The article gave a brief synopsis of His message to the gathering. He said God is real, a loving and compassionate God who cares for us. He'd said everyone needs to turn to God in prayer, to seek guidance and courage in making the right choices in their lives, to find strength and comfort in facing life's challenges and sorrows and to express their thanks and joy for the many blessings God has bestowed on them. He'd emphasized the Golden Rule and the need to love one another. The article stated He'd used a few parables to illustrate and expand on His message.

The article reported that at the conclusion of His message, a voice in the crowd had yelled out, "Is abortion a sin?" Although initially, the article continued, it appeared as if the preacher was going to ignore the question, He suddenly turned and raised His hands to silence the crowd of mostly students.

The article reported the man had then spent several minutes describing the miracle of conception and birth, calling it one of God's greatest gifts and blessings. Then the article stated that the young man had posed several questions to the group, prefacing them with the statement, "Would the loving and compassionate God I have told you about believe it was a sin to abort a pregnancy if . . .." The man followed this question, the article continued, with many of the thought provoking questions that are voiced and debated in the public discourse on abortion. He prefaced each with the same question, the article said, going on to list His follow up questions: the pregnancy endangers the life of the mother, conception is the result of incest, conception occurs during the violent rape of a woman, modern technology reveals a baby will be born with severe birth defects, a woman's physical and/or mental health will be adversely impacted by the pregnancy?

The article reported the preacher had then posed other questions to the crowd. "Should there be laws to govern when a pregnancy can be legally terminated? Should a woman be required to prove certain circumstances exist before she can request an abortion?" The reporter stated that the preacher had addressed those questions by digressing into another of God's blessings, freedom of choice. As he began to expand on what he described as a gift of God, the article reported, there had been a smattering of applause, quickly followed by an enthusiastic ovation and cheering by well over half of the audience.

The article said the preacher's expression had become stern as He held up his hands to quiet the crowd. He was quoted as having said, "God has given us the ability to make choices in expectation we will make the right decisions in regard to abortion and other matters by turning to Him for guidance, courage, and support. Please remember what I said in prefacing my answer to the question. Childbirth is a miracle. A woman's decision to bear a child to be adopted by a loving, caring family is a wonderful act of love."

The article went on to say that this latter statement appeared to leave the crowd confused. It seemed as if the preacher was delivering a mixed message. "Had He meant to take a side in the Roe versus Wade debate?" the reporter asked. In providing an answer to the question He'd been asked, rather than providing an answer that would calm and diffuse the passion and anger the question provoked, He'd further inflamed it, the reporter concluded.

I shook my head, wondering if the reporter had heard or seen something he hadn't mentioned in the article. Based on what had been reported, I thought that the young preacher had skillfully and sensitively addressed an extremely divisive issue and that His remarks should have had the opposite effect. The man in my opinion, had not been attempting to dodge the question or to further confuse the issue. More power to Him, I thought. At the same time I was wondering what the reaction of Ann Arbor's religious leaders would be. As I read the footnote to the article, I thought it wouldn't be long before that reaction was known. The preacher and his followers had arranged for a meeting with them tomorrow morning, Tuesday, at the St. Francis of Assisi Church on Stadium Boulevard. The article said the meeting would be open to religious leaders of all faiths.

I had Beth read the article. Her reaction was similar to mine. She'd chuckled as she later said, "Jesus' first visit to the world sparked a great deal of controversy, too. It'll be interesting to hear what results from that meeting."

Chapter VI

Tuesday morning's *Detroit Free Press* ran an article titled "Preacher Resembling Jesus Visits Ann Arbor." The article told of the man's appearance at Ann Arbor's Farmers Market on Saturday morning. His appearance and dress resembled the images of Jesus we have from paintings and movies the article stated. I skimmed the paragraph describing His meeting with several hundred students on the U of M Diag. I found the following listing of the various groups He'd visited and spoken to over the past forty-eight hours very interesting, amazing in its number and diversity. They ranged from the Ronald McDonald House to an Alcoholics Anonymous meeting, from U of M's Mott Children's Hospital to the Sisters of Mary Convent in northeast Ann Arbor, from the Washtenaw Country Jail to the Pittsfield Township Senior Citizen Center, from Planned Parenthood to Catholic Social Services.

What really caught my attention, however, were the paragraphs describing the group of followers He'd recruited to help coordinate these visits. As of Monday evening, the article stated, their number totaled fourteen. Ernie Smith, the former street person, appeared to have been the spokesperson for this group. He was quoted as saying the group had met with Jesus for a cabinet dinner meeting at the Campus Inn on Monday evening. When asked if the man had identified himself as Jesus or claimed to be Jesus, the article said Mr. Smith had laughed and was quoted as having said, "No, He didn't.

He hasn't, but we all believe He looks like what we'd envision Jesus would look like and says what we'd believe Jesus would say. We wanted to address Him by some name. He seems to have graciously accepted our choice of calling Him Jesus. He hasn't said we shouldn't or suggested we address Him by another name."

The article continued by quoting Mr. Smith's description of the group of followers who had been recruited. "We're a very diversified group. There are six women. Three are African Americans, one of whom is fairly well known as a leader in the Muslim community. We have an Asian, I believe he's Korean. There are two Hispanics. One of the men is openly gay. Our ages range from eighteen to seventy five. We come from all walks of life, some University professors, some business people and some hourly wage earners. We even have one Jewish young man, David Epstein. He was initially a little reluctant about joining the group as he's very active in his synagogue. Then Jesus reminded him He was also Jewish."

Mr. Smith had been asked what commitment had been made by these followers or cabinet members, what the preacher was demanding of them. Mr. Smith was again quoted as having answered . . . "We all realize we've made a life changing decision. He gave us a day or two to consider our decision. Most didn't need it. As to how long we'll be involved in directly working with Him, He's said it could be as short a time as a few months. As to how long He expects us to work for Him, that is for the remainder of our lives."

The article concluded by stating the man had plans to meet with community religious leaders at 10:30am this morning at St. Francis of Assisi Catholic Church in Ann Arbor.

As I finished reading, I handed the newspaper to Beth. She'd been patiently waiting, watching my reactions as I'd been reading. I told her I thought she'd find it interesting, explaining that it was the first time I'd read or heard anything about the followers this man had recruited other than Ernie.

After reading the entire article, Beth asked me if I'd picked up on the fact the man had apparently recruited twelve Christians among His followers. "I realize maybe He's just getting started and He could be recruiting additional people, but two of the fourteen aren't Christians. Makes you wonder if there's special meaning in the number twelve, doesn't it?"

I'd nodded in response. Several thoughts occurred to me. One was why these people were being referred to as followers or cabinet members rather than disciples. Another was wondering if there was or would be a Judas in the group.

Chapter VII

I had attended a meeting at the Washtenaw United Way office on Platt Road Tuesday afternoon and had turned the radio on as I was driving home and caught the five o'clock news. The main story was about the meeting of community religious leaders at St. Francis. The meeting had begun shortly after 10:30 a.m. and had been scheduled to be concluded by noon. The meeting didn't end until 2:30pm. The staff at St. Francis had ordered box lunches a little before one o'clock when it appeared the meeting wasn't going to end anytime soon. About seventy-five attendees had been expected, but over double that number showed up. A couple dozen of them left early, a handful making quite a show of storming out.

For the most part, however, the newscaster reported, the attendees were in awe over what the young preacher they'd come to hear had to say. One minister in attendance said that the time had passed quickly, that he felt he'd only been there less than an hour. His comment made me think of Whitney Stratton's similar reaction when she'd heard the man speak at the Ashley parking structure.

The major action resulting from the meeting was a decision to have the man address the general public this coming Thursday afternoon. That event was tentatively being scheduled for 3:00pm at Crisler Arena, home of Michigan basketball with enough seats to easily accommodate over ten thousand people.

I greeted Beth with this bit of news as I came in the door. She smiled and replied that she was already privy to that news and that it had been confirmed the site would be Crisler Arena. "I've checked our calendars, Mike. It looks as if neither of us has a conflict Thursday afternoon. Should we go?"

Beth had a broad grin on her face as she'd asked the question. She knew how much I'd been intrigued by the young man, she knew what my answer would be.

Beth went on to tell me that there had been several news stories on TV about the meeting.

"I think the *Free Press* article stirred up the interest of all the local Detroit channels. They weren't allowed to get their film crews inside the church, but they stayed around and interviewed several attendees following the meeting. Most were positive, a few negatives. I'm sure they'll be showing their interviews again on their 6 o'clock news shows. Remind me to turn the TV on in a few minutes. Which channel do you prefer?"

I told her to decide, that any of them would be fine.

"You might want to check out the editorial page of this afternoon's *Ann Arbor News* before we switch on the news," Beth suggested. "There are a few letters to the editor that I think will be of interest to you."

I smiled as I reached for the paper. Usually I was the one who was suggesting something she should read. I immediately opened the newspaper to the editorial page. The first letter to catch my attention was titled "Beware of False Prophets." The writer was dismayed and angered over how many Ann Arborites seem to have been won over by this strange preacher in our midst. Citing a couple of biblical passages, he warned the man's appearance was the work of the devil. As seemingly proof, he stated that the man's answer on the Diag on

Sunday afternoon to the question of whether or not abortion was a sin should be proof enough. Stating the man was guilty of blasphemy, he urged readers to rise up and force him out of town. The letter was signed by a Stephen R. Rommano.

Well that's one view I thought as I glanced on down to another letter titled "Facts Not Opinions." The letter writer criticized the *Ann Arbor News* reporter who had written the article "Abortion Dialogue on the Diag" for inserting his opinion in the article. The writer stated that she'd been on the Diag when the preacher had answered the question about whether abortion was a sin. She believed that nothing He'd said was meant to be controversial, rather the opposite. The reporter, in injecting his opinion, was the one who was provoking controversy. Just the facts in the future, she'd concluded.

The third letter, and the last on the subject of the preacher, was titled "Why Ann Arbor??" The writer began by saying he'd encountered several people over the past couple days who believed the mysterious man preaching throughout the city was actually Jesus returning to the world with His message of love. In the writer's opinion, this was a preposterous belief. If Jesus were to actually return, why in heaven's name would He choose Ann Arbor as the place to make his initial appearance, the writer asked. "With all the troubled spots in the world where Christ's message was most urgently needed, with the many people in the world in dire straights, starving and dying, who needed to be comforted, why on earth would Jesus come to Ann Arbor?" The writer concluded by suggesting this preacher might be a Man of God, with a message people should hear. "But to think this preacher is Jesus is just far fetched and ridiculous."

I looked up and saw Beth staring at me; I could tell she was waiting to hear what my reaction was to these letters. I smiled and told her they hadn't changed my opinion about wanting to attend the event at Crisler Arena on Thursday. She returned my smile and replied she was hoping that would be my reaction. She then picked up the remote control and turned on the TV. She chose *Channel 7*, the *Detroit ABC* station for the 6 o'clock news.

    The news began with an update on hurricane Delores which was gaining in strength. The good news was that it was altering its direction. The storm had been originally forecasted to batter the northern Florida east coast. It now appeared it might avoid landfall altogether. There was also news of a major oil find in China and an update on Friday's coming election in England. Following a commercial break, the lead story was coverage of the meeting of religious leaders in Ann Arbor. The television screen showed a picture of St. Frances of Assisi Catholic Church as the newscaster provided some background. He explained that *Channel 7*'s camera crew and reporter had patiently been camped outside the church for several hours. They had been previously advised the meeting would conclude by noon. In fact, the newscaster said, the meeting didn't draw to a close until sometime after 2:30 p.m.

    The newscaster went on to say a participant had exited the church around 2:00pm and *Channel 7* had been able to get an exclusive interview with him. The screen showed a tall man coming out of the main entrance, dressed in a dark suit and wearing a cleric collar. Initially he'd seemed hesitant when approached by the *Channel 7* reporter. But then he stopped and glared into the camera and launched into an angry tirade. "This is the work of the Devil. What is taking place in there," he screamed as he pointed back to the church, "is sinful. The Bible warns us to beware of false prophets. This man is evil! He's using syrupy talk to seduce us, to corrupt us. The news media should be doing its job and exposing him as a fraud and an agent of the Devil." The man's eyes appeared glazed and he was nearly frothing at the mouth as he shouted, "You should find out who this preacher really is. Find out where all his money is coming from, the cash to pay his daily bills at the Campus Inn, the cash to pay for the sandwiches from Zingerman's today. And while you're at it, you should also check to see whether this man has a twin. Whether the Devil has more than one person involved in this treachery. How else do you explain his meetings with so many groups these past few days? Ending one meeting and then appearing clear across town with another group minutes later."

The reporter appeared stunned. His mouth had kept opening as he'd tried to interrupt the man, probably to question him about his identity and what was taking place inside the church. But the man was not about to be distracted as he continued his outburst.

"I think it's absurd that so many seemingly intelligent people are being so easily deceived into believing this man could be Jesus. We need to turn to God. We need to unmask this charade. We need to remove this man from our presence, get him out of Ann Arbor. Now!"

The man raised his arms in frustration and then rudely shoved the reporter aside. He'd stormed off in the direction of the parking lot next to the church.

The lead newscaster then appeared on the screen. He seemed to be as stunned as the reporter who had been attempting to interview the man. "As you've just seen," the newscaster said, "the reaction to this man's appearance in Ann Arbor is not all positive. About a half hour after our reporter's confrontation with this yet to be identified man, the meeting at St. Francis of Assisi Church in Ann Arbor ended. We were informed that the participants had agreed not to grant the media interviews other than to announce that the man would be speaking at 3:00pm on Thursday in Crisler Arena on the U of M campus."

The screen then showed people streaming out of the main entrance of the church. You could see a number of them waving off reporters and shaking their heads in response to requests for interviews. One voice was heard above the commotion shouting out the question, "All we really want to know is whether or not those of you who've heard and seen him think this man is Jesus Christ." The *Channel 7* news reporter seen earlier had positioned a mike in front of a man who I recognized from a recent photograph in the *Ann Arbor News*, the new minister from the United Methodist Church on State Street. The man smiled as he said to the reporter, "We all realize that's a question everyone is asking and that we'd be asked. There was certainly no consensus among those of us in attendance today. It's one of the reasons we agreed we wouldn't speak to the media. Those interested in an answer should be at Crisler Arena on Thursday and form their own opinions. I will say, however, that nothing was said by this man today to answer that question. He didn't personally make that claim."

The screen flashed back to the lead newscaster who said, "That's the latest from our crew on the scene in Ann Arbor. We'll keep you informed of any new developments as they occur. Next up, the latest word on a proposed new bond proposal coming out of

Lansing."

As a commercial came on I switched off the TV. I asked Beth what her thoughts were. She grinned as she replied, "I'm as excited about going to hear the man on Thursday as you get before a Notre Dame vs. Michigan football game. I can't wait. Have you any idea who that man was who was so angry and worked up?"

I shook my head before replying that I thought the last man was the new minister at United Methodist Church. We discussed the subject a few more minutes before turning our attention to what we'd have for dinner.

Chapter VIII

There was an article in the following day's *Detroit Free Press* about the meeting in Ann Arbor. The only thing new was the identification of the man whose critical outburst has been aired by *Channel 7*. The station and the *Free Press* had received several phone calls from viewers who recognized the man. He was identified as Stephen R. Rommano. I thought the name sounded somewhat familiar. It quickly dawned on me it was the name I'd seen on the letter in last night's *Ann Arbor News* which had been so critical of the preacher. It made sense, I thought. Many of the same thoughts had been expressed in both instances.

The man was identified as a former fireman who had retired two years ago with a medical disability. Callers had described him as a community activist who frequently attended Ann Arbor City Council and Washtenaw County Commissioners' meetings. One caller was quoted as saying, "He's nothing but a rabble rouser." The article went on to say the man had not been in attendance at the meeting at St. Francis of Assisi church. It was presumed he'd entered the church through a side door and then come out the main entrance, giving the impression he'd been attending the meeting. Several callers had been critical of *Channel 7* for having given the man so much airtime. The article quoted the general manager of *Channel 7*, apologizing to its viewers. "Our reporter was deceived into believing Mr. Rommano had attended the meeting. He was wearing a cleric collar and had come out of the main door of the church. The fact that other attendees were refusing to grant interviews resulted in our featuring of Mr. Rommano's comments in our coverage of this major story. The one-sided viewpoint which resulted was not intended."

In the *Ann Arbor News* there was also a feature article on the meeting. The thrust of this story was the concern being voiced by a number of people over the University of Michigan allowing Crisler Arena to be used as the site for Thursday afternoon's gathering. Separation of church and state issues were being raised. The question was being asked as to whether the University of Michigan Regents had been consulted or given their approval to rent Crisler Arena for this purpose. Questions were also being raised on how this preacher's followers and other community religious leaders had been able to make arrangements for the Arena's use so quickly. The manager of the University of Michigan's athletic facilities was quoted as saying, "We didn't make any special price concessions for this rental. We have already been paid the full amount in advance. We viewed it as an unexpected revenue opportunity and acted quickly to take advantage of it. There is a long history of outside groups renting this facility. The only requests made by the 'Friends of Jesus' were that we not operate the concession stands and that we make free water available for the attendees."

The weather report indicated that Thursday's temperature might top 90° and there was 60% chance of afternoon showers. I suggested to Beth that we take an umbrella with us tomorrow and get there early because of potential problems with parking and having to walk a ways. She was in agreement and said she'd phone the Hanson's to tell them we'd be by to pick them up around 2:00pm. Beth had spoken to Joy earlier in the day to invite Jerry and her to join us.

Chapter IX

We arrived at Crisler Arena around twenty after 2 p.m. The parking lot next to Crisler was already filled. We decided it would probably be best if I dropped the three of them off before trying to find a parking space. After they'd found seats, Jerry was to come back out to the south entrance to meet me and lead me to the seats.

I first drove around the streets to the east of Crisler. There wasn't a parking place to be found. I ended up parking in the Pioneer High School lot and hiking back to the Arena. The weather was gorgeous. The earlier forecast was in error. There wasn't a cloud in the sky and the temperature was in the low 70°s.

Jerry met me and explained that all of the seats in the lower blue section had already been filled by the time they'd arrived. We found ourselves in the yellow section, only about ten rows from the top. It was like old home week, seeing and greeting numerous friends as Jerry led me to the seats. The crowd appeared to be largely middle-aged and older, not surprising I thought considering it was mid-afternoon on a work day.

By a quarter to three nearly every seat had been filled and people were still streaming in. Five minutes later, an announcement was made over the public address system to inform everyone due to the size of the crowd, we'd be moving next door into the University of Michigan football stadium. The stadium is lovingly nicknamed the 'Big House' with a seating capacity of over one hundred thousand. It's filled every Saturday in the fall when Michigan plays at home.

In about ten minutes the four of us were comfortably seated on the press box side of the field, about thirty rows up and near mid-field. We gazed in amazement as the stadium continued to fill. Friday's newspapers estimated that seventy-five to eighty thousand people witnessed the event.

At about a quarter after three the young preacher came out of the tunnel across the field and walked to the center of the stadium. He was dressed the same as He'd been at the Farmers Market when I'd first seen Him, His white robe gleaming in the sunlight. People were still coming into the stadium as He began speaking. Though the crowd had completely quieted down as He began, it was still amazing that we could hear every word He was saying as He spoke in a normal conversational tone. I wondered if He was using some type of new technology to amplify his voice.

He began by thanking those in attendance for coming and thanking God for the opportunity to speak to them. He reaffirmed that God did exist, a loving, compassionate and caring God who deserved our praise and gratitude. He then emphasized that God was also a forgiving God and as forgiven people we were also commanded by Him to forgive as well. He stressed that forgiving someone was not always easy. Forgiving someone did not mean forgetting the wrongs they'd done. It did not mean letting bygones be bygones and wiping the slate clean to begin a relationship anew. Rather, forgiveness is motivated by love, love of our families, love of our friends, love of strangers and love of our enemies.

He explained that a loving and forgiving God did not mean that God could not be angered or that God did not punish sinners. He continued by saying God truly forgives and has blessed his children with the ability to truly forgive their fellow man. Again, He stressed that this was not always an easy thing to do. But with God's guidance, encouragement and support it could be done and God demanded it should be done. As I glanced around I could see people nodding in approval and seemingly as captivated as I was by the Man's words.

He, next, quoted from the Bible, not reading, but from memory. He quoted from Ecclesiastes. "For everything there is a season, and a time for every matter under heaven: a time to be born, a time to die; a time to plant, and a time to reap what is planted; a time to kill, and a time to heal; a time to break down, and a time to build up; a time to weep, and a time to laugh; a time to mourn, and a time to dance; a time to throw away stones, and a time to gather stones together; a time to embrace, and a time to refrain from embracing; a time to seek, and a time to lose; a time to keep, and a time to throw away; a time to tear, and a time to sew; a time to keep silence, and a time to speak; a time to love, and a time to hate; a time for war, and a time for peace."

He then reviewed each line, often using short parables to illustrate His points. I looked down at my watch and was shocked to see it was a few minutes past five. I held up my wrist and nudged Beth. She seemed equally surprised to see the amount of time that had elapsed since He'd begun speaking. Like us, everyone in the stadium appeared to be concentrating on His every word. It was as if He was personally addressing each of us. I was being energized by His words.

A few minutes later He asked us to bow our heads in prayer. It was a simple, yet complex prayer, mentioning not only the many areas of our respective lives, but also the numerous troubled spots in the world in need of love and reconciliation. It expressed thanks to God, while also asking for His help and guidance. It was a very ecumenical prayer.

After this prayer, He suggested that following His benediction we should all greet and embrace those around us with the message "God loves you" and the response "And He forgives."

His benediction, though brief, was very moving and challenging. He gave it in about six languages and I was reminded of what Mary Stratton had told us about her daughter Whitney telling her He'd used various languages in the parking structure when He'd spoken there on Saturday.

What followed was an amazing sight to behold, complete strangers were grasping hands and hugging one another. As Joy embraced me she whispered in my ear how happy she was Beth and I had persuaded Jerry and her to join us. As I glanced around I was hard pressed to find anyone not wearing a smile. After slightly over two hours of complete silence, the noise was almost deafening. After shaking their hands and embracing several more people, I turned to stare at the spot where the preacher had been standing, expecting to see people swarming around Him. However, there was no sign of Him.

As we were leaving the stadium, Jerry commented that the crowd reminded him of one which had just witnessed a stunning come-from-behind victory for the Michigan football team. It was true, the goodwill and happiness was contagious. Everyone seemed to have been uplifted and energized by what they'd heard and witnessed.

On the drive home, Joy said there was one thing that troubled her about today.

"Did you notice there was no reference to the Lord, to Jesus Christ the entire afternoon? Christ is the main focus in our church service. We pass the peace of Christ. We celebrate communion in remembrance of Christ. Our statement of faith is all about Christ and His sacrifice to grant us all salvation. I had the feeling that this man, whoever He is, and He certainly is impressive, is presenting to us a case for God and His worship and glorification, which leaves Jesus out of the picture. I'm not sure I'm comfortable with that. I understand the need to reconcile all faiths and the need to remove barriers which serve to prevent this. But does this mean we're expected to forget about Christ, forget about our biblical heritage? Those are troubling questions."

"They certainly are, Joy," Beth replied after a few seconds. "I'd be surprised if Jerry and Mike didn't also have them. I know that I do. At the same time though, I'm finding myself grappling with an even larger question. This man's followers appear to be convinced this man is Jesus Christ. As He spoke today, there's no question that in the back of my mind I was asking myself, could this be true? If He truly is, that changes everything."

Nodding his head, Jerry agreed saying, "It surely would. Maybe it explains why Ann Arbor's clergy seem to have been reticent in challenging this man. If the possibility exists, even though remote, that He is in fact Jesus, they might be hesitant to challenge or criticize Him. We've been taught that Jesus' return will be accompanied by Judgment Day. When Jesus first came into the world, the religious leaders of the day turned on him. Let's not make the same mistake a second time, might be their thinking."

"But that was all foretold in scripture," Joy said. "Jesus came to die for us, for man's sins. His pain and suffering and death were prophesied."

"That's all true," Beth said. "But I think your husband makes a valid point. You've been pretty quiet, Mike. What are your thoughts?"

I smiled before replying. "My thoughts might cloud the issue even more," I began. " I think we all would agree that God works in mysterious ways. What about the possibility God has sent His son, Jesus Christ, back to earth for an unscheduled visit? An appearance that wasn't foretold in the Bible? Does this make any kind of sense?"

Beth laughed, "I knew when I asked you to tell us your thoughts, you'd come up with something like that. What are you always saying, 'think outside the box?' But why would God have done this? And there's also the question that the letter writer asked, Why Ann Arbor??"

"Good questions," I answered. "I did say God works in mysterious ways. I still very much question whether or not this man is Jesus. I'm still open to the possibility that He is. Today, just now, was truly one of the most memorable days in my life. We were witnessing something very special. It was miraculous how the Man's voice projected in that cavernous stadium. His voice wasn't loud, He wasn't shouting to be heard. And yet, we had no trouble hearing every word He said. Maybe I'm just imagining what I want to believe. The God He describes is the kind of God I want to believe does exist."

I'd smiled again before I concluded by saying, "I think all four of us are probably going to have a restless sleep. Lots of questions, lots of possible answers."

Chapter X

The Hanson's joined us for a very relaxing dinner at the Travis Pointe clubhouse. We had an abundance of news to share with one another, some of which was relating the latest exploits of our respective grandchildren, and steered away from further discussion about the questions that were still foremost in all our minds.

Beth and I watched the news before retiring. The national news media had picked up the story of what was taking place in Ann Arbor. Coverage focused on the massive size of the crowd and the fact that everyone could hear the speaker clearly, rather than on what He'd actually said. There were, however, several shots of the crowd embracing and greeting one another following His talk. Several spectators had also been interviewed, none of whom we recognized. All were very enthusiastic and appreciative of having had the opportunity to be there to see and hear the speaker. When asked their opinions as to whether or not the man was Jesus, most backed off by responding that it was "too soon to tell" or "the jury's still out." All agreed, however, that the man had held them in awe for over two hours with his stirring positive message and skilled delivery. Two of those interviewed said they were inclined to believe the man is Jesus Christ. In both instances the reporter had followed up their answers with the question "Why do you believe God picked Ann Arbor for Jesus' return?" The man responded by saying, "I've no idea, but I'm sure glad He did." The woman replied, "Maybe for the same reasons my husband and I decided to return to Ann Arbor for our retirement."

It took me a while before falling to sleep. One thing I was thinking about was an article I'd just read in the *Ann Arbor News*. Catholic Social Services and Planned Parenthood, two unlikely allies, were teaming up to explore whether they should jointly be involved in a program to assist women interested in carrying their pregnancies to full term and giving up their babies for adoption. The article had said that forty years ago Catholic Social Services had been the major agency involved in adoptions taking place in Washtenaw County. The aim of the program was to basically take the cost factor of a pregnancy out of consideration in a woman's decision regarding childbirth. Prenatal care, delivery and the hospital stay would be arranged on a gratis basis. A place to stay with room and board could also be arranged for no cost. The tentative plans called for simultaneously beginning programs in Ann Arbor and Toledo, Ohio, so the option for a woman to move to another community during the pregnancy would be possible. The C.E.O. of Catholic Social Services was asked if adoptions would be limited to Catholic Families. He'd said no and stated that nearly ninety percent of the clients served by the agency weren't Catholic. He said the mission statement which already had Board approval, called only for a placement in a loving, stable and safe environment. He'd gone on to say this definition could encompass single parent and same sex households. He'd also pointed out that a birth mother of a particular faith might request the agency attempt to place the child in a household of the same faith.

One reason I'd found the story so interesting was my having remembered reading that Planned Parenthood and Catholic Social Services were two of many organizations the preacher had visited.

I wondered if He had perhaps played a role in getting these two adversaries to work in conjunction with one another to explore the need for and the feasibility of such a program. My guess was He had.

Chapter XI

Friday's *Free Press* and *Ann Arbor News* had articles about Thursday's stadium event, including many photos. I was pleased to see that both papers featured fairly lengthy summaries of what had been said by the speaker. There were even short articles about the event in the *USA Today* and the *New York Times*.

The *Ann Arbor News* had a short article about the controversy over the University having allowed its facilities to be used for religious purposes. There was clearly mixed sentiment in the community over the issue, with passionate opinions being voiced by those on both sides. The Manager of Athletic Facilities had been asked if the same "Friends of Jesus" group was to ask to rent the stadium or the arena again, what the University's response would be. He'd avoided an answer by replying the group hadn't made another request and nothing had occurred to lead him to believe it would.

On the Letters to the Editor page there was one titled "He Practices What He Preaches." The letter writer had been present outside the Campus Inn when "Jesus" confronted Stephen Rommano, the author of the letter so critical of Him that had previously been published in the *Ann Arbor News* and the man who had been interviewed by *ABC News* in front of St. Frances of Assisi Church. The letter writer stated that "Jesus" had lashed out at the man, harshly criticizing him for his behavior. Then, however, "Jesus" had forgiven Mr. Rommano and embraced him. The letter writer said that he'd heard "Jesus" stress the need to forgive more than once in his talks. "He practices what he preaches" was the final sentence in the letter.

I nodded, thinking the letter would be even more meaningful for those who had heard the man speak yesterday. He'd elaborated on the topic of forgiveness then. I was also intrigued to see the writer referring to the man as Jesus. The media was having a hard time with its coverage in identifying the man, avoiding referencing Him as Jesus as the letter writer had done. I was having the same difficulty in my conversations about Him, referring to Him as that young preacher, that Jesus look-a-like, that man whose followers called Him Jesus, etc. etc. Currently, I felt uncomfortable calling him Jesus. Maybe that would change. I had empathy for the news media. Just as it might be premature to reference Him as Jesus, it would also be premature to call Him that Jesus imposter.

Another letter also caught my eye. It was titled "Good Questions." The letter writer, while conceding that the man appearing on *Channel 7*'s coverage of the meeting of religious leaders at St. Frances of Assisi Church earlier in the week might have been the wrong man to have voiced the questions about the man several people were calling Jesus, the questions were good ones. "And while the news media is trying to get the answers to them," the letter continued, "it should also try to determine why the man is seemingly dodging their interviews." The writer then stated her own opinion of why, saying she believed the controversy which resulted from His answer to the question about abortion made Him fearful of being asked other tough questions. She gave a few examples, suggesting that while the media was asking questions, it should see what He had to say about same sex marriages, women and married men as priests in the Catholic Church, evolution and U.S. involvement in the mid-east. The letter writer was a Carolyn Miller.

As I finished reading the letter, I pondered over her allegation that interviews were being avoided. I remembered seeing quotes from His followers saying His whirlwind schedule of meetings with groups hadn't allowed time for Him to be interviewed. I'd also heard rumors He was no longer staying at the Campus Inn, that He'd thought his presence there was creating problems for Campus Inn with the swarm of reporters and the number of cameras outside waiting to confront Him. I asked myself that if this man was truly Jesus, wouldn't He want to be interviewed? Wouldn't He want to get His message out to thousands rather than just addressing small groups? I glanced at the letter again and the questions the woman had suggested He be asked. Maybe she was right, maybe with His message of reconciliation He was trying to avoid getting into potentially controversial areas.

Beth, who had been on the phone, interrupted my thoughts as she informed me that she'd been talking to Kristi Cloverdale. "Tom's written a letter to the *Ann Arbor News*. She wants us to be watching for it. She thinks we'll find it interesting. It's Tom's answer to the question raised in a previous letter, the letter titled 'Why Ann Arbor??' I'm sure you recall it, we discussed it."

I acknowledged that I certainly did and then said, "So Tom thinks he has the answer. I'm curious. Maybe you should call her back and ask them to fax us a copy. What do you think?"

Beth smiled at me as she replied, "There's no question Tom's very articulate, being an English professor and all. But I'm sure you'd agree, he can be a real screwball at times. You've heard him express some crazy views, too. I'm probably as curious about what he's written as you are, but I think we can wait though, and just watch for his letter to appear."

Chapter XII

Later that afternoon as I drove toward home, I'd turned the radio on. I usually always have it tuned to 950 AM, the all news station. I'd just run a couple errands for Beth. My attention perked up as the announcer gave a recap of an accident that had occurred around noon on State Street, just north of Hill.

Over twenty people, mainly children, had been injured, a few quite severely, when a driver lost control of his vehicle as he tried to swerve to avoid a piece of scaffolding that had fallen into the street from the construction site on the east side of State Street. I could easily visualize the scene, having been watching the rise of the Gerald Ford School of Public Policy Building on the northeast corner of State and Hill.

The announcer explained that the vehicle had veered over the curb on the west side of State Street and rammed into a group of mostly children who had been heading north toward the dorms for lunch following morning sessions at the U of M athletic complex.

This was big business in Ann Arbor during the summer months, bringing hundreds of middle school and high school students into town for week long sessions of coaching in a wide variety of sports. I'd often driven past these youngsters as they filed to and from the sport activities.

"Twenty one people, six girls, thirteen boys and two adult males had been taken to University of Michigan Hospital," the announcer continued. "We've just been informed that nine of the children have already been released. Their injuries were fairly minor.

One of the adults who was injured is the man who spoke yesterday in Michigan Stadium. We've been informed He'd been invited to speak to some of the kids on their final day of instruction. He'd been hiking up State Street, surrounded by a swarm of children, when struck by the vehicle. He's suffered major injuries and we will keep you updated. The other injured man is Ernie Smith, who is a follower of the man who began preaching in Ann Arbor last Saturday. He's expected to be released in the next hour."

I switched the radio off as the announcer turned to another story. I hoped the young preacher's injuries weren't that severe and wouldn't be permanent. I hoped the same for the youngsters who were still hospitalized. I also wondered how the tragic accident would affect what the man had done and was doing. He'd certainly made a major impact on the community in just a short period of time. I thought if He were to be hospitalized for any length of time, it would probably give the news media the opportunity to interview Him. I also was thinking that there were probably a considerable number of people in town who were thinking that God may have intervened and brought about an end to this man's actions and claim of being Jesus.

When I arrived home, I learned that Beth hadn't been aware of the accident. I filled her in on the details. She'd glanced at the clock and suggested we catch the story in a couple minutes on the 6 o'clock news.

I poured Beth a glass of wine and made myself a cocktail before turning on the TV. The accident was the feature story. I was already familiar with most of the details. Beth and I could easily relate to the accident scene being shown as the newscaster described what happened. The picture changed to the emergency room entrance to U of M Hospital as the announcer told of the injuries. Two more children, now up to eleven, had been released. She described the children still hospitalized as having a few broken bones, some severe bruises, a couple cracked ribs, a few cuts and in two instances, mild concussions. Doctors expected all to be discharged by sometime tomorrow.

Beth and I exchanged glances and I flashed her a thumbs up sign. We were both relieved to learn the youngsters hadn't been more seriously injured. The anchorwoman continued by saying one of the two injured adults had been released just moments ago. The other injured man was currently undergoing surgery and she didn't have any information concerning the details of his injuries. She then went through a lengthy explanation of who the latter man was, concluding by saying he was the man who had spoken to the huge crowd at the U of M stadium yesterday afternoon and the man His followers were calling Jesus.

The anchorwoman told viewers the station had a reporter on the scene at U of M hospital interviewing the parents of one of the boys who was still hospitalized. The father was extremely angry, saying they hadn't sent their son to Ann Arbor to learn about religion. He'd been there to improve his skills at soccer. "I don't know who was responsible for inviting that preacher down to speak to the kids, but I'm sure going to find out. We were told our son was following on the man's heels when the car struck him."

The man's wife tried to soften her husband's criticism by saying, "We realize this was a freak accident. We aren't blaming the man for what happened, for our son's injuries. We just think it was wrong for him to be involved with the youngsters."

Chapter XIII

The morning newspapers both ran front-page articles on the accident. The *Ann Arbor News* and *Detroit Free Press* articles were quite similar in content up until the *News'* concluding paragraphs. Both stories had stated that medical personnel had declined to comment on the extent of the injuries of the man who was still hospitalized or the surgery he'd undergone. The *News* had pulled a coup of sorts in quoting a nurse who had been present for the man's surgery. She'd requested that the paper not reveal her name. Though she had declined to say anything about the man's injuries or the surgery, she'd vividly described the many scars on the man's body from previous injuries. She was quoted as having said, "I was in awe. In addition to the scars on his hands and feet, his back is covered with scars. Not only that, but he had a large scar on his side near his waistline. I'm not all that religious, but I do remember the story of Doubting Thomas. If you saw the movie 'The Passion', these are the scars you'd expect to see on Christ's body. I think this man may really be Jesus."

The article said their reporter had questioned one of the doctors who had performed the surgery on the man and asked him if could either affirm or deny the nurse's statement. He refused to do so.

The article concluded on that note, with no attempt to editorialize or expand on the implications of the unidentified nurse's statement.

Later in the day, a beautiful one, warm and sunny, Beth and

I decided to take a walk around our neighborhood. The Hanson's spotted us from inside their condo, as we were passing by, and came out to flag us down.

Following a brief conversation about the accident and the article in the *Ann Arbor News,* Jerry suggested to Joy that she fill us in on what she'd learned during a phone call with her close friend, Mary. Joy began by saying this information was second hand, maybe even third hand. "Mary has a friend who knows a woman who works in the billing office at the U of M hospital. The woman had told her friend about the confusion when the man who had spoken at the stadium was being admitted. It began as they were attempting to obtain His name, a name to register Him under. They finally decided to use the name Jesus with no last name. Insurance was another problem. The man, Ernie Smith, who was also being admitted, said he'd be paying cash to settle his charges and he'd be paying cash for Jesus' charges, too. The woman who had related this said she'd ended up with a pile of currency on her desk, a stack of bills totaling over twelve thousand dollars. She was instructed to find a safe place to store it and any difference after the final charges for the two men were known would be addressed later. It was the first time anything like that had happened since she'd worked there."

"Wow!" exclaimed Beth. "Did the woman pass along any information on . . ." Beth hesitated before adding, "Jesus' injuries or his surgery?"

"A little," Joy replied, "The injuries were serious. She'd heard that one of the witnesses to the accident had said that the man had turned as the car came over the curb and stepped in front of a couple of the youngsters to shield them. He had absorbed the full impact of the vehicle."

Beth and I cringed as we pictured the scene.

"Again, this is only what she'd overheard, the rumors around the hospital," Joy said as she continued. "Many of His organs—his kidneys, spleen, pancreas, gall bladder and all—had been crushed. There were doubts about surgery, if it could be successful, if the man would survive it. She had heard that the man had become conscious for a few minutes and one of the physicians had explained the extent of His injuries to Him. He'd nodded and told the doctor they should go ahead with the surgery, that God would be looking after Him."

Joy paused for breath before continuing, "The woman had heard there were four doctors involved and they'd thought it might take at least ten hours to complete the surgery. It actually took less than half that time and they're cautiously optimistic about the results. It's thought to be a miracle that the man has survived with such major injuries."

I told Joy and Jerry we were glad they'd stopped us and shared this information with us. I suggested tomorrow's newspapers would probably verify what the woman had said.

"There's one other piece of news that also might interest you," Jerry said. "Joy and I ran into coach Samuels last night."

Jeff Samuels was one of the assistant football coaches, liked and respected by players and fans. He was the offensive coordinator.

"He was working with the youngsters yesterday when . . ." Jerry hesitated as Beth had done earlier, "When Jesus came to talk to the kids. He said the youngsters' response to Him had been very enthusiastic. When Joy and I asked Jeff if he'd heard what was said, he said he had. The man had emphasized to the kids that God loved them. That God had blessed them with bodies and minds, which would allow them to accomplish great things. He told them they were a very privileged group with opportunities that other children could only dream about. He stressed that with all these privileges also came responsibilities, that they should take care of their minds and bodies and not abuse them. He also said they should try to be positive role models for their brothers and sisters, for friends and for strangers. He said God wanted and expected them to use their talents to create a better world, a more loving and caring world. He told them God was present in their lives to guide and support them. And if they should sometimes stumble or make bad choices, God was also there to comfort and console them. Jeff said it was a simple message, only lasting about ten minutes. He spoke to these youngsters as adults and in Jeff's opinion, not only did He get his message through to them, He had them all fired up."

"That's good to hear," responded Beth. "Mike and I saw on TV the agitated father of one of the kids who had been injured. It doesn't sound to me that he could be finding fault with anything that was said."

"That was my reaction, too," Jerry replied. "Jeff also mentioned he'd been as impressed with what the man hadn't said as what He had. The words drugs, booze and tobacco were never mentioned. It wasn't a morality lecture. The man didn't give them specific directives on how to behave. He'd simply told them to love God, to love and respect themselves and to love the world and all people."

I'd been focusing on every word Jerry was saying. I could see that Beth was also enthralled with what we were hearing. I'd once again thanked Jerry and Joy for sharing all these details with us.

Then Beth smiled and said we also had a bit of news to pass on to them. "It's not nearly as fascinating as what we've just learned from you, but Kristi Cloverdale told us Tom has written a letter to the *Ann Arbor News*. It's his answer as to why God and this man, Jesus, might choose to come to Ann Arbor. It's in response to the letter that appeared a few days ago titled "Why Ann Arbor??" in which the writer raised doubts about this man being Jesus."

"I recall it," Joy replied to Beth. "Did Kristi say when Tom's letter is going to be published?"

Beth shook her head. "No, I don't think they've been told. Kristi did say the *News* had phoned Tom to verify whether he'd actually written the letter."

"Well, we'll be on the lookout for it," Jerry said. "If you see it, let us know. Knowing Tom, I'm sure we'll find it interesting."

Chapter XIV

During the remainder of the day and evening Beth and I frequently discussed all that had been happening and all we'd been learning about the man we were still reluctant to call Jesus. I'd teased Beth, saying I'd noticed her hesitation when she'd identified the man as Jesus.

I was up early the next morning and immediately went out to get the newspaper. I have a habit of pulling out the advertising inserts before sitting down to read them. One of the flyer inserts caught my eye. It was an announcement about an upcoming appearance of the preacher on Wednesday evening at Hill Auditorium. The University of Michigan Musical Society was promoting this event as a fund raiser for its Youth Education Programs. There would be a hundred dollar charge for tickets, tax deductible, with all proceeds going to UMS.

My initial reaction was this had been planned before the tragic accident on Friday. The flyer insertion was probably in the works and it had been too late to pull. However, after reading the *News'* follow up article on the accident, I discovered I'd been wrong in my assumption. The concluding paragraphs quoted Ken Rector, the Executive Director of the Musical Society. He said that in speaking to the preacher's followers, he'd been assured the man would be available to speak on Wednesday evening as scheduled. He also said that at the preacher's request, two hundred of the tickets would be free. The box office would be open at 8:00am on Monday, for both ticket purchases and for obtaining free tickets.

I glanced at the flyer again and saw tickets could also be purchased by phone. I'll discuss it with Beth, I thought. I know I'd like to attend. I set the flyer aside, planning to put it up on the refrigerator as a reminder to phone the next morning.

Beth was now up as well and came over to where I was sitting and handed me a cup of steaming coffee. As I was thanking her, she asked if I'd seen Tom's letter in the paper. I told her I hadn't had a chance to get to the editorial page yet and I handed her the flyer.

She showed her surprise as she read it. "Do they really think He'll be recovered enough to appear on Wednesday?"

"Hard to believe, isn't it?" I replied. "But Ken Rector's quoted in today's paper saying the man's followers have assured him that He will be. Want to go?"

"Try to keep me away," she giggled. "You'll get tickets? Maybe the Hanson's would like to join us again. I'll check with them."

I turned to the editorial page. Tom's letter wasn't there. However, there were two other articles of interest in the paper. One was about the preacher's visit with the youngsters on Friday. The details were very similar to those related to us by Jerry. The article also mentioned the concern raised by some parents over the fact the preacher had been invited to speak to the youngsters. One of the coaches was quoted as having said, "If we'd had 'Bo' there giving much the same message, those same parents would be heaping praise on us. Hard to figure." I smiled, picturing "Bo", Michigan's former football coach, addressing the kids.

The article ended with quotes from some of the kids who had

been tailing the preacher up State Street just prior to the accident. One young girl had asked Him why God would let hurricanes do so much damage. She told Him her grandparents lived in Florida and she was scared they were going to be hurt in one of those storms.

The girl and one of the boys with her said He'd answered by saying perhaps they, or some of the other youngsters He'd spoken to, might someday, using their God given talents, come up with answers on how to control hurricanes. They said He told them about how much of the testing of the vaccine which had virtually eliminated the dreadful disease of polio in the world had taken place right here in Ann Arbor. He also told them a man in Ann Arbor seemed to be on the threshold of discovering how salt water could inexpensively be converted to fresh water. He smiled and said the fact they lived in Michigan, which was surrounded by the Great Lakes, might make them think that was no big deal, but the benefits to millions of others in the world would be enormous. They said He challenged them to do the things, little things as well as big things, to help make a better world for everyone including the young girl's grandparents. He'd told them God would be counting on them.

The other article was a short one, telling how a group had gathered outside the U of M Hospital on Friday and Saturday night to pray for the injured preacher. The article explained that what had begun with a handful of people, mainly His followers, had soon blossomed to over hundreds. On Saturday night it was estimated over a thousand people participated in praying for the preacher. The main article on the accident had only mentioned that everyone who had been injured had been discharged by early Saturday evening with the exception of the preacher who had suffered serious injuries. The article gave none of the details Beth and I had learned from Joy. It only said though the man was still listed as critical, doctors were guardedly optimistic over the success of the major surgery which had been necessary.

Chapter XV

A little after 9:30am on Monday, I placed a call to the University Musical Society to order tickets for Wednesday evening's event at Hill Auditorium. The Hanson's had been delighted to be asked to join us. Jerry had given me his credit card information to pay for their tickets. I kept getting a message saying all operators were currently busy with other customers and that I should call back later. It was nearly an hour later before I was able to speak to someone.

I was disappointed to learn the event had already sold out. The woman explained that the free tickets had gone in a matter of minutes and that those requiring a hundred dollar donation had all been sold by 10:00am. I told her I'd been trying to phone the ticket office for over an hour. She apologized and said I wasn't the only one who had told her that, a number of people were disappointed and angry. She asked me if she could put me on hold for a minute or two. She came back on the line in a matter of seconds, excitedly telling me arrangements had been made to have the man speak again on Thursday evening.

I gambled that the Hansons would also be available to join us then and immediately ordered the four tickets. The woman advised me that we should plan to arrive early, by 7:00pm, to pick up the tickets.

I immediately informed Beth who volunteered to phone the Hansons with the change in dates. "Ken Rector must be ecstatic," Beth said. "It's a real windfall for UMS. I bet he'd had doubts over whether they'd be able to fill Hill Auditorium with the hundred-dollar charge. Now it appears they'll do it twice."

I'd joked in response to her saying, "Who knows, maybe they'll have to switch to the stadium again." Beth smiled back at me and said, "I doubt if that's going to happen, but I'm still impressed over how many people are willing to fork over a hundred dollars apiece just to see and hear the man."

I agreed with her and also suggested that maybe a number of those who had been at the Stadium would be coming to see and hear Him again as we and the Hansons were. I was thinking that if that were true, Ken Rector might have to give some thought to hosting a third event and perhaps even doubling the contribution required for tickets.

Beth phoned the Hansons, but there was no answer. She left them a voice mail. Beth and I both had luncheon plans and didn't get back to the house until shortly after 4:00pm I'd stopped at the curb to pick up the *Ann Arbor News*. Before even continuing into the driveway, I opened the paper and checked out the editorial page. Tom's letter was there, more than just a letter actually. It was probably three or four times the length of a normal letter and was presented as a guest editorial beneath the other letters. The *News* did this fairly frequently.

I was just ready to push the button to lower the garage door as Beth drove in the driveway. I waited for her, holding up the newspaper saying Tom's letter was in it tonight. She smiled as she said, "Who is going to get to read it first, me or you? Should we flip a coin?"

We ended up spreading the newspaper out on the island in the middle of the kitchen so that we could both have first dibs. Leaning over, we both began to read.

Tom had begun by stating his letter was not being written to give credence to the belief of some people that Jesus had returned to earth in Ann Arbor. Rather, he stated, he wanted to build the case as to why God or Christ might choose Ann Arbor for His return and answer the earlier letter writer who had questioned "Why Ann Arbor?" Tom went on to state that when he'd first heard about this preacher's appearance, he'd expected that stories would appear about the man's appearance in other cities in the U.S. or somewhere else in the world. After stating he was surprised that hadn't occurred, he suggested that with all the recent publicity about the preacher's arrival in Ann Arbor, it still might.

Tom went on to spell out some of the reasons Jesus might choose Ann Arbor for His return. The relatively small population of less than one hundred fifty thousand meant the news of His appearance would be widely known in Ann Arbor in a very short time. Ann Arbor was internet savvy; the University had been a pioneer in this area. News from Ann Arbor circulated instantly throughout the world. Tom cited The Consumer Confidence Survey and The Economic Forecasts as examples. He described Ann Arbor's diversity, stating that sixteen different nationalities had been represented in his granddaughter's class last year at Angell Elementary School. With the presence of the University, there was a constant flow of people and ideas from all over the world coming to town. But the flow out of Ann Arbor was also enormous with many residents staying for a relatively short time.

What they learned in Ann Arbor would spread to all four corners of the world.

Tom was tongue in cheek with some of the reasons he was giving and I chuckled as I read on. He stated Ann Arbor had a liberal bent; Kerry and even Gore stickers could still be spotted on many cars. Ann Arbor was definitely not a bastion for the religious right wing. He suggested that Ann Arbor also had far more skeptics than most communities. Therefore, if Jesus and His message were to be embraced in Ann Arbor, chances were they'd be welcome in most other communities in the U.S. as well.

Throughout his letter, Tom kept referring to the diversity Ann Arbor offered. Intellectual diversity. Racial diversity. Asians represented the largest minority with also a sizeable population of Hispanics and African Americans. All religious faiths were also represented. Tom mentioned a place of worship on Packard Road which is a combined church and synagogue—St. Clare's and Temple Beth Emeth —where Episcopalians and Jews both engage in worship.

Tom also mentioned Ann Arbor being in the forefront of communities addressing issues such as the homeless and the environment. He pointed out the city's and the University's readiness to tackle new challenges and told of the opportunities the new Life Science Center brought to the area.

In closing, Tom stated the question wasn't "Why Ann Arbor?" now, but rather how long the man some were calling Jesus would stay in Ann Arbor. He stated that everyone should take full advantage of the man's presence in our community and attempt to see and hear Him and draw their own conclusions as to whether or not this was the Second Coming of the Messiah.

Beth and I finished reading at the same time and glanced over at one another. I remarked that I thought Tom must have had fun writing the letter.

"It's not surprising that it's well written," I said, "And he certainly does cover some points I wouldn't have considered. What's your take?"

"I think what surprises me the most about it is the feeling I had as I read it that Tom is so open to the possibility this man may really be Jesus," Beth answered. "I really didn't expect that from him. I realize he stated at the beginning that the letter wasn't intended to build a case for the man being Jesus, but that's the impression he's given me."

"I tend to agree," I replied. "As I was reading I kept thinking what my reaction would be if we hadn't known Tom was the author."

Beth laughed, "Probably that one of the man's followers had written it. Oh look, the message light is blinking. I'll check and see who its from."

There were two messages. The first was from the Pollards wondering if we'd be available to play a round of golf with them Friday afternoon and then join them for dinner. The second was from Joy saying that, yes, they'd be free on Thursday evening to join us at Hill Auditorium. She said that they'd be glad to drive and she'd get back to us. She also asked if we'd had a chance to read Tom's letter yet, explaining it was in tonight's paper. She said Jerry and she were curious to know what we thought of it.

"We can let them know on Thursday," Beth said. "You know

Mike, I just had a thought. The timing for this man's appearance in Ann Arbor is ideal, just after the Summer Festival and before the Art Fair. He's the featured story with virtually no competition, maximum exposure and coverage."

I smiled and quipped, "You're absolutely right, Beth. The only show in town. Tom should have mentioned that in his letter. The perfect place to come, the perfect time to do it."

As I was talking I'd folded the newspaper back in place. The headline of one of the front-page articles grabbed my eye: "A Miraculous Recovery." The article reported the preacher who had been seriously injured in Friday's accident and undergone several hours of surgery had made a remarkable recovery. Though still hospitalized, doctors believed He would be released late Tuesday or early Wednesday. Two of the surgeons who had participated in the operation were quoted. One said, "It's a miracle the man's alive today following such massive injuries." The other was quoted as having said, "His recovery is nothing short of amazing. None of those of us involved have ever witnessed anything like it."

Just below this article was another short one which stated the *Ann Arbor News* had just learned the preacher was going to be featured in a segment on "60 minutes" this coming Sunday. The article reported one of the man's followers, Ernie Smith, had also informed them that "Jesus" had agreed to be interviewed by reporters from six major newspapers: *The New York Times, The Washington Post, The L.A. Times, U.S.A. Today, The Detroit Free Press,* and the *Ann Arbor News.* Mr. Smith was quoted as saying, "Although we'll be limiting the interviews on Thursday morning to just these six publications, all have agreed to make their stories available without charge to other news media. The article concluded with an editorial statement saying how pleased the *Ann Arbor News* was to be chosen to be one of the newspapers in this select group.

As I read the article, I couldn't help but recall reading about criticism over the preacher's refusal to be interviewed, questioning what the man was trying to hide. I wished I could eavesdrop on the interviews.

Chapter XVI

On Tuesday evening Beth and I had an early dinner at Zanzibar and then headed over to the Michigan Theater to see a movie we'd both wanted to see. Following the movie we walked across the street to browse through Borders.

We ran into Brad Babcock as we were strolling down one of the aisles. After some small talk, Brad commented that he hadn't seen us since the dinner party at our house.

"Seems like ages ago," he said. "You and the Strattons' daughter had just had your initial encounter with this preacher who's been creating such an uproar, Mike."

I nodded, recalling some of our conversation. Brad was continuing. "One of my biggest concerns about this man is who's behind Him, the person or group who seems to be supplying Him with a seemingly unlimited supply of money, cash no less. Does this trouble the two of you?"

Beth and I agreed we'd also had some thoughts on the subject, that it was a valid question to be asking.

"I'm sure the question will come up when he's interviewed," I suggested. "You're aware aren't you, Brad, he's agreed to be interviewed by six newspapers on Thursday?"

Brad nodded, "Tory and I have tickets to see him at Hill on Wednesday. We've been keeping close tabs on this guy. I don't think there's been an article that's been written about Him that we haven't read." Brad smiled, "I was about to say we can't get Him out of our minds, but it might be more apt to say I can't get Him out from under my skin. I know He's been saying some positive things. But you realize Tory and I are staunch Catholics. What He's been saying, what He's been preaching, could have an enormous impact on The Church. I confess I'm concerned and more than a little confused. How about you two, what are your thoughts?"

I glanced at Beth before attempting to answer his question. Brad noticed and asked if we had different opinions, "No," I answered. "I think Beth's and my thoughts are pretty much in sync. We're both still open to the possibility this man is Jesus. Maybe even leaning in that direction. Of course, we both have questions, too. We're going to Hill on Thursday night along with the Hansons. We're also waiting to read what He has to say in those interviews, hoping they'll answer most of our questions."

"So you two really believe this guy could be Jesus, Jesus Christ!" Brad exclaimed. "I find that hard to believe, you're both so intelligent." Brad was smiling, "I guess what troubles me most about what you've said though is that I think I might be on the same page as the two of you. I'm sorry that Tory has been so vehement with her snide comments about the man. You don't know how lucky you are to have compatible thoughts."

The sad expression on Brad's face quickly vanished as he said, "Hey, it's our turn to initiate getting together. Expect a call soon. I admire you two, I'm glad we ran into each other."

During the drive home, we talked about our conversation with Brad. I asked Beth if I'd been correct in assuming she was in step with me when I'd answered Brad's question as to what our thoughts about the preacher were. She at first teased me, pretending she was angry, saying I was being chauvinistic in speaking for her. Then she grinned and grabbed my hand and whispered, "I'm glad you're my partner."

Chapter XVII

Beth received an interesting e-mail from Joy Hanson early Wednesday morning. It was titled "Jesus Identified?" It began with a brief explanation about the mysterious preacher who had first appeared in Ann Arbor, Michigan in mid-July and whose followers were calling Him Jesus. The e-mail stated that this man bears a striking resemblance to Johnathon Tyler, one of the stars in the popular afternoon soap opera "General Hospital". There were photos of the two men; the preacher in a robe with His long hair and beard, Johnathon Tyler's photo was from a scene in the show. Beneath the latter was an altered photo of Tyler picturing him with a beard and longer hair. He was dressed in a robe similar to the one the preacher was wearing. This was followed by a second photo of the preacher, minus the beard and long hair and dressed in attire similar to that worn by Tyler in the initial photo.

There was no doubt the two men resembled one another. If not twins, at least brothers or relatives. Their facial expressions, in addition to their physical builds, were almost identical. Studying the photos again, I questioned whether I'd be able to identify who was who if I wasn't already aware.

The e-mail went on to say that Tyler had vacated his condo a few days before the preacher first appeared in Ann Arbor and no one appears to have seen him since. The e-mail asked the question of whether Tyler could be performing the acting role of his life, impersonating a preacher that his followers thought was Jesus.

Beth and I both had the same reaction. What a let down if this in fact was true! Had we been conned? What a major disappointment! We'd both believed we were possibly being witnesses to one of the most major happenings in history, the second coming of Jesus. There was a pit in my stomach as I said to Beth, "Let's hope this isn't true and that the resemblance is just a weird coincidence."

Beth nodded in agreement. There were tears in her eyes. We both seemed to mope around the house the remainder of the morning.

Early that afternoon we received a second e-mail from Joy though, titled "Tyler Found". Johnathon Tyler had been found vacationing, actually on a fishing jaunt, in New Zealand. He was on a two-week trip, heading home on Thursday. He knew nothing of any similarities in his appearance with the Ann Arbor preacher and didn't even have any knowledge about the man prior to being informed.

Beth's reaction, mine too, was one of elation. "What do they say?" Beth exclaimed, "What a difference a day, or a few hours, makes. I'd been so devastated and angry, too. I feel as if I have a new lease on life. I'm all fired up once again about being at Hill tomorrow evening."

I agreed with her, saying I had the same feelings. I'd smiled as I asked her what the two of us had learned from this incident, if anything.

She'd mulled my question over for few seconds before replying, "One thing I think is that perhaps both of us are getting too emotionally involved with .... Jesus. I can't remember ever feeling as depressed as I was before Joy's latest e-mail. Maybe we have to step back a little and see how this all plays out. Hearing Him on

Thursday and reading the newspaper interviews will give us a great deal more information to digest and mull over."

"We'll have the '60 Minutes' segment we'll be seeing, too," I said. I'll give Joy and Jerry a call and see if they've been on the same roller coaster ride that we have been on today."

Chapter XVIII

The *Ann Arbor News* had a short article reporting the preacher who'd been injured in the accident on Friday had been released from U of M hospital early this morning. Once again, hospital personnel were quoted as saying the man's speedy recovery was miraculous.

There was also an article about tonight's and tomorrow night's appearances by the preacher at Hill Auditorium. The article reported both were sellouts and gave a guesstimate of how many dollars UMS would net for its youth programs.

The article also reported that UMS had attempted to sell television rights and radio broadcasting rights for tonight's event. Those negotiations fell through, however.

Beth and I watched the 10 o'clock news. Jesus' appearance at Hill was the lead story. The announcer began by saying the preacher had spoken in Hill Auditorium to an enthusiastic, standing room only, crowd for close to an hour and a half. The announcer then introduced the station's reporter on the scene with live coverage. The picture showed the reporter positioned on the steps leading into Hill Auditorium with a microphone in her hand. There were only a few people milling around behind her, some still filing out of the building.

The reporter said the highlight of tonight's program came early in the evening when the preacher acknowledged He was indeed Jesus Christ. He'd done it indirectly, she reported. Following a gasp from the audience, He'd then explained the reason why He hadn't done so earlier. The reporter said that even though His followers had been referring to Him as Jesus for sometime, the man Himself had never made that claim before this evening.

The man said His hesitancy over revealing His identify was because He wanted to get His message out to people of all faiths. He was fearful of losing many opportunities to do so if He approached people as Jesus, He was afraid many doors would then be closed to Him. He was fearful if He was seen only as Christianity's main spokesperson, people would turn away before listening to what He had to say.

As the reporter continued, I recalled reading about the many groups the man had spoken to. I remember being somewhat surprised at the time by the fact He was being welcomed in a number of places of worship which were non-Christian. His delay in identifying Himself had indeed worked, I thought, even though it had only been for a short period of time.

"Those who were in attendance tonight to hear Him talk seem to have come out with more questions than answers," the reporter continued. "They've said the man assured them God does exist, a loving, caring God. A God who was not a creation of man as some people would have them believe. He said there was but one God, the same God for all people and for all religious faiths. A God who was sometimes called by different names, but the same God.

"He said God is understanding of the fact people have chosen diverse ways in which to worship Him. He stressed, however, that religious places of worship should be open to all who truly believe in God. They should be inclusive rather than exclusive places of worship, He emphasized. He said God did not discriminate and people shouldn't either. Rather, He said, people need to focus on that which they share in common, their belief in the same God and what that means, rather than emphasizing their differences and zeroing in on the beliefs that divide them.

"That's just my take on what was said this evening," the reporter continued. "The man who calls Himself Jesus did indeed speak at length, covering many subjects. Following His closing prayer, the crowd gave Him a standing ovation. Still many left Hill, scratching their heads. This is Judy Norton reporting for *Channel 7 Action News.*"

The lead announcer thanked Judy and then went on to another story.

I looked over at Beth. Reading my mind she said, "You want to know my reaction, what I think?"

I nodded and she continued, "The major news, as the reporter on the scene said, is that the man has now acknowledged He is truly Jesus Christ. Does He now expect everyone to believe that He actually is? Does He expect His word alone is sufficient evidence for everyone to now have faith that He is? I still have reservations, I don't know about you. As far as what He was reported to have said, I don't find any fault with it. But I'm more concerned than ever over what He hasn't said, what He hasn't explained. For example, as Jesus is He still claiming the only way to the Father, God, is through Him, His son? Is there a heaven? Is there an after life? Is this second coming going to be accompanied by a Judgment Day?"

Seeing my startled expression, Beth smiled as she continued. "And I'm just scratching the surface with these questions, I'm just getting warmed up."

I laughed and told her she was probably not alone in raising those questions.

"You know what His message reminds me of, Beth? An experience of mine as a youngster on Mackinac Island. Our family went there for a week in the fifties."

Beth smiled and raised her eyebrows. "I know," I said, "a long time ago and about the same time you were being born. There was a group in existence headquartered on the island. It was called the M.R.A.; Moral ReArmament. I guess you'd call it more of a movement than a religious group per se. It's founder as I recall was a man named Frank Buchman. I believe he was a Lutheran minister, born in a little town in Pennsylvania. He believed the major religions in the world shared some common values, similar beliefs in how people should live their lives in a way that would be pleasing to God. He was concerned people weren't living their lives in this manner, that they'd lost or compromised their moral values. The result was conflicts and wars. He believed the only hope for peace in the world was for people to change. He fervently believed this was possible, that people could change and rearm themselves with moral values. If individuals could change, communities could change, nations could change, the world could change.

"His proposed solution was to have people live their lives governed by four absolutes: honesty, purity, love and unselfishness."

Beth was smiling and interrupted me. "For being up there for only a week and being just a youngster at the time, I'd say this man really made an impression on you. You're talking as if you're an expert on . . ." She hesitated before saying, "M.R.A."

"Moral ReArmament," I responded with a grin. "It actually wasn't being exposed for just a week. My father got caught up in M.R.A. for a couple of years. He had several of Buchman's books around the house and I believe he sent the group quite a bit of money. We never actually met the man. We did see movies of him speaking, though. The group staged first class musicals and plays at the Grand Hotel to dramatize Buchman's message as to how people could change and what this could mean for the world. They were usually followed by a film clip message from Mr. Buchman along with discussions.

"One of his quotes that I still remember was, 'There is enough in the world for everyone's need, but not enough for everyone's greed.' He was a very devout Christian who believed the four absolutes I mentioned were demonstrated in the life of Jesus Christ. And if we could follow Christ's example, we could indeed see His Kingdom On Earth become a reality."

Beth was nodding as she listened, "Does this M.R.A. still exist Mike? I'm surprised I never remember hearing or reading about the group."

"No, I believe the movement slowly faded away and ended a few years after Buchman's death. At its zenith though, the movement attracted major media attention, more overseas than in the U.S. Several countries awarded Buchman their Peace Prizes. Even though Buchman said and believed that people could still practice their own religious faiths while taking this major step to alter their lives, he had his critics and the movement generated a great amount of controversy. This saintly man was posing a threat to others. Though his was a philosophy of reconciliation which would lead to a more peaceful world, he was taking on the establishment—business leaders,

leaders, government leaders, and religious leaders—telling them they had to change. Frankly, I'm a little surprised that the ecumenical message this man now claiming to be Jesus has been preaching hasn't resulted in more controversy. Maybe it will start after those interviews tomorrow or after more people have had the opportunity to hear Him. Those thoughts of mine led me to remember Frank Buchman and M.R.A.

"Although M.R.A. isn't around any longer, one legacy of Buchman's survives in Alcoholics Anonymous. I believe the organization has a twelve-step plan to lead one to a life of sobriety. The program was derived from Buchman's teachings."

Beth was impressed, "I hadn't heard that before either. You've made it sound as if he was a very exceptional person. I'm surprised we don't hear more about him, especially with the state the world's in, much in need of reconciliation."

"Well, I'm just happy to have had an opportunity to tell you about the man," I told Beth. "You're usually the teacher with me on the learning end. Feels good for me to be on the lecturing end."

Beth laughed, "As if this was the first time! You know that's not true. You know a lot more about a whole lot of things than I do."

"Maybe that's because I have a few years up on you in experience," I answered with a chuckle.

Chapter XIX

Thursday morning's *Detroit Free Press* had a banner headline: "Ann Arbor Preacher Proclaims He's Jesus." The article gave a detailed recap of what had transpired since the man's appearance at the Ann Arbor Farmers Market a week ago Saturday. And indeed, much had. From the meeting with Ann Arbor's religious leaders at St. Francis of Assisi Church, to the huge crowd who'd come to hear Him at the U of M Stadium, to the State Street accident and to the standing room only crowd which had jammed Hill Auditorium last night to hear Him say that yes He was Jesus Christ. The article also mentioned His choice of followers and the numerous meetings He'd had with diverse groups during His brief time in Ann Arbor. The scars on the man's hands, feet and body were also referred to and their similarity to the scars one might expect to see on Christ. The recap concluded with the description of His miraculous recovery from the life threatening injuries He experienced in the accident.

The article's account of what "Jesus" had said in Hill Auditorium was very generalized, classifying His remarks as a very ecumenical message for all faiths.

The article concluded with details of the arrangements for the Thursday morning interviews the man had agreed to have with representatives of the six selected newspapers. Rather than holding a general news conference with the reporters, "Jesus" would be meeting separately with reporters from each of the papers. Sessions would be limited to fifty minutes each with no restrictions on the number of questions or subject matter. The *New York Times* would be the first to interview Jesus at 8:00am this morning. I glanced at my watch, this first interview was scheduled to begin in just a few minutes. The article stated that following a ten minute break, the second interview would begin and they'd continue in this fashion until all six were completed.

The *Free Press* said that in addition to its own reporters' article, the entire article from the *New York Times* would also appear in tomorrow morning's edition.

I explained this to Beth as I handed her the paper. "Wouldn't it be fun to sit in on some of those interviews?" I said. "Are they allowing spectators?" Beth replied.

I shook my head no. "Just the reporters," I answered. "They don't even state where those interviews will be taking place. No doubt for that reason, to keep eavesdroppers out. My guess is the Campus Inn. But they could be anywhere."

"Do you think maybe we should be flipping a coin to decide who's going to have the first look at tomorrow's paper?" Beth asked with a smirk.

"Probably a good idea," I answered. "But maybe better yet, why don't I give you the first go at the *Free Press* article while I'm reading the *New York Times* story. The *Free Press* indicated they'd be publishing that article, too."

"Fine with me," Beth replied. "Just as long as the two don't appear on the same page or printed back to back. If that happens, do you still want to give me first dibs?"

In hopes neither of these would be the case, I nodded and said, "Of course. I'm always out to please you. And besides, I want you to be the first to see if the *Free Press* used any of your suggestions."

Beth had gone into the *Free Press* and *Ann Arbor News* web sites to submit questions she believed should be asked of "Jesus" during the Thursday interviews. Both publications had invited this input. Though she and I were both hopeful many of her questions would be addressed this evening at Hill Auditorium, we were still curious to see if the reporters did pick up on her suggestions.

Chapter XX

Joy and Jerry and Beth and I were in our seats at Hill half an hour before the scheduled start of the program. The auditorium was already half filled. Our first indication tonight was not going to be a rehash of last night was seeing over a dozen chairs on the stage. My initial thought was that Jesus had invited the reporters who'd interviewed Him earlier in the day to join Him on stage and participate in some fashion. Then it dawned on me that the chairs were probably there for His followers. I counted fourteen. Except for Ernie Smith, these men and woman had been maintaining a low profile, definitely not in the spotlight with "Jesus". I shared my thoughts with Beth and the Hansons and they agreed that my assumption was probably correct. Joy commented we'd know for sure in a few minutes. And we did. At about 7:25pm a group of men and women filed in across the stage and seated themselves in the chairs. I recognized Ernie Smith and a couple others whose photos had appeared in the papers, identified as "Jesus'" followers.

A short time later, "Jesus" strode onto the stage. His followers stood and began to applaud Him, joined in a second or two by a very enthusiastic audience. He'd held up His arms, and with an engaging smile on His face invited everyone to take their seats. Once again, like in the Stadium, He seemed to be using no mechanism to project His voice. Yet I could hear Him clearly, and I expected that was probably true for every person in the audience, regardless of where they were seated.

He began by thanking everyone for coming. He thanked UMS and Ken Rector for making Hill Auditorium available and those who'd made contributions to the UMS Youth Education Fund. There was a warm smile on His face and a sparkle in His eyes as He continued, saying He believed everyone was probably aware that last night He had identified Himself as Jesus Christ. This remark was greeted with smiles and a few chuckles as you'd have to have been dead or sleeping not to have been aware. He went on to mention the series of interviews He'd had with representatives from several newspapers earlier in the day. He said He didn't want to steal their thunder this evening in repeating some of the questions He'd been asked and what His answers had been, that everyone would have an opportunity to read about them in tomorrow's newspapers. He mentioned that quite often the media tended to sensationalize and frequently provoke controversy in its reporting of the news. This statement was also greeted by a few smiles and chuckles. He cautioned the audience not to over react to a single quote or blurb, but to rather thoughtfully reflect on the full context of His answers.

He said He'd been asked if He had any plans to do something extraordinary this evening or sometime in the future to verify or prove He was truly Jesus Christ. He said that those who'd come this evening expecting to see a sign of some kind, doves flying from the ceiling or a miracle or two performed, would be disappointed. "Some of you", He said, "already believe in your hearts and minds that what I've said is true, that I am indeed Jesus. Others of you still have doubts, you're still waiting to be convinced. My hope is that my words and actions over the coming days will eventually lead you all to embrace my message, and not only those of you here this evening, but every man, woman, and child throughout the world. God's Kingdom on Earth can become a reality."

He was interrupted at that point by a shout from a man in the balcony. "How long do you plan to stay here on earth?"

Jesus smiled prior to answering the question. "For that answer my friend, you'll have to buy a newspaper tomorrow." The audience also responded to this answer with laughter and smiles.

"This evening," Jesus continued, "I want to introduce you to some of My followers." Smiling again, He'd said we could observe for ourselves they were a diverse lot. Men and women, young and old, all shapes and sizes, all colors. But all shared something in common. Each of them was attempting to emulate Him in word and deed. "They are a reflection of their love of God," He'd said.

"Everyone of them believes in the loving, caring God I've told you of who they can turn to in prayer. A God who will provide them with the confidence and courage to do His will. A compassionate God they can turn to for consolation in times of sadness and stress.

"Each of them loves God. They also love and respect themselves. And all of them also love and respect their fellow human beings without regard to sex, race, color, economic status, particular faith or sexual orientation. All of them have enthusiastically agreed to take time from their busy lives and travel the world over the next six months. They'll be delivering God's message, the message I've been preaching, throughout the globe. They'll soon be leaving Ann Arbor in pairs. Their task is to demonstrate God's love to all people.

"What is this message? Simply that we are all God's children. And that with God's guidance everyone can play a role in creating God's Kingdom here on Earth, a world filled with love, a world at peace. God's message is one of reconciliation, in our personal lives, in our communities, in our countries, in our world. A world where people of all races and faiths, joined together by their love of God, can live and work together in peace and harmony."

Jesus emphasized that change begins with individuals and that if they can change and truly reflect the love of God in their personal lives, then families can change, neighborhoods can change, cities and countries can change and the world can change. "Change is difficult," He said. "But God is also forgiving. The patient and kind God I've told you about can guide us if we open our hearts and minds and truly listen to Him."

He then explained that the lives of His fourteen followers had been changed by God. Over the next half an hour Jesus proceeded to individually introduce them to the audience, providing details and insights about each of them, often with a touch of humor.

The evening had concluded with a very moving prayer by "Jesus", a portion of which was asking God's blessing for these men and women, reinforcing them for the task they were undertaking. Following the prayer, Jesus asked the audience to give His followers a warm Ann Arbor send off with a rousing round of applause.

As people filed out of the auditorium, it was relatively quiet. Though friendly, people appeared to be in thoughtful reflection, still contemplating what they'd just heard and seen. Joy turned and asked Beth and me what our thoughts were, if the two of us were among those who firmly believed this man was Jesus Christ.

"I think we both want to be," Beth replied. "I can't speak for Mike, but I'm not quite there yet. I realize that in order to get your message through to people, you have to simplify it. But one of my thoughts is that He's oversimplifying, maybe being too idealistic. He came close to saying those followers of His are without sin. I always thought confession of sin and God's forgiveness of our sins were basic to our Christian religion. And I can't but help feeling sorry for those followers of His. His charge to them is so awesome. I worry that they're doomed for failure."

Joy appeared to be somewhat surprised by Beth's answer. I'm sure she hadn't anticipated such a lengthy one. Joy looked over at me, no doubt wondering if I was going to second Beth's thoughts. However, before I could speak, Jerry spoke up.

"Did the rest of you notice there was no mention of the existence of evil the entire evening? Though I guess I'm one of those who's never believed in the Devil per se, I realize there are evil people and evil thoughts and ideas at work in the world. We see and hear of evil acts being committed nearly every day. Shouldn't His message have included something about how to combat evil?"

"I think Beth and you are both getting into questions He may have addressed in those interviews this morning," I volunteered. "I'd suggest we all wait until after we've read the papers tomorrow before getting sidetracked. You've both raised good questions, let's hope the reporters asked them, too."

Though Beth was the most reluctant, all three seemed to agree that my suggestion was probably a good one. We switched the subject and engaged in small talk on the drive home. After dropping off the Hansons, however, Beth returned to the main subject.

"Mike, I couldn't help but think about what you told me about Frank Buchman and the M.R.A. as Jesus was speaking this evening. I didn't bring it up in front of Joy and Jerry, thinking you were probably a little tired and not anxious to get into the lengthy explanation which would have been necessary. But seriously, weren't you having some similar thoughts tonight?"

I smiled as I replied, "Yes, I definitely was. There's almost an eerie similarity in the beliefs and goals of M.R.A. and Jesus' message this evening. You said earlier you thought His message was maybe too idealistic. I had the same thought. But you also said you truly want to believe He's Jesus. I do too."

Chapter XXI

    Beth and I were both awake by 6:00am Friday. She started the coffee while I went out to check to see if the *Free Press* had been delivered yet. It was there. The interview with Jesus was the feature story. I smiled as I read in a box near the masthead that the *New York Times* interview with Jesus appeared on page 8. I wouldn't have to wait; we could both begin reading right away.

    After pulling out the section containing page 8, I handed the paper to Beth. She grinned, well aware of our previous agreement.

    Two reporters' names appeared in the byline for *The Times* story, Robert Shipman and David Goldberg. The article began with a description of the setting for the interview. The reporters stated that prior to the interview, the two had been uncertain what their reactions to the man who claimed to be "Jesus" would be. Following the interview, however, both were in total agreement. The next paragraph was full of superlatives. Jesus was characterized as having a brilliant mind, superb communication skills, and appealing charisma or aura. The article stated they'd been as impressed by His demeanor, sincerity, common sense reasoning and delightful sense of humor as they'd been by His thoughtful answers to their questions. The second paragraph concluded with the reporters expressing their hopes this article would do justice to the man and His answers and convey in some fashion the emotions they'd experienced during the interview. They described themselves as being held spellbound for nearly an hour, enjoying a few short parables in the process.

I was surprised by this preface to the article. The *New York Times* generally took great pride in just reporting the facts on its news pages and leaving opinions for their editorial pages. This was a departure from that practice. It certainly set a positive tone for readers.

The article took up nearly a full page. There appeared to be over twenty questions that had been asked. The questions were in bold print, followed by Jesus' answers.

The first question was actually two. "What prompted this visit? Does it mean Judgment Day is near at hand?"

Jesus had answered saying, "We agreed this unforetold return was necessary for there to be any hope for the world to be saved from destruction, any hope for establishing God's Kingdom here on Earth. And no this does not necessarily mean Judgment Day is near at hand. Only God knows that exact timing. I pray that this return will be successful in bringing peace and reconciliation to the world."

I paused and read His answer again. He'd referred to "We". Did "We" mean the Father, Son, and the Holy Spirit, the Christian belief in the Trinty —three in one? I wondered if the reporters would pursue that question.

The second question was an unexpected one for me. "One of the best selling books in recent years was Dan Brown's "The DaVinci Code." In this fictional work, allegations were made that You married Mary Magdalene and fathered a child with her. Is this true?"

Jesus had smiled, the article stated, before replying to the question. He said He was aware Dan Brown had written several best sellers and acknowledged him as a skilled writer with a very vivid imagination. No, He'd answered, this is not true. "Though it is true I was very fond of her and she of Me. We were soul mates. However, except for a few shared embraces and kisses, we were never physically intimate. I regret she didn't experience the joy and miracle of bringing a child into the world."

The next question was somewhat of a follow up one. "What would You say to those members of the Roman Catholic Church and other faiths who are currently urging changes which would allow married men to serve as priests?"

I cringed as I read this question. It was a very volatile one. Emotions ran deep on both sides of the issue. The question was a hot potato. Jesus had been preaching reconciliation. What answer could He give to avoid being divisive?

Jesus had answered by first saying He had boundless admiration for those men and women who had taken vows of celibacy and chastity in dedicating their lives to God. He expanded on this, praising them for their selfless commitment, marriage to the Church and desire to emulate the example He had set for them in leading a life of purity and love.

He had then proceeded to ask a series of questions. "Should the current shortage of priests necessitate a change in a dogma which had served the Catholic Church and other faiths well for many centuries? Is it in the best interests of a religious body to have practices and rules that do not permit many of its best and brightest to marry and have children, to pass on their genes to future generations? Do the distractions of having a family hinder a priest from fulfilling his commitment to devote his life to serving God, a total commitment of his talents and energy? Should those who are among the most ardent in seeking to love God and all God's children not teach and instruct their own children? Would the loving and compassionate God whom I have described demand all who would truly serve Him to not marry or have offspring? Would God not welcome and bless all who turn to Him without regard to their personal decisions in respect to marriage and children?"

The article stated Jesus had then said that while the ways people choose to worship and praise and serve God can greatly differ, God's love was always present. God's command is to love Him and convey that love to others through one's thoughts, words, and deeds.

I paused for a minute and then reread the questions. Had Jesus answered the reporters' questions with His questions? Was He in effect saying the Catholic Church could elect to keep its dogma if it so chose, but there were valid reasons to make a change? He had seemed to make it clear that God was not demanding there be a change, but that there were reasons to make a change.

I read on. The article stated Jesus had smiled and said though the question hadn't been asked, perhaps it was a good time for Him to comment on whether women should serve as priests in the Catholic Church. He began by saying there were many other religious groups as well with restrictions or limitations on female participation.

Once again, He asked a series of questions. "Should the traditions and practices which evolved in a male dominated society with women in a subservient position still be followed? Was I sending a message by including a number of women among My followers? Is it wise for a religious faith to exclude or place restrictions on participation for half its members, depriving it of their talents and skills in leadership roles?"

He'd concluded by saying while the U of M would probably never field a football team of half women, He believed a more prominent role for women would soon become a reality in almost all religious faiths. He'd added that many changes had already occurred or were in the process of being made and more were to come.

"You're pretty deep in thought over there," Beth said. "Are you learning anything? Any surprises?"

I looked up, smiling. "Are you through reading the Free Press article already? I'm barely halfway through this one. And yes, I think I'm getting more convinced by the minute Jesus is who He says He is. Give me another twenty minutes or so. But how about you, learn anything?"

"As a matter of fact, I have. Do you know what His two favorite hymns are?"

As I shook my head, Beth giggled and said, "He has a sense of humor. After answering He loved so many and it would be difficult to single out a favorite, He said his two top choices were probably 'Jesus Loves Me' and 'What a Friend We Have In Jesus'."

I laughed and asked if that was all she learned. With a more serious look on her face she replied, "He was asked if God had sent hurricane Katrina to punish New Orleans and Biloxi. He said no. His answer was similar to the one He'd given to those children prior to the accident on State Street. Remember? A girl was concerned about her grandparents in Florida?"

I nodded as Beth continued, "He said that evil exists in the world and that evil things happen that are not of God's making or choosing."

"Was he asked if there is a Devil?" I asked. "Not directly," she answered. "You'll be able to read his complete answer after you're done reading that *New York Times* article that seems to be taking you so long. I think the *Free Press* asked some good questions. One is about gay marriages. I think Jesus might be asking for trouble with His answer, even though I'm in one hundred percent agreement with it. He said God would rejoice in those unions and bless them as He does marriages between a man and a woman. I know some people are going to be saying that goes against Biblical Scripture, but He addresses that in His answer. He says to remember the Bible was written by men and that even though they may have been directed and guided by God, men sometimes err or seek to express their personal views. He also touched on the many translations there have been of the Bible and some of the discrepancies and contradictions one finds in the Scriptures."

"So, is He saying the 'Word of God' might not really be the actual word of God after all?" I asked. "That maybe there's a need to have fresh start, a new Bible?"

Beth laughed, "I don't think He's suggesting or recommending anything like that. But that is an interesting thought, maybe assembling the world's leading religious leaders and Biblical scholars and having them take that project on. You'd better get back to your reading Mike. I'm anxious to see how the two articles differ, how many of the same questions were asked."

"And whether His answers were the same," I replied with a grin.

The next question the *Times* reporters had asked was, "How can the account of the creation of the universe in the Book of Genesis be reconciled with Darwin's theory of evolution?"

Jesus had smiled and complimented the reporters on the timeliness of this question saying He was aware of the theory of Intelligent Design, which currently had its proponents. He'd said He was also aware of the latest scientific research on the origin of life, which appeared to reinforce Darwin's conclusions.

"The central question," Jesus was quoted as saying, "is whether the scientific explanation of the origin of life leaves room for or can include the actions of an unseen higher being, God? The theory of Intelligent Design seeks to answer this question by alleging that there are holes in Darwin's theory and that the complexity and diversity of life goes far beyond what evolution can explain and this clearly points to the hand of a higher being at work in the world. I think nearly everyone would agree that the Biblical account of creation in Genesis is a simplified somewhat poetic version of creation. And that Earth was not formed thousands of years ago, but billions of years ago. Accepting those premises, some have alleged that Adam was the first human being with whom God made spiritual contact. Some go so far as to allege that this world is but one of God's experiments, that many planets similar to earth exist in the universe."

Jesus had smiled again, the article stated, and said if He were to continue on as He was, reciting all the theories and arguments concerning this question, the reporters wouldn't have time to ask any additional questions. The article said He'd winked as He joked, saying perhaps that wasn't a bad idea.

Once again the article quoted Jesus. "In answering your question, I'll reiterate what I've been preaching since my arrival. There is a God. God is real, not a figment of men's imaginations as some suggest. Millions of people serve as witnesses to this fact, having felt His presence in their lives, having communicated with Him through prayer. God created man in His own image. The how and when are thought provoking questions, ones for which we may never know the answers. God works in mysterious ways. But I repeat again, God loves every man, woman and child on the face of this earth. Millions have experienced His love. We need but open our hearts and minds and listen to Him to establish His Kingdom here on Earth."

I glanced up and saw Beth was staring at me and I hurried and skimmed through some of the other questions and answers. However, two in particular drew a more focused attention from me. The first of these dealt with the difficulty of a rich man entering the Kingdom of Heaven, referencing the camel and the eye of a needle analogy. The intro ended with the question, "Are the doors of Heaven open to a Bill Gates?"

I chuckled, the reporters had been stymied. They'd chosen to say doors of Heaven rather than Gates of Heaven. I was also thinking most people would need no explanation as to who Bill Gates was. The founder of Microsoft had amassed a personal fortune. He was one the richest men in the world. Perhaps the richest. I was also aware of his charitable giving through the foundation he'd set up. He, by far and away, ranked number one in terms of dollars in sharing his wealth with others. Literally millions of people have benefited from his generosity.

Jesus' answer was brief, the shortest of any He'd given so far. He was quoted as having answered, "Yes, if he truly loves God and seeks God's guidance."

I was a little disappointed with His short answer, no mention of whether Bill Gates had to surrender all his wealth. However, maybe the parables in the Bible only meant that a rich person would find it extremely difficult to give up his or her worship of wealth and the perks that wealth provides. Extremely difficult to make their love of God the number one priority in their lives.

The second question that had drawn my attention was, "For your return to Earth, why did you happen to first come here to Ann Arbor?"

The article stated Jesus had chuckled, joking that A2 came at the top of the alphabetical list of places He'd considered. I smiled too. "A" squared was sort of an insider's lingo and I was pleased Jesus was aware of this abbreviation for Ann Arbor. I don't know if I was surprised or not as I read Jesus' answer. Many of the reasons he gave for having chosen Ann Arbor were the same as those Tom Cloverdale had suggested in his letter to the *Ann Arbor News*. The article stated the two reporters had even pitched in with an added reason, "close proximity to a major airport and even a train station in town from which He could quickly journey to other places." The article said Jesus had simply smiled and shaken His head. I wondered if the reporters had heard about how Jesus had appeared at various places in Ann Arbor, miles apart at virtually the same time. The article didn't indicate if they'd asked why He'd shaken his head.

"Finally done?" Beth asked as she handed me the *Free Press* article. "Before we discuss any further what we've read, I'm anxious to see what's kept you so entranced for so long."

I handed her the page I'd been reading, telling her, "I bet you'll get engrossed, too. If you hadn't been sitting there chomping at the bit, I'd have liked to have had even a few more minutes to digest it."

She laughed and asked me if I wanted a refill of coffee? I shook my head no and told her I thought I'd take a break and drive over and get a copy of *USA Today*.

Chapter XXII

Though the articles in all three papers were similar in content, tone and approach, the *USA Today*'s format gave it a more sensationalized flavor. Single sentences, attempting to summarize Jesus' answers, appeared in boxes in bold print to the right of the feature story. Although the sentences were fairly accurate, I thought they gave the impression He'd given simple answers to some fairly complex questions. I'd been impressed over how thoughtful His answers had been. I hoped the *USA Today* readers would take time to read His complete answers.

There'd been several questions asked by reporters of the *Free Press* and *USA Today* which hadn't been covered by the *Times* article. Jesus had been asked about capital punishment, cloning, alteration of genes and euthanasia. In all cases, I thought His answers were very reflective of the loving and caring God He described. Like a Monday morning quarterback, I'd been ready to second guess the reporters with a whole slew of questions they should have asked. But I'd been pleasantly surprised, their questions seemed to have fully covered all the foremost issues being debated today.

During breakfast Beth and I had a very lively discussion, voicing our respective opinions about Jesus' answers as reported in the three papers. We were mostly in agreement. However, Beth was more concerned than I was over the fallout she was foreseeing from His answers on the more controversial issues.

"He's going to be upsetting a whole bunch of people, faithful believers, God fearing people. He seems to me to be distancing Himself from the Biblical text that quotes Him, which says that the only way to the Father is through Him, His Son. You read his answer about other religions. He's saying they can have the same access to and acceptance from God as Christians."

"I realize that," I replied. "But He said from the start He returned to the world to reconcile people, bring peace and establish God's Kingdom here on Earth. I don't believe and I don't think you do either, that everyone in the world is going to enthusiastically embrace our Judeo-Christian beliefs and convert to Christianity. Our Bible is never going to be accepted by everyone, including the vast majority of Jews. And Jews are ostracized in the Mid-east, not viewed as God's chosen people. Uniting the world in peace and harmony is not going to be an easy task. But it has to start somewhere and Jesus is saying we can all unite under a common God."

"Now, you're starting to preach," Beth said.

"No, I don't mean to. I guess I'm just not as concerned about the reaction to some of His answers as you are. I understand and agree with what He's attempting to accomplish."

"And you're suggesting I don't," Beth replied. "I do. But don't you agree it would be wrong to scrap two thousand years of Christian beliefs and heritage, forget about the Bible?"

"He's not saying we have to do that, Beth. Denominations within the Christian faith, Jews, Muslims, Hindus, Buddhists, and others can all continue to worship God in their own way. He's just asking them all to accept, forgive, and love one another with guidance from their common God."

"I hear you, but I still think Jesus should be putting a meeting with the Pope at the top of His agenda. You're saying nothing has to change. But Heavens, Mike, a number of His answers were a direct challenge for the Roman Catholic Church to change."

"True, but He was careful not to say those changes had to occur right away. He seems to be sensitive to the fact some changes take time."

"That may be true in regard to allowing priests to be married and even having women serving as priests, but aren't you forgetting His answer about abortions?" Beth asked. "He sounds pro-choice to me, directly counter to Catholic Doctrine and the Right to Life supporters."

"I haven't forgotten," I replied. "But remember, He also made it very clear that a woman's decision to terminate her pregnancy should only be made after much soulful thought and seeking God's guidance. His answer to the question about divorce was very similar. He said God has blessed us with the freedom to make choices in our lives, hopefully decisions that will be pleasing to God. He doesn't believe legislators or religious groups should be attempting to define the facts which must be present for an abortion or a divorce to take place."

"Mike, understand me. I'm not questioning His answers. I agree with what He's said. My concern is His main message is very apt to be lost in the furor some of His answers are going to bring on. I wonder if He's truly aware of the likely storm of controversy He's launching. He says He wants to reconcile people and bring peace to the world. I think He's getting off to a very questionable start."

I smiled. I'd seldom seen Beth so intense, so emotionally fired up. My smile further infuriated her.

"Look at the two of us sitting here, Mike! Embroiled in a heated debate! And the two of us usually see eye to eye on about everything. Can't you picture what's going to happen between people who aren't in general agreement to begin with? I wish I had the same amount of confidence in Jesus that you apparently have. I really don't think He's aware of how His answers are going to incite people. His answer about gay marriages is going to delight one segment of the population, but it's an inflammatory issue for a major segment."

"I understand your point of view, Beth. I really do. And you're probably right. But if Jesus asked for your advice now, what would you tell Him? That He shouldn't have been so honest in His answers to the press? That He should have dodged their questions and asked them to turn to the Bible for answers? Or structured His answers in a way . . .?"

"I give up!" Beth exclaimed, standing and raising her arms. "You say you understand what I'm saying. I don't think you've actually heard a word of what I've been saying. I'm going to take a break. Maybe stroll over to the Hansons, see what their thoughts are. Maybe they'll hear me out."

She was out the door before I could stop her. I grimaced. From feeling so uplifted and inspired a few minutes ago, I was now in the doldrums. How and why had I been so insensitive to Beth, to her thoughts and feelings? She was right! If Jesus was prompting this confrontation between us, imagine some of the other heated arguments taking place at this moment.

I turned on the TV. The major story on every station seemed to be about Jesus and the articles in this morning's papers. If He wanted to gain the spotlight, He'd succeeded. But now that He had the attention of the nation, would people calm down long enough to hear His central message. One station was reporting on Jesus' followers. Except for two who'd stayed with Him in Ann Arbor, Ernie Smith and a young single woman, Ginny Roberts, the others had scattered to various countries. They were reported to be attracting large crowds. The accompanying pictures bore this out.

I clicked off the TV; it was time to take a shower and hopefully clear my head.

Chapter XXIII

Beth was gone for over two hours. I was on the phone when she returned. I'd called Tom Cloverdale. He and Kristi were apparently out and I was leaving a voice mail message, saying that Jesus had apparently read Tom's letter in the *Ann Arbor News*. I told him Jesus' answer to the question of why He'd come to Ann Arbor in this morning's *Free Press* was nearly verbatim to his letter.

Beth had a smirk on her face. I smiled back and quickly walked over to her and grabbed her in my arms in a bear hug. We embraced for several minutes, saying nothing, before sharing some long kisses. As we stepped back from one another we both began to apologize. We kept interrupting each other and finally ended up holding hands and laughing.

I didn't ask her about the Hanson's and she didn't volunteer any details of her visit with them. Neither of us mentioned our earlier discussion. We both chose to ignore it, pretend it never happened. We discussed other subjects including our plans for the evening, the Strattons had invited the two of us and three or four other couples to their house for dinner.

Beth was immersed in household chores for the next few hours and I did some yard work and straightened up the garage. Shortly after 3:00pm I saw the *Ann Arbor News* being delivered.

The News featured its interview with Jesus on its front page. Most of the questions asked by the *News* reporters were similar to ones in the other articles Beth and I had read earlier. However, there were some new subjects covered. One question asked, "The Catholic

Church frowns on its members participation in Crop Walks because a portion of the proceeds are used to furnish condoms to control the spread of AIDS in Africa. Do you agree with its stance?"

Jesus had prefaced His answer by saying He was fearful several of His answers to questions He'd been asked this morning might be highlighted and construed to create the impression He was opposed to much of the Catholic Church doctrine. This, He said, was far from true. He praised the Catholic Church in glowing terms for keeping its members focused on God. On the specific question, He said He was aware in many instances of the Catholic Church encouraging participation in Crop Walks, while directing its members to ask that funds raised through their participation be allocated to groups involved solely in providing food to those most in need. As far as the more controversial question as to whether condom use should be encouraged, He'd said in instances where man's increased knowledge, made possible through God, could be applied to eliminate suffering in the world or enhance people's health and well being, God would want this knowledge used.

Then, the article stated, Jesus had boldly taken the question a step further by asking, "Does God believe in birth control?" Once again, as He had in other answers, Jesus said, "God has endowed men and women with the ability to make choices in their lives, choices that will hopefully be pleasing to Him. A woman's right to plan her family, plan her pregnancies, is among those choices."

Wow, I thought. Jesus certainly wasn't hesitating about stepping into the middle of a very controversial issue. As Beth had questioned this morning, was Jesus fully aware of what He might be getting into, what the consequences of some of His answers might be?

A question a little later in the article asked, "Here in the U.S. we believe in the separation of church and state. How do you view the actions of those who seek to remove all references to God in our public life? Those attempting to have the reference to God removed from our pledge of allegiance, our currency, in schools, at athletic events and other public forums including governmental bodies?"

Jesus had begun His answer, the article stated, by saying not just in the U.S., but throughout the world, all people worshiped one God, the same God. The God given ability, which allows people to make choices in their lives, included a choice not to believe in Him. However, He said, that should not empower non-believers to restrict the right of others in their private and public worship of God, in their seeking of God's guidance in prayer. God would be offended and angered by the acts of some atheists to remove all public references to Him. He emphasized, however, that God didn't stop loving those non-believers.

The final question in the article asked Jesus if He thought His return might meet with the same results He'd encountered during His initial visit to Earth? Did He have fears about being physically harmed or killed?

Jesus had responded saying He was aware His answers to some of the questions He'd been asked would upset and anger some people. He'd also said He realized some would view Him as one of the false prophets the Bible had warned of who would appear before His second coming and the end of the age. But no, He had no fears of being harmed or killed. He said He was confident God was present to protect Him. He said He hoped His message of peace and reconciliation would be heard, understood and embraced by all. And yes, He was fearful controversy over some subjects might prevent this from happening. He repeated, there was but one God; a loving, compassionate and forgiving God, who would guide and protect Him. A God who was anxious to see His kingdom on Earth become a reality.

Next to the feature article, there was also a short one reminding readers Jesus would be appearing on "60 Minutes" Sunday evening. Some were predicting the number of viewers might break all time television records. Beth and I already had planned to be home and be among those tuning in.

Beth came downstairs just as I was finishing up with the *News*. I told her a little about what I'd been reading as I handed her the newspaper.

"So you think He may have addressed some of my concerns?" she asked.

"Just maybe," I replied with a smile. "At least I don't think there's anything He's reported as having said that's going to get us in a heated discussion again. I hope not."

"Me too," Beth answered. "But stick around, I may have some questions." Beth plopped down in her favorite easy chair and began to read.

Chapter XXIV

Beth and I arrived at the Strattons shortly after 6:30pm. We were surprised to see so many cars parked in the street. We'd been led to believe this was going to be a small dinner party with only two or three other couples being invited.

In response to Beth's question, Mary winked and explained we'd soon be learning why they invited so many to come this evening. She said Rob was out on the porch bartending and pointed us in that direction. The Strattons and ourselves had many friends in common, a number of whom were already present. We greeted several as we were making our way out to the porch.

Rob greeted us warmly. I asked him if he wanted some help with his bartending chores. After checking on his supply of ice, he said it would be great if I could spell him for a few minutes while he went out to the garage for another bag of ice and some more tonic.

I poured a glass of wine for Beth and then proceeded to fill drink orders for several others. More guests were continuing to arrive. Rob returned just as I was beginning to take a breather and make a drink for myself. He thanked me for filling in and glanced at his watch.

"If you're game, I'm going to ask you to pitch in a few minutes longer, Mike. Mary and I are going to be making a special announcement at 7:00pm on the dot. It won't take over five minutes."

"No problem," I replied. "I'm doing fine. I've been able to find everything I've needed thus far. What's up? Are you going to be announcing you'll be running for City Council after all?"

Rob was often very critical of some of the things the Ann Arbor City Council did. My retort was always the same, saying he should run for a seat. He'd say no and tell me I should be the one to get involved now that I was retired and had the time. Rob had grinned following my question and shaken his head no. "Keep your drink handy though, we'll be having a toast."

A few minutes later Rob and Mary announced their daughter, Whitney, was engaged. They introduced Whitney and her fiance, Lance Parish.

"You all probably want to know a little more about this young man who thinks he's worthy of our daughter," Rob said with a twinkle in his eye. "Lance is an Ivy Leaguer, a graduate of Princeton. He's here at Michigan working on his MBA. Don't hold it against him, but he was born and raised in Columbus, Ohio."

The crowd laughed and one of the attendees yelled, "Go Bucks!" Everyone there was well aware that Columbus was the home of the Ohio State Buckeyes, one of U of M's major football rivals.

"He's already assured me, though, he's a true blue Michigan fan," Rob said. "Right Lance?"

The tall and handsome young man standing next to Whitney grinned and then yelled, "Go Blue!" to the delight of everyone. Rob proposed a toast to the newly engaged couple. Following the toast, a woman in the crowd called out, "How long have you known him Whitney? How did you meet?"

Smiling, Whitney replied they'd met on a blind date. "Exactly eight weeks ago today." She could see people were somewhat stunned to learn of this short courtship and quickly added, "We both seemed to immediately know we were meant for one another. Then Jesus came to town and we thought the world might soon be coming to an end. So we decided to move quickly."

People were nodding their heads and smiling as Whitney grabbed Lance's hand as she was speaking. As they stared into one another's eyes, it did indeed look as if they were meant for one another.

"Have you set a wedding date?" another woman asked.

"We're working on it," Lance answered. "Sooner rather than later, we hope."

"Have you thought about asking Jesus to perform the ceremony?" another person asked.

The crowd was buzzing in conversation, discussing just how special it would be. I heard the woman next to me say, "They'd have to move quickly; there's no telling how long He's going to be here in Ann Arbor." The man next to her, maybe her husband, remarked, "I'm actually surprised He's still here."

Whitney was holding up her hands to silence the crowd.

"Believe it or not, we have thought about asking Him. When I mentioned the idea to Mom, she nearly fainted. For some reason she thought having the wedding next week might be a bit much."

It was a joyous occasion. Guests lined up to personally speak to and congratulate Whitney and Lance. It was over half an hour later before Beth and I had an opportunity to chat with them. Beth asked Lance if his parents were here. I sensed what Beth was doing. We both realized if they'd been present, they'd have been introduced during the announcement of the engagement. Beth's question was a polite way of asking why his parents and siblings, if he had any, weren't present. He answered that his mother was seriously ill, hospitalized in Columbus. His father and younger sister were at her bedside and he'd be driving back to Columbus tonight to be with her. We both told him we were sorry to hear that and said we'd include her in our prayers.

Whitney told me her mother had mentioned I'd been at the Farmers Market the morning Jesus had first appeared in Ann Arbor. She asked if we'd been following Jesus in the news and had an opportunity to hear Him yet. We explained we'd seen and heard him at the Big House and at Hill. Beth told them I'd spent nearly the entire day reading and re-reading the articles about Him in today's papers. After a short conversation about our reactions to Him and His answers to the many questions He'd been asked, Whitney lowered her voice and asked, "Want to hear the latest rumors about Him that we're hearing on Campus?"

Beth and I both smiled as we nodded, leaning closer to hear.

"Well," she whispered, "the rumors are that He's currently in Salt Lake City at the Mormon Tabernacle. He's supposed to be meeting the Pope at the Vatican tomorrow. And on Sunday He'll be in the Mid-east for at least three stops."

I glanced over at Beth. If the rumors were true, it appeared Jesus was acting on the suggestion Beth had made this morning. Immediately meeting with the Pope and other religious leaders, personally delivering His message and perhaps calming the waters.

"There's another rumor afloat too," Whitney continued in even a lower voice. "Ginny Roberts is in U of M's hospital." Seeing the blank stares on our faces, she explained: "She's one of Jesus' followers. She stayed here in Ann Arbor along with Ernie Smith, the former homeless man who's become the leading spokesperson for Jesus."

Beth and I both nodded. We both knew about Ernie, we just hadn't remembered Ginny Roberts as the name of the young woman who'd also remained behind in Ann Arbor as Jesus' other followers journeyed abroad.

"Rumor has it a group of people confronted Ginny and attempted to get her to confess that Jesus was having an affair with her, sleeping with her. She was being roughed up as Ernie Smith appeared on the scene. He saved her from being injured more seriously and took her to emergency at U of M's hospital."

Beth and I were both wide-eyed. Just a rumor we knew, but maybe true. Beth asked if they'd caught or been able to identify the ones who'd assaulted her.

"I haven't heard, I don't think so. I heard Ernie's injuries weren't serious, though. Just some minor cuts and bruises."

Several people were standing behind us, waiting to greet and congratulate Whitney and Lance. We thanked Whitney for sharing the rumors with us and once again expressed our best wishes and congratulations.

Chapter XXV

During the drive home Beth and I discussed the rumors Whitney had told us about.

"I hope she's right about what Jesus is doing," I said. "But I also hope the one about Ginny Roberts is false. But as you suggested, Beth, some of Jesus' statements were likely to offend a great many people. It wouldn't surprise me if some were motivated to attempt to discredit Him. But if the other rumors are true about His going to visit various religious leaders including the Pope, you have to be pleased. It's what you were hoping for. Going to Salt Lake City would be a great start."

"I agree, Mike. I've read that the Church of Latter Day Saints is one of the world's fastest growing religious sects. For all their success, we really don't hear that much about the Mormons.

"I think Jesus is playing it smart in visiting them first. It'll be good preparation before visiting the Pope. The Mormons also have limited roles for women in the Church."

"Remember the article I was reading in the airline magazine and showed you on our last trip?" I asked. "The one describing the new conference center the Mormons have built in Salt Lake City? How impressed we were, a huge facility with beautiful landscaping of its roof? I know we said at the time we should plan a visit to see it sometime."

"I remember," Beth replied. "That could well be where Jesus is meeting with the Church Elders today, providing the rumor

Whitney heard is true, of course. I wonder if His visit will attract media coverage. It should. But this is the first we've heard about it. Maybe He's hoping to keep a low profile and keep everything hush hush until He's talked to a number of religious leaders. That way he could possibly avoid controversy over why He chose to visit some before others."

"I think you might be right, Beth. There are enough controversial subjects for Him to address without adding to them."

"It was fun being included at the Strattons this evening," Beth said, changing topics. "Lance seemed very nice and Whitney was just glowing, Rob and Mary were bursting with joy, a happy occasion for everyone."

"Too bad Lance's parents and sister couldn't be there," I said. "I wonder how serious his mother is, whether it's a life threatening illness?"

"You must have been talking to Rob when I asked Mary that question," Beth replied. "She didn't go into all the details, merely saying Lance's mother was still undergoing tests, but the prognosis was not at all good. She said they already thought there might be a need to advance the wedding date. They were originally thinking next spring."

"Maybe an earlier date would give them an opportunity to have Jesus involved," I commented. "I wouldn't be at all surprised if Whitney tries to arrange it. Talk about a memorable wedding, that would be it!"

"You haven't forgotten we're playing golf with the Pollards tomorrow afternoon have you?" Beth asked.

"No, and staying on at the club for dinner. The weather is supposed to be beautiful, should be fun."

Chapter XXVI

As I was going out to the curb the following morning to get our newspapers, I noticed Joy across the way retrieving theirs. We waved at one another and I called out and asked her to wait up. I walked over toward her as she came to meet me. I told her first about Whitney Stratton's engagement. Though she and Jerry didn't know Whitney well, Joy seemed pleased to hear about some of the details of the party and the young man she'd chosen to marry.

I then explained that Whitney had told Beth and me about a couple rumors which were circulating around campus. Holding up the newspaper, I said maybe there'd be something in this morning's papers to verify them. I then proceeded to tell her about our conversation with Whitney. As I knew she would be, Joy was delighted to be informed. She asked if Beth and I were planning to watch "60 Minutes" tomorrow evening. I quickly answered we definitely were.

"I was going to call you," Joy said. "Would the two of you like to come over to our place for a light supper and to watch it?"

I told her that sounded fine to me. I said I'd check with Beth to make sure we didn't have a conflict, but I was fairly certain we didn't. Joy suggested we come over around 6:00pm and that she'd plan on seeing us then unless she heard otherwise from us.

I glanced at the *Free Press* front-page stories as I headed back to the house. I didn't see any that related to rumors we'd heard from

Whitney. With a cup of coffee a little later, I thoroughly read both papers, still finding no mention of the two subjects.

The *Ann Arbor News* had a full-page story, however, about Jesus. The title was, "A Busy Two Weeks." Accompanying the article was a listing of the many groups, organizations and places Jesus had visited since his arrival in Ann Arbor. There had to be over a hundred. I was aware of many of them from previous articles or hearing about the visits, but nevertheless the listing was very impressive.

The article stated that Jesus had experienced a warm reception on nearly ever occasion. Sandy White, President of Washtenaw United Way, was quoted as having said. "We think His visits and message resulted in a first for United Way. Three agencies over the past two weeks have returned a portion of the funds we had allocated to them. It wasn't because they couldn't put the dollars to good use. Rather, all three believed they were at fault in not using the money for the purposes they'd promised United Way they would. And that's not all that's happened. One of the services United Way provides for the community is to act as a sort of clearing house to match individuals interested in volunteering their services with agencies who can best use them. In a normal week we might have half a dozen inquiries. A week ago that number jumped by over tenfold to over sixty. This past week we've had over one hundred and fifty people contact us. It's been sort of a minor miracle. Virtually overnight getting over fifty thousand dollars to fund requests we previously couldn't fund and having over two hundred more people volunteering to help others in Washtenaw County."

The joint project of Catholic Social Services and Planned Parenthood was also referenced in the article along with several other examples of different agencies making plans to work more closely with one another for better and more efficient results.

There were several articles in the *Ann Arbor News* about next week's Annual Ann Arbor Art Fair, suggesting it was going to be the best ever. In recent years I'd made it something to avoid, but Beth relished it, always attending at least once.

As Beth and I were finishing lunch and preparing to head out to the golf course, we had a phone call from Joy. Beth spoke to her for nearly twenty minutes. I finally started pointing to my watch to indicate to Beth we should be thinking of leaving.

During our drive to Barton Hills, Beth related to me the details of her conversation with Joy. Joy had made a few phone calls after I'd told her the rumor about Ginny Roberts being assaulted, probably to the same sources from whom she'd garnered information about Jesus after the accident on State Street. Ginny was at U of M's hospital and yes, she'd been the victim of a vicious attack. Some men and at least one woman had confronted her in the parking structure not far from the Bell Tower Hotel. She and Ernie Smith and Jesus had been staying there.

"They had a video camera," Beth continued. "They were attempting to get Ginny to admit to having an affair with Jesus and film her confession. She'd told them that it wasn't true. She tried to get away from them. One of the men slammed his fist into her abdomen and another shoved her down. She was kicked a few times as she struggled to get up. The woman in the group had a container of acid of some sort and threatened to . . .Watch out!" Beth yelled.

I'd been so absorbed in what Beth was saying, I hadn't noticed the car pulling out in front of me. I slammed on the brakes and swerved, barely avoiding a collision. After we'd composed ourselves and said a prayer of thanks for not having gotten into what could have been a serious accident, I asked Beth to continue.

"Ginny had screamed for help and in the resulting commotion some of the acid splashed on her face. Fortunately she'd been able to shield her face a little with her arm. Ernie Smith had heard her screams and come to her rescue. Another person who'd heard her screams had dialed 911. However, her assailants had quickly fled, minutes before the police arrived on the scene. Ernie had been more concerned about aiding Ginny than pursuing them. The police immediately took her to emergency at U of M's hospital. She had acid burns on her arm as well as her face."

"Do they have any idea who was involved?" I asked. "Can she or Ernie identify them?"

"Joy didn't know. She did say that it initially appeared Ginny was going to be scarred for life. Did I mention she'd had her arm broken too? They twisted it as they tried to force her to confess to her sin."

"The rumor Whitney heard was really accurate then," I said. "I sure hope they catch the ones responsible. What a tragedy! I'm surprised there wasn't any news about it on this morning's papers."

"Joy did mention the hospital had been keeping a tight lid on the incident, afraid of a media frenzy if news was to get out. Its first priority is to treat Ginny's injuries. I'm sure that the details will eventually leak out. But I haven't mentioned yet one of the most startling things that happened. Jesus had appeared at the hospital around 11:00pm last night. He came to see Ginny Roberts and He spent considerable time with her. The buzz around the hospital this morning was about the miracle that took place. All signs of the acid burns on her face and arm have vanished. She won't be disfigured after all. Her arm was set and is in a cast and she'll be in the hospital for a day or two, but her most serious injuries have been healed."

"That's wonderful!" I exclaimed. "In addition to seeing her at Hill Auditorium that night, I've just seen one photo of her, a group shot at that. But I do remember thinking what a beautiful young lady she was. And I'd say this is another verification He's who we were already fairly certain He was, at least I was."

Beth smiled, "Me too. While I still have a few questions and concerns, I think we're witnessing a world-altering happening. I prayed for Jesus last night. I hope this incident doesn't force Him to postpone His meetings in Rome and the Mid-east."

Chapter XXVII

While waiting to tee off, Beth and I brought up the subject of Jesus with the Pollards. After Chip had dribbled his opening drive, Ruth lectured us about religion and golf not being a good mix and ask that we not spoil our round with talk about this man who claims to be Jesus. She added that in her opinion, He was getting too much attention and publicity anyway.

"Why you can't turn on the TV or radio without hearing about Him," Ruth said. "And the newspapers! I think this is getting overblown. What do you think?"

Beth replied for both of us, "Mike and I would argue that point. But that's one of the blessings we have in this country, isn't it? We can strongly disagree with one another and still be friends. We believe He's who He says He is and are privileged to have seen and heard Him in the flesh."

That was the last reference to Jesus during our day and evening with the Pollards. Although I can't say I wasn't sorely tempted to try to persuade Ruth to change her views. I had the feeling I was betraying Jesus by saying nothing. Still I'd kept my mouth shut and Beth did as well.

The weather had been ideal for golf. Beth ended up shooting a ninety-four, two strokes better than her previous low round of the season. I ended up with an eighty-eight. Anytime I'm able to break ninety is a successful day for me. The Pollards both struggled. Chip, who supposedly has a sixteen handicap barely managed to break a hundred. And Ruth picked up her ball on several holes. We did have an enjoyable time with the Pollards, however. Our conversation was mostly limited, however, to U of M's building plans, our respective grandchildren, and the Art Fair.

Sunday's *Ann Arbor News* had a brief article about Ginny Roberts. Describing her as one of Jesus' followers, the article stated she'd been mugged in the parking structure near the Bell Tower Hotel where she'd been staying and that her injuries resulted in her being admitted to the U of M hospital. There was no mention about what may have prompted the attack. The impression being given was that it was possibly an attempted purse snatching. The article stated the police were still trying to piece together the details of what had occurred and the identity of her assailants was unknown. The article did mention Jesus had visited her at the hospital and that it was thought He'd returned from an out of town visit to do so. The final sentence was a zinger, which I thought was totally uncalled for. "There has been speculation about the close relationship of Jesus with Ginny Roberts."

Although nothing was directly said about the rumor of an affair by Jesus with the young woman, the implication was clear. I was shaking my head. The article had completely failed to communicate the viciousness of the assault, the horrible nature of the criminal act. The perpetrators might even find some justification for their action in the tone of the article. I hoped that maybe one of the *News* enterprising reporters would delve into this story so everyone would know the true facts.

My disgust with the *Ann Arbor News* quickly turned to admiration, however, as I read the feature editorial. The thrust of the editorial was an admission by the *News* that its staff was surprised and somewhat baffled by the fact Jesus' answers to the many questions He'd been asked in the Thursday interviews hadn't sparked more controversy. After more reflection, however, the editorial said the *News* believed this was because people in general, were ready to change some of their long held attitudes and beliefs and Jesus was now giving them a reason to do so.

"His answers in many instances are a breath of fresh air," the editorial continued. "It is human nature to hold on to one's basic beliefs, whether they be religious or political. Jesus' appearance on the scene is prompting all of us to re-examine some of these, to determine whether the loving, caring God He's described would mandate that we hold fast to practices and beliefs which in many instances are in conflict with logic and common sense."

As I continued reading and finally reached the final sentence, I couldn't help but feel the *News* might be jumping out ahead of many of its readers by so boldly endorsing Jesus. The final sentence said, "The *Ann Arbor News* wishes to go on the record in saying we enthusiastically welcome Jesus to Ann Arbor, we embrace the thoughts He's communicating and we hope we can play a role in getting His message out to the rest of the world."

I told Beth about the *News* editorial, telling her she should definitely read it. "I think you'll be a little surprised. It's a pretty daring move, I'm sure they'll be plenty of criticism and a few repercussions."

Beth smiled, "As much as when the *News* endorsed Bush for President in 2004? Remember all the letters to the editor that provoked? Here in the liberal capital of the Mid-west, knowing Ann

Arbor voters were likely to support Kerry by as much as a three to one margin. That took guts!"

Chapter XVIII

Shortly after 6:00pm Beth and I headed over to Joy's and Jerry's. They had always been marvelous hosts. Their version of a light supper was quite a spread. I think the buffet Joy had prepared had enough food to feed a dozen people and there was just going to be the four of us. As Jerry fixed us drinks, Joy asked us if we'd read the article about Ginny Roberts in this morning's *News*. Joy was still worked up about it, particularly furious over the last sentence. Her reaction was much the same as ours had been.

"If the *News* doesn't come up with the full story in the next couple of days, I'm going to write a letter spelling out all the details," Joy said. "Since I spoke with you I've also heard Ernie Smith had injuries. Not serious enough for him to be hospitalized, but major none the less."

"Do any of you think the *News* might have been asked to play down the story?" Beth asked.

Joy thought for a moment before replying, "I probably could be convinced into believing that if the article hadn't ended the way it did, implying Ginny Roberts was having an affair with Jesus."

"I think I'd answer you the same way," Jerry said.

"Did the two of you happen to read the *News'* editorial about Jesus?" Beth asked.

Joy's frown turned to smile as she quickly replied, "Yes! Now that was right on! But why slam Jesus in the one article when they're making such a glowing endorsement on the editorial page. How do you figure?"

I grinned, "You've heard the expression, the left hand didn't know what the right hand was doing, haven't you? That's what probably happened here. Beth and I were as surprised and delighted about the editorial as we were disappointed and angry about the article. I just hope people will take the time to read it. I have to admit I frequently never get as far as the editorial page, especially on Sunday."

There was a play-off in the golf tournament and "60 Minutes" was delayed by about twenty minutes. *CBS* had been hyping its interview with Jesus for the past two days with enticing teasers, touting some of the more controversial questions Jesus had been asked. The interview was shown in the final half hour of the program. The opening story was about New Orleans, analyzing what had gone right and what had gone wrong since the devastating hurricane Katrina disaster. The second story was a report on the test results for a new drug not yet on the market. Initial tests were showing it reversed Diabetes. Jerry made a note of the name of the pharmaceutical company involved, joking that he might want to phone his stock broker first thing Monday morning to buy some shares. Joy cautioned him, suggesting he'd never had much luck in the past trying to get into the market ahead of everyone. To the two of us she added, "The big boys seem to have an edge, Jerry's usually buying in at the high price."

Jerry smiled, "Wait a minute, Joy. We've had a few successes. Remember RIM with its Blackberry? We more than tripled our investment. And how about . . ."

Joy laughed, "I'm not saying you haven't had some winners. I'm just suggesting it's a short list. I'm just expecting you to bat a thousand." Winking at Beth and me she added, "He's perfect in everything else he does."

The "60 Minutes" interview with Jesus didn't' disappoint, it was a fascinating half hour. I'd thought some of the question the newspaper reporters had asked were toughies, but many of the ones now asked of Jesus were potential bombshells.

Following the initial chat, which allowed Jesus to articulate and clarify his basic message, Jesus was asked about stem cell research. He'd answered in a very deliberate way, saying God shared the excitement and optimism that man's increasing knowledge in this field would soon result in miracles, relieving pain and suffering and improving the quality of life. "I foresee," He said, "a day when full recovery from crippling and paralyzing injuries becomes possible with the discoveries this research results in. I also believe man's ingenuity will allow this research to proceed ahead without a need to destroy life in the process. This is the controversy, the area in which good, dedicated and God guided men and women disagree. I believe if both sides work diligently and honestly with one another, many ways will be found to reconcile their differences, solutions which can be embraced by all, answers which will be pleasing to God."

The next question was an equally challenging one, "Should gays or lesbians be ordained as priests, pastors, or rabbis?"

Jesus began his answer emphasizing there was but one God for all people regardless of their nationality, race, religion, or sexual orientation. He then asked a series of questions. "Does this mean God would say each and everyone should be allowed to serve in a religious leadership position? If the answer is no and I say it is, whom would He exclude? A known child molester? A mentally deranged person? A drug addict?"

"Yes," Jesus continued, "there are many cases where common sense dictates a person should not serve in a religious leadership role and God would agree. Any case where the individual would present a danger to those he or she was ministering to. Should the ban apply to women? In previous answers, I've said no as would God. Now to your specific question, should the ban apply to gays and lesbians? There have been many studies which have shown that they present no greater risk to others, including children, than heterosexuals. The evidence is overwhelming. Why then should they be excluded? Because of certain passages in the Bible, written when homosexuality was viewed as a life style choice rather than a matter of genes. I've often answered questions by saying God has blessed men and women with the ability to make choices in their lives. People should have the right to choose who they desire as their religious or political leaders. But they should do so knowing God wants us to love another, to accept one another and to include one another. God would not include gays and lesbians on his exclusion list."

The four of us exchanged glances. I believe we all sensed Jesus' answer was not going to go down well with many and be accepted at all. He'd made it very clear, a definite right and wrong question. It would be wrong to exclude gays and lesbians. I could sense the interviewer was somewhat surprised by Jesus' answer. Possibly, he might even be second-guessing himself. Asking himself if he was perhaps even crucifying Jesus with his choice of questions.

One of the next questions was whether man should intervene prior to the birth of a child to alter or change genes that govern the development of certain physical traits. It certainly didn't appear the interviewer was easing up on his questions. This was another timely issue, only recently had man acquired the knowledge to make this possible. It was a controversial subject. One side believed a child was God's creation and man should not tinker in this area. It feared it might lead to cloning or the creation of a master race. The other side believed if man was able to determine in advance if a child might be born with a major physical impairment and had the means to alter this result, it was the humane and just thing to do. To save a child from a life that in all likelihood would be filled with agonizing pain and suffering warranted the intervention.

    Jesus had begun His answer in acknowledging there were many devout individuals and groups sincere in their belief man should not intervene in the creations of God. "Their strong beliefs in some instances apply to genetically altered foods and animals in addition to human beings. But God has given men and women the ability to increase their knowledge, to discover cures and procedures that will benefit all mankind. The polio vaccine is but one example."

    Jesus then briefly touched on the huge advances that had been made in genetic research in recent years. He then asked several questions, an approach He often used in answering questions put to Him. "If God has allowed man with His guidance to be able to discover which genes contribute to severe birth defects, would God not want that knowledge used to alter the genes so that these results could be avoided? Does God want a child to come into His world with missing appendages, eyes which can't see, ears which can't hear, a voice which can't speak, or a disease such as cystic fibrosis, when the means to prevent this from occurring exists? Does God want to place parents and siblings in the often traumatic position of caring for a child with severe birth defects when there are ways to avoid it?"

Jesus then said, "Some believe for everything that happens in the world, God has a reason. That hurricanes, tornadoes, earthquakes, droughts, and floods are of God's making. I would say to them, that that is not true. Things happen in His world that God does not want to happen. Though, it is true that adversity, the pain and suffering of some often brings out the best in others. And though it's also true God can and does punish sinners, the loving and forgiving God I describe is not a vengeful God. Bad and sad things happen, big and small. A young child drowns in a swimming pool, a child is hit by a car while chasing a ball into the street, children playing with matches start a fire injuring or killing themselves and scores of others. God does not orchestrate these events, but the compassionate God I describe is there to comfort and console all His children in times of sorrow.

"I can tell by the expression on your face," Jesus told the interviewer, "that you think I'm digressing, taking too much time to answer your question. But what I'm saying is that the question is not whether man should use his knowledge to alter genes, but when and in what instances. If man can use his knowledge to genetically alter food to alleviate famine, should he not do so? If man can prevent a child coming into the world with severe birth defects or a crippling disease, should he not do so?

"However, should man intervene to prevent the birth of left handed children? To alter the sex of a baby? To alter the color of hair or eyes? To prevent the birth of a mongoloid child or a midget? As I've so frequently said, God has given man the ability to make choices. But this God given capability should not be exercised with impunity; people should turn to Him for guidance. People should act responsibly to protect their children from the type of tragedies I mentioned earlier. People should act responsibly in making choices. Does God want man to discover the means to better control weather? Man can use this knowledge for good or evil. Do I believe that terrorists have already discovered the means of managing weather and are responsible for the recent rash of major natural disasters in the world? No, but I repeat, man should use its knowledge in ways that are pleasing to God."

Jesus concluded His answer saying there were many questions and challenges ahead as men and women decided how best to apply their increasing knowledge of genetics. He said God believed people could come together in a spirit of love and mutual understanding to reconcile their differences over these difficult choices "God has created a diverse world, it is one of its joys and beauties. In bringing about God's Kingdom here on Earth, man would be wrong to try to change this diversity."

Jerry quipped, "Guess that means he's opposed to cloning." Joy smiled, as she put a finger to her lips to tell him to be quiet.

The interviewer next asked Jesus if He'd spoken to any of the world's religious leaders yet in that some of His answers ran counter to the doctrines and beliefs of many religious bodies. Jesus said He hadn't yet, but planned to do so in the very near future, possibly even prior to the telecasting of this interview. "I'm definitely not avoiding or bypassing them," He said. "Their cooperation is essential if I am to succeed in bringing peace and reconciliation to the world—God's world."

Even though *CBS* had had no advertising breaks during the

interview, time was running short. The interviewer's final question was, "In hindsight, are You still happy with Your choice of Ann Arbor for the initial stop for Your return?"

Jesus' face lit up with a broad smile and He quickly answered a resounding, "Yes." He's probably also happy to see the interview come to a close, I thought.

"Wow!" Joy exclaimed. "What you think?"

"He's impressive!" Beth responded. "There's no doubt about that. And I can't find fault with His answers. Although I think He was a little nebulous with some, using questions to have viewers come up with the answers He was seeking. I'm still worried that some of His answers might be disillusioning some of His most devoted followers. I sure hope the rumor was true and He's meeting the Pope today. Maybe He already has."

Jerry and I looked at each other and I gestured for him to be the next to answer Joy's question.

"I guess I'd second what Beth just said," Jerry began. "I want to tune into some of the talk shows tonight and hear what some of the commentators have to say. Personally, I think He did a beautiful job of handling several very tough questions. He wasn't out to antagonize or belittle anyone. As would be true of anyone, I'm sure that after the interview He had additional thoughts about some of His answers and how He could have improved on them. But knowing that millions would be watching and hearing Him, I give Him high marks."

The three turned to me and I smiled, "What can I add?" I asked, " I mean to improve on Beth's and Jerry's comments. I totally agree, but I have to admit I'm probably a little prejudiced. His answers dovetail with many of my own thoughts and beliefs. I wasn't feeling challenged by anything He said. No, I take that back. I guess I was asking myself what I could do, steps I should be taking, to help Jesus turn His message into a reality."

Joy grinned, "I didn't realize I was with such astute and articulate people. Yes, even you Jerry. I really don't have anything to add. I was impressed as you can all tell. I have been saying prayers for Him. Now I'll pray even harder."

Chapter XXIX

Beth and I crawled into bed rather early and clicked the TV on. Joy and Jerry were probably doing the same thing, switching channels frequently to get a variety of views. There was no doubt the "60 Minutes" interview was the major story of the day. Early on we'd been told preliminary surveys were indicating it had been one of the most watched moments in the history of television. I smiled to myself, wondering how many viewers were now watching "Desperate Housewives" instead of the talk shows that were commenting on the interview. We normally watched "Desperate Housewives", but not tonight.

I thought all the talk show producers had done a good job of lining up people to interview, ones who were likely to offer conflicting views. Somewhat to my surprise, I found that most of the more conservative guests being interviewed, whom I would have anticipated being critical of some of Jesus' answers, were, if anything, more receptive to those answers than those being interviewed who were generally more liberal in their thinking. The latter, I would have thought, should be overjoyed; Jesus was seemingly endorsing many of the ideas the Democratic Party had been advancing for years.

I smiled to myself as I thought of one explanation. Democrats had been critical of the religious right core of the Republican Party for years. If the religious right embraced Jesus' answers, Democrats would be deprived of several of their main campaign issues. Roe vs. Wade, for example, would no longer be one of the most divisive issues separating the parties. It seemed funny. Religion was one of the core reasons that united people, and yet it was also one of the major factors that sparked divisions.

The commentators and guests weren't limiting themselves to just the questions and answers shown on "60 Minutes". The ones reported in the newspaper articles, as well as earlier statements that Jesus made, also came into the discussions. The feedback was generally very positive, although one of the guests on *Fox News* lambasted the public and news media for blindly accepting that this engaging man was Jesus. He cited several Biblical passages that warned of false prophets appearing on the scene before the second coming of Christ.

One of the most discussed subjects was the position Jesus had taken in regard to gays being ordained. Many of the commentators and guests were sympathetic to the difficult position that it created for the Catholic Church. Many of them spoke about the millions of dollars that had been spent in recent years to settle public and private claims of sexual abuse by priests, in most cases, involving young boys. Regardless of the evidence showing homosexuals were no more likely to become sexual predators than heterosexuals and with some studies showing even less so, the recent costly turmoil would make the Church very reluctant to change its stance against gays entering the priesthood.

Some argued the Catholic Church would have never found itself in the position of being sued for the actions of a few priests if it had acted openly and decisively in denouncing their conduct and immediately barring them from further service as priests. The desire to avoid unfavorable publicity, the motivation to forgive and rehabilitate the offenders, and the concern that many of the charges might be false, combined to turn the situation into a disaster that the Church never wanted to risk occurring again. Critics of what had occurred say the answer is for the Church to have a plan in place to address problems of this nature as they happen rather than ousting or banning gays from the priesthood.

I couldn't help but think the discussions about gays serving as priests was jumping way ahead of what I believed was the current position of the Catholic Church. Didn't it view homosexual behavior as a sin? Didn't it prohibit homosexuals from receiving communion? Debating about whether they should be allowed to serve communion seemed out of context.

One of the other subjects over which there was considerable discussion was communion in general in light of Jesus' return. However, the vast majority agreed that communion, in addition to being done in remembrance of Christ and the sacrifice He made for our sins, was also an acknowledgment of Him as the Son of God and the opportunity for participants to re-commit their lives to Him. During these discussions, I couldn't help but recall Beth's comments after we'd taken communion that morning. She'd said she'd felt a little different about receiving communion now that we'd seen and heard Jesus in the flesh. She'd been motivated to pray for Him and His current mission in addition to acknowledging His previous sacrifice and expressing gratefulness.

After an hour or so, I'd asked Beth if she'd seen and heard enough. She nodded, saying she was really surprised Jesus wasn't provoking more controversy. I told her about the thought I'd had about how the general acceptance of what Jesus was saying might alter the political divisions between Democrats and Republicans. She'd laughed and responded that thought had also crossed her mind.

Just as I was about to switch off the TV, programming on the channel we were tuned to was interrupted for a news flash. There was confirmation Jesus had been in Rome earlier today meeting with the Pope. Unidentified sources were quoted as having said the meeting had lasted for nearly six hours and another meeting had been scheduled for the near future. The Vatican was not providing any details about what had been discussed, only verifying that a meeting had taken place. The current whereabouts of Jesus was not known, although there was speculation He was remaining in Rome and a second meeting might take place as early as tomorrow. The announcer said the meeting was unusual in its length and that no one could recall anyone having had an audience with any Pope lasting that long.

"Our timing was good," Beth said. "I'm glad you left the TV on long enough so we could hear that news. I know I'll sleep a little sounder tonight knowing He's been in contact with the Pope."

I smiled as I leaned over to kiss Beth good night. "I know you've been worrying about that, His meeting with the Pope. I would be surprised if we didn't hear some further details tomorrow morning about what actually took place."

"I'll keep praying for Him," Beth replied as she reached over and gave my hand a squeeze.

Chapter XXX

The banner headline in Monday morning's *Detroit Free Press* was "Jesus Visits Vatican to Meet With Pope." The article contained little new information. The two had met privately and sources described the meeting as cordial. Although the fact another meeting had been scheduled was mentioned, there were no specific details. The article said a number of people were speculating the Pope might summon Cardinals to Rome in the very near future to brief them about the meeting or meetings, if a second one was to take place prior to the special conclave.

The front page also contained an article about a meeting Ernie Smith would be having that afternoon in Detroit with over three-dozen African American church leaders. The article also stated that Ginny Roberts, another follower of Jesus, had been discharged from the U of M hospital Sunday evening.

Another article provided an update on some of Jesus' other followers. The two currently in South Korea were scheduled to address a crowd expected to number over fifty thousand on Tuesday evening. The team in Russia was receiving a warm reception, not only from church goers and religious leaders, but from government officials and the general populace as well. Thousands had turned out to greet the two followers of Jesus on their arrival in Sydney, Australia, on Sunday. In South Africa, the two followers had received a standing ovation after addressing a mixed audience of nearly five thousand on Saturday. The team planning on visiting China was caught up in red tape. They were hopeful of getting the necessary clearances to enter the country and to meet with various groups within the next few days.

Monday's *Ann Arbor News* also had stories on the same subjects. The *News* reported Ginny Roberts had been released from U of M hospital without providing any additional details on her injuries or what had prompted her attackers. I thought of what Joy had said about writing a letter to the *Ann Arbor News* if the paper didn't publish the full story of the assault. Perhaps it was better it didn't. Often times, publicity about a crime being committed prompted copycat occurrences. Maybe Jesus or His followers had requested that the *News* not highlight the story of the assault and the *News* was complying. I wondered if I should be contacting Joy with my thoughts, advising her a letter might do more harm than good. I decided to give it a little more thought, maybe discuss it with Beth, before phoning Joy.

The *News* also had a story about Jesus' Vatican visit. There were few details, only quotes from a few people who alleged they had seen Him. The story ended with a paragraph stating there were unsubstantiated rumors Jesus had left Rome for the Mid-east for meetings with the Shiite Grand Ayatollah and other religious and political leaders in Iraq and meetings with similar leaders in Iran. It was thought that Taylor Williams, a leader in the Muslim community in Ann Arbor, and David Epstein, a devout Jew from Ann Arbor, were accompanying Jesus on these visits. If the rumor was true, I couldn't help but wonder what the reception would be like. The fact they had even arranged for audiences with these leaders was a major accomplishment in itself. I quietly voiced a prayer.

Chapter XXXI

Beth and I ran several errands Tuesday morning and both heard the news on our car radios of the assassination attempt on Jesus in Israel. Jesus had been meeting in Jerusalem with a large group of Muslim and Jewish leaders. A man had entered the hall and darted toward Jesus, yelling in Arabic. As he'd raised his arm to fire a shot at Jesus, the man standing to the right of Jesus lunged in front of Jesus and was struck by the bullet. Security guards immediately fired at the would be assassin and several bullets found their target. He was killed along with the man who'd shielded Jesus. The guards had immediately surrounded Jesus and quickly escorted Him out of the meeting room.

The announcer went on to say that the person struck by the bullet intended for Jesus had been identified as David Epstein of Ann Arbor, Michigan, who was a law professor at the University of Michigan and a follower of Jesus. David Epstein had been accompanying Jesus on this Mid-east trip. The man who'd fired the shot that struck Epstein and who later was killed in a hail of bullets had not been identified as of yet. He was thought to be an Islamic terrorist.

I pulled into my drive and saw the garage door was up. Beth was getting out of her car. She must have been just ahead of me. She called out, asking if I'd heard the news, saying that someone had tried to shoot Jesus. I told her I had and we quickly went inside and turned on *CNN News*.

The newscaster was describing David Epstein as thirty-two, unmarried, and the sole Jew among Jesus' followers. He'd been raised in White Plains, New York. He'd received his undergraduate degree from Dartmouth and his law degree from the University of Michigan. He had served on the Law School faculty at the University of Michigan for two years and had taken a six month leave of absence. The newscaster explained that a reporter was now with Mr. Epstein's grieving family in White Plains and the screen changed to show a devastated couple sitting on a sofa, clinging to one another in tears. A young woman was sitting next to them, holding the older woman's hand.

The reporter introduced them as David's parents, Joseph and Rosalie Epstein, and sister, Martha Seidman. The reporter expressed her condolences and said she realized they must still be in shock over David's tragic death. She asked them when and how they'd learned of their son's death. David's father's lip was trembling as he started to answer her. He shook his head, unable to get the words out. His mother, however, spoke in anger, tears in her eyes.

"Taylor Williams phoned us about three hours ago. The man he and David believed is Jesus, the man whose life our son saved, hasn't been in touch with us yet. This didn't have to happen! This shouldn't have happened! We begged David to reconsider. We pleaded with him not to get involved."

The woman was sobbing and becoming hysterical as she continued in a high pitched voice.

"If that man is really Jesus, why didn't he bring our son back to life? Our son didn't deserve to die!"

The daughter hugged her mother, patting her on the back,

stroking her hair.

"This has been extremely hard on us as you can see," the daughter, Martha, said to the reporter. "My brother was very committed to his Jewish faith. He believed God was directing him, giving him a once in a lifetime opportunity to make a difference in the world. He was doing what he believed he should be doing."

I glanced over at Beth. Like me, she had tears in her eyes. The screen had switched back to the lead newscaster again who said *CNN* would now be taking us back to the scene in Jerusalem. The reporter at the scene there began with a brief recap of the event, which had occurred a few hours earlier. This was followed by an interview with a person who'd witnessed the shooting. He described the chaos that followed the assassination attempt. Another person interviewed spoke in anger saying the world would now understand the terror Jews faced on a daily basis.

"These extremists are evil men," he shouted. "The only thing they know is violence. They don't want peace and reconciliation. If it were to come, their lives would lose meaning, they'd be left with nothing to protest, nothing to die for."

There was a commercial break. When the news came on again, *CNN* had turned to a story about two missing teenagers who'd been mountain climbing in Colorado. We switched the TV off. We both felt a little depressed. I asked Beth if she thought we'd ever see the day when peace came to the Mid-east.

"I just don't' know," she replied. "As you well know, I've always seemed to be the pessimistic one in comparison to your seemingly perpetual optimism. But this time I was really hopeful, really confident Jesus could pull this off. Now I just don't know. I'll continue praying, I do know that."

Chapter XXXII

The *Ann Arbor News* featured an article titled "One Question Still Not Answered". The thrust of the story was with all the questions Jesus had been asked and answered, it still wasn't known where His financing was coming from, who were the individuals or groups providing the substantial funds necessary to pay for the expenses of Him and His followers who were traveling to all parts of the world. The article stated that payments had been made in cash, initially. A huge sum for the rental of the stadium, for example. Now Jesus' followers were using both cash and debit cards. They seemed to have a plentiful supply of the currency in use in the countries they were in. When His followers were asked where their funds were originating from, they more or less shrugged their shoulders, answering they didn't know, but money wasn't a problem. Inquiries to the financial institutions who'd issued the debit cards had garnered no new information. There were high balances in all the accounts with continuous deposits flowing into them. But if the banks knew the source for them, they weren't revealing it.

The article went on to say the News was unaware of any instances where Jesus or His followers had asked for funds, passed collection baskets or plates for voluntary contributions, or sought special concessions for fees or charges. The article concluded by saying if and when Jesus returned to Ann Arbor, they'd attempt to get an answer to this puzzling and troubling question.

Beth and I decided to take a walk around the neighborhood before dinner. We agreed it was a more healthy choice than perhaps overindulging in cocktails with the mood we were both in. As we were finishing our walk we ran into Jerry Hanson who was picking up his mail. He commented that it had certainly been an interesting day news-wise and asked us what we thought about the latest developments. "About the assassination attempt on Jesus?" Beth asked. "The interview with David Epstein's parents?"

"Well, yes," Jerry replied. "But maybe you haven't heard the most recent news. Did you hear they've identified the would be assassin? Rather than being an Islamic terrorist as first thought, it's been determined he's Jewish. A fairly well known member of a militant right wing group. He was disguised as an Arab. There's speculation he wasn't acting alone, that he'd had help getting access to the hall. That he'd also have had help in his escape following the shooting. They believe he'd been very confident he wouldn't be caught or identified. That people would conclude a Palestinian was involved. Blame the Palestinians and punish them."

Beth and I glanced at one another. If what Jerry was telling them was true, role reversals had occurred. Jews were the villains rather than the Muslims. I think we both were seeing the implications as Jerry continued, a possible uniting of Christians and Muslims against the Jews.

"There was quite a squabble following the shooting over who would take possession of the would be assassin's body and attempt to identify him. They reported Israeli and Palestinian security personnel had engaged in a heated shouting match. There was also a strong rumor circulating suggesting that the man wasn't dead, that blanks had been fired. This was later proved false, he had been killed in the skirmish. Eventually, a joint custody agreement was reached. The Jews were actually the ones who were quickly able to identify the man after his disguise had been removed. The man's name is Jacob. I can't recall just now what they said his last name was, something like Somel."

"No, we hadn't heard any of this," Beth said. "Thanks for bringing us up to speed. We've been out walking for the past hour. We'll get the TV on as soon as we're home."

Jerry held up his hands as Beth and I started to leave. "I haven't told you the other story that's been on the news. Jesus appeared in White Plains about an hour after the *CNN* interview with David Epstein's parents and sister. He met with them for over an hour. No one's saying what was said during the meeting, the parents and sister are saying it was a private conversation and they intend to see it remains private. But the real shocker is the sister's, Martha Epstein Seidman, decision. She's announced she's going to become a follower of Jesus. Take her brother's place."

"Wow!" I exclaimed. "Slow down Jerry. Give us a chance to digest all this. I feel as if I've been gone a few days, or even weeks, and am now just catching up on the news."

"I agree," Beth said. "As you said, Jerry, its been a very interesting day news-wise. Would Joy and you care to come over for a cocktail? Not dinner, Mike and I are just having leftovers.

"We'll have to pass," Jerry replied. "We're going out tonight." He looked down at his watch. "As a matter of fact we're due to meet friends in about forty-five minutes. I better get a move on."

Chapter XXXIII

We'd turned the news on as soon as we were home. Not surprisingly, the two new developments Jerry had told us about were being discussed on nearly every channel. Jerry had done a good job of briefing us. There were a few new details. Israeli police were in the process of questioning two men who were suspected of also being involved in the shooting. The Israeli government was trying to distance itself as far as possible from the militant group Jacob Somel had been active in. Spokespersons were expressing hope the action of one or possibly a few evil men would not set back the positive moves that had recently been made to bring about peace and reconciliation between Palestinians and Jews and the Arab world in general.

A number of Palestinian and other Arab leaders were being interviewed. While most appeared to support the Israeli position, it was sad to see so many who were condemning Israel and the Jews and almost gleefully taking delight in the fact a Jew had been responsible for the assassination attempt on Jesus and the death of one of His followers.

One interesting statement was made by one of the commentators involving those who had been meeting with Jesus prior to the incident. To a person, the commentator said, all were expressing genuine interest in having the dialogue with Jesus continue. Though supplying no specific details, the attendees were saying the meeting prior to the assassination attempt had begun to create an atmosphere of togetherness, understanding and cooperation, which none had experienced in the past.

Though the President had expressed his sadness over the incident and the death of David Epstein and endorsed the Israeli position that this should not alter the road to peace, several Senators and Congressmen were saying it was time to take a good look at the massive amount of financial aid the U.S. was currently providing Israel.

There was no question Israel was going to end up with a black eye, I thought. It was now a question of how permanent the damage would be to the entire peace progress in that volatile area of the world. Hopefully, the cries for retaliation against Israel would soon cease. The charge that Jews were responsible for killing Jesus once before and were attempting to again would not be embraced by many. Was the door still open for Jesus to lead the world to peace and reconciliation? I hoped so and would pray so.

The other story concerning Jesus' visit to the Epsteins' home was also receiving major news coverage. One of the questions being asked was how He'd managed to get there so quickly following the assassination attempt. Had the military, U.S. or another country, provided Him the transportation, the use of some type of high speed secret jet to carry Him half way around the globe in so short of a time? If so, who had authorized its use? It would have had to have been done within a short time after the attempt on His life.

Some were speculating Jesus had the power to transport Himself from one place to another without using conventional means of travel. There were several facts being used to support this speculation. The fact Jesus hadn't been seen in any airports even though He was showing up in many parts of the world, the fact that in Ann Arbor Jesus seemed to be able to make an appearance across town within minutes of a previous meeting and the fact many of His followers had been sighted using conventional means of travel.

Even more thought provoking and amazing to me was hearing the results of Jesus' visit to the Epsteins'. One channel had filmed the Epsteins' home. Dozens of relatives and friends were coming to visit. Though the Epsteins had declined requests for interviews, they could be seen in the background greeting their guests. They were hardly recognizable from the devastated couple and the angry grief stricken woman in the case of Rosalie Epstein, I'd seen interviewed earlier in the day. They appeared to be relaxed, almost serene, as they greeted people. I knew they had to be saddened with the loss of their son. Yet, as I noticed their smiles, I could tell they were now celebrating David's life with joy. I wondered what Jesus had said to comfort them. I wasn't that familiar with Jewish traditions. I did know, however, home visitations with the family of the deceased continued for a number of days. Beth and I had attended several. I wondered what Jesus had said to them to give them the strength and courage to welcome their guests so warmly.

The other amazing thing that had happened was the quick commitment of David's sister to take her brother's place as a follower of Jesus. Newscasters provided some background on Martha. She was employed in a senior position with a leading marketing and advertising company in New York City. She'd been married for seven years. Her husband was in the stock investment industry, employed by one of the major firms. The couple had one child; a four year old daughter.

Martha had agreed to a brief interview with the news media.

She said she'd be teaming up with Jesus in about ten days. The delay, she explained, would give her time to make the necessary arrangements at work and with the care of her daughter so nothing would suffer during her absence. She'd made a commitment to be involved with Jesus through January. She declined to discuss her reasons for making this commitment and also declined to tell them any details of her conversation with Jesus.

Beth and I discussed these new developments as we watched various channels. I told her she'd been somewhat psychic in predicting something like the assassination attempt might happen; that Jesus might stir up such a furor it might prompt something of this nature. Beth smiled, knowing I was intending my comment to be a compliment.

"I know I said that, Mike. But the more details we learn, the more it makes me think Jesus wasn't even the intended target of the man's wrath. I believe his main goal was to discredit the Palestinians, Muslims in general; to get Christians to rally around Israel. Maybe he didn't even intend to necessarily injure or kill Jesus. What do you think?"

I pondered for a few seconds before answering. "I think you may be right, Beth. Maybe silencing Jesus wasn't his main objective. Still, Jesus is attempting to reconcile the world. There are some who have no interest in seeing that come about. I'm a little surprised though that no one has suggested what you have. They certainly have covered every other aspect."

"True, Mike. But they might be hesitant about suggesting it, not wanting to be seen as trying to excuse the man's actions in some way. If David Epstein hadn't been killed and a shot had missed Jesus,

I think a number of them would be suggesting what I have."

"Maybe, but those are big ifs and that's not what happened. Israel authorities say they've brought in a couple other people for questioning, though. Maybe they'll be able to piece things together and discover you're right on target once again."

"Darn it, Mike. There you go again! I don't care if I'm on target or not. I'm just anxious to see questions asked so we can get to the truth of what that man's intentions were."

"You think it's that important?" I replied. "What difference does it make?"

"That's the problem, Mike. Don't you see that makes a huge difference?"

I merely shrugged my shoulders. Though I understood the point Beth was making, I wasn't enjoying being portrayed as stupid. I buttoned my lips. I wasn't going to give her the satisfaction of knowing I thought she was right, as usual.

Chapter XXXIV

Beth had plans to pick up Kristi Cloverdale at 8:00am on Wednesday so the two could be among the first to arrive at the opening of Ann Arbor's Summer Art Fair. This had been a standard ritual for the past five or six years. They'd be able to find a parking place and avoid the later crowds. The Art Fair brought thousands of people to Ann Arbor every year. It was indeed a happening, one I usually was able to avoid.

That's not really true, though. It seems as if every year Beth finds something she claims to need my advice on. I usually end up joining her for a trip back down to the carnival like setting. I'm convinced her telling me my opinion is needed is just a ploy to recruit another pair of hands to carry her purchases.

As she'd left, she told me she should be home at about 1:00pm for lunch and asked if I'd be home them. She'd winked, saying she might find something she'd need me to go back and see. I have to compliment her though, she usually gets a great deal of her Christmas shopping done at the Art Fair. I told her that I'd plan to be home by 1:00pm.

I actually returned home around 12:30pm. I thought I'd surprise Beth and score a few points by getting lunch ready. I set the table and found a container of Italian vegetable soup to heat up. I was just putting out cheeses and crackers when Beth arrived.

She came through the door lugging three bags of goodies. I could tell by the smile on her face that she'd had a very successful morning. She was a little surprised to see that I had lunch nearly ready and complimented me as she gave me a kiss.

"But I just have to show you some of my purchases before we have lunch, Mike. You'll never guess what the hottest selling item is this year—I bought one for you. Maybe you'll never wear it, but I knew you'd be disappointed if I didn't get you one."

She was giggling as she reached down into one of the bags and pulled out a T-shirt. She laughed as she shook it out and held it up in front of her. The front of the shirt had the words "Why Ann Arbor?" in bold lettering. She quickly flipped the shirt over. On the back were over a dozen answers to the question. She was right, I would never have guessed this would be this year's hot item.

I grinned as she continued talking. "They come in all colors. I picked this white one out for you. I thought it was a little more conservative than some and you might even wear it someday. They also had posters with the same copy in calligraphy. I probably should have gotten one of those for you instead of this shirt."

"Oh, no," I said, "the shirt is perfect. Thank you! And I might wear it. The perfect time would be if we get a chance to see and hear Jesus again."

As I was speaking, I read the script on the back of the T-shirt. "Why Ann Arbor?" appeared at the top of the list of reasons for why Jesus might have chosen to first appear there. The next line was "Takes Pride In Its Diversity" with "Age, Race, Religion, Nationality and Lifestyle" in parentheses under the line. Below, additional reasons were listed: *An Educational Hub • Top Ranking Graduate Programs • A Diverse Student Body • Many International Scholars • Providing Knowledge Worldwide • State Of The Art Research Facilities • A World-Class Medical Center*

• *A Culturally Rich Community* • *Technology Savvy* • *A Skeptical Populace* • *Connected To The World* (I smiled as I read the last one.) • *A Center Stage Between AASF And AAAF.*

Nearly all could have been lifted from Tom Cloverdale's letter, but this last one wasn't. Beth and I had come up with the thought that Jesus wouldn't have any competition for attention between Ann Arbor's Summer Festival and the Ann Arbor Art Fair.

"Kristi must have been delighted when you spotted the T-shirts," I suggested to Beth.

She laughed as she answered, "That's an understatement! Kristi went bonkers. She bought at least a half-dozen of them in a variety of colors and also a couple of posters. She thinks Tom may have a stroke when he sees them. By the way, you'll be interested in what Kristi told me about Tom. You remember that he'd begun his letter by emphasizing he wasn't intending to validate Jesus, to reinforce the preacher's claim of being Jesus. According to Kristi, Tom regrets having said that. That he's become a true believer. He's even thinking of writing another letter to the *Ann Arbor News* listing the reasons everyone should now believe the man is Jesus."

"That is interesting, Beth. For some reason I've never thought Tom was very religious. I've always thought of him as more of an agnostic, questioning whether there is a God or a future life. I'm delighted to hear he's acknowledged Jesus. I know Tom has a huge following in academic circles. Who knows, maybe he can be of help to Jesus."

"I thought the same thing as Kristi was talking," Beth replied. "Sometimes a person who hasn't been previously identified with a specific faith can have more of an influence on others' beliefs and thinking than one who has."

"What about Kristi?" I asked. "Did you get any sense of where she stands in her thinking?"

"Maybe a little. I could tell she was a little embarrassed as she told me about Tom, maybe a little concerned because he'd changed his thinking so quickly. I did tell her that you and I were fairly certain the man was truly Jesus. I also mentioned we liked the answers He'd given to some of the more controversial questions He'd been asked. She said they'd pleased Tom and her, too. I think she was a little surprised by me telling her that, Kristi and Tom probably view us as their most conservative friends."

I laughed, "I wouldn't be surprised if that was true! I sense they know I don't see eye to eye with them on a number of political issues. And that probably isn't going to change. But that doesn't change my delight in learning Tom's become a believer in Jesus and His message."

Chapter XXXV

Around 3:00pm Beth and I took a stroll through the neighborhood. We both commented on how perfect the weather was for the Art Fair with the temperature in the high seventies and low humidity. It seemed as if every year there was at least one day of heavy showers during the Art Fair. That wasn't going to happen today, there was hardly a cloud in the sky. Beth had given me the option of going back down to the Art Fair with her or taking a walk around the neighborhood. I was pleased to have the option and quickly opted for the latter. She had persuaded me to wear the "Why Ann Arbor?" T-shirt, however, suggesting it might be one of the few times I'd wear it. Fortunately, or unfortunately, we didn't meet anyone during our walk until we were near the end of it and passing the Hansons' home.

Joy and Jerry came out of their front door with grins on their faces. We immediately understood why as we observed that Jerry had the same shirt on as I did, only a different color.

"We saw you heading out for a walk earlier," Joy said as they approached us. "We spotted the shirt you were wearing Mike. I picked one up for Jerry this morning, too, as you can see."

"And I told her I'd probably never wear it," Jerry said laughing.

"He actually said he doubted if anyone under the age of thirty would be caught wearing one," Joy said. "Then, a few minutes later, we saw you wearing one, Mike."

"Wearing it wasn't my idea," I quickly said. "When Beth gave me the option of going back to the Art Fair with her or going out for a walk, I considered myself lucky. The least I could do was to give in to her request that I wear this shirt."

"It looks good on you!" Joy said, smiling. "And I was able to talk Jerry into putting his on after we'd seen you."

"Savor the sight of the two of us now, ladies," Jerry said, "I don't think you'll see us together wearing them again soon. Right, Mike?"

I nodded as Beth said, "Keep them handy, though. I'm sure there'll be another occasion to wear them. Kristi Cloverdale told me this morning that we'd all be hearing from her soon with an invite to come to their home for dinner. It would be fun if you two showed up in those shirts then."

"From what you've told me about Kristi buying several of these shirts for Tom," I said to Beth, "I wouldn't be at all surprised if he showed up at the door wearing one."

"Come to think of it, there might be another perfect time to wear them," Joy suggested. "That group of African American Church leaders who Ernie Smith met with a couple of days ago is planning on having Jesus speak in Detroit at Comerica Park. They're trying to copy the success UMS had at Hill Auditorium by making the event an optional fundraiser. They're still working on a date that would fit Jesus' and the Tigers' schedule. It might be fun for the four of us to go."

"I hadn't heard about those plans," I responded. "I'm sure we'd be game for it if we don't have a conflict on the date. Right, Beth?" She agreed.

"They're planning the event as a way to bring about racial harmony in the Greater Detroit area. They hope to get a true cross section of people attending—all races, faiths, and ages. And it all ties in with Jesus' basic message. That's one reason they think He'll agree to appear."

"That all makes sense," I said. "I hope they'll be able to pull it off. They'll have to be a little creative in determining where the donations are going to end up, though. I think, for example, if its limited to the United Negro College Fund, it'll defeat the purpose."

"I agree," Joy said, "And from what I've heard, the organizers do, too. They hope to have all the details spelled out by this coming weekend. There's a short article about it in this afternoon's *Ann Arbor News*. You probably haven't had a chance to see the paper yet."

Beth and I acknowledged that we hadn't. I asked Joy if there'd been any other news of interest in the paper we should be on the lookout for.

"As a matter of fact, yes," Joy replied. "*Time Magazine* is going to be publishing an interview with the Pope in this coming week's issue. As I'm sure you're aware, this is maybe a first. Popes don't make it a practice to hold news conferences or grant interviews to the news media. Frankly, I can't recall when it's been done before. The Pope's made an exception in this case so he'd have the opportunity to squelch some of the rumors that have been circulating concerning his meeting with Jesus. As you know, there had been speculation prior to the meeting that it would be very confrontational, that Jesus and the Pope would be at odds on several issues. And the four of us have discussed the fact that many of the published statements of Jesus appeared to attack long held Catholic beliefs and doctrines. Rumors following the meeting implied the meeting had been tense with much heated discussion.

"According to the *Ann Arbor News*," Joy continued, "the Pope told *Time* the meeting with Jesus couldn't have gone better. He's described the meeting as cordial, enlightening and very productive. There was no animosity. There were no arguments. Just a frank discussion about the challenges facing the world and the Catholic Church.

"The article is going to quote the Pope as saying how impressed he was with Jesus' vast knowledge on a broad range of subjects and issues."

"That is interesting Joy," Beth said. "Especially in light of the negative rumors and comments we've heard and read about. It should be a fascinating article; we'll look forward to reading it. I'm relieved to tell you the truth. As Mike would tell you, I've been concerned that a major conflict with the Catholic Church might torpedo everything Jesus is seeking to accomplish. I'm delighted to learn that maybe I've been wrong to worry."

"Maybe not all wrong, Beth," I said. "It appears Jesus has gotten off on the right foot with the Pope and I'm pleased to hear that. But even though the two may greatly admire one another and are very respectful of one another, they might end up at odds when they get down to the details. I realize I've been the one who's been saying Jesus appears to be sensitive to the fact that long held beliefs and attitudes won't change overnight, but Jesus' message is clear. Change is necessary and it must occur. I'm still worried whether the Catholic Church and other religious bodies are going to be up to His challenge. I truly pray they will be, but I have my doubts."

"I think we all do, Mike," Jerry said. "Still you'd have to agree, what we've heard about the *Time* interview, thus far, is optimistic news. I'm with Beth; I can't wait to read the complete article. Do you happen to know when that issue will hit the newsstands Joy?"

"Not for sure, I think on Monday. I think the News gave the exact date, we can check. I do remember reading that *Time* was going to publish twice as many copies as normal, however."

Chapter XXXVI

The evening news shows reported Jesus had met with the same group of Jewish and Muslim leaders He'd been meeting with when the assassination attempt had been made. The meeting had taken place in Jerusalem earlier in the day and there were still no details as to what had been discussed. Although a few of the previous attendees had not come to the meeting, citing security concerns, a small number of Christian leaders had been invited and the total number in attendance was virtually the same as the previous meeting.

There was also news of three more arrests related to the assassination attempt on Jesus. All were Jewish and members of the same militant group as the man who'd been killed. The prompt investigation and arrests by Israeli police were doing little to lessen the cries for the entire Jewish community to be held accountable and punished for the assassination attempt.

There were rumors Jesus had individually met with the two men who'd previously been arrested. There were conflicting stories regarding the purpose of the meetings. Some were saying He'd gone to forgive them. Others were suggesting He'd been able to persuade them to divulge the names of their accomplices and this had led to the arrest of the additional three men.

There was also news of a meeting scheduled in Bombay where Jesus would be addressing several hundred Buddhist and Hindu religious leaders. The mere fact such a meeting had been orchestrated was being viewed as a minor miracle.

True to her word, Kristi Cloverdale had phoned to invite us for dinner a week from Friday. Beth had asked her what Tom's reaction to the T-shirts had been and she'd said he currently had one on and loved the fact she'd bought them.

As we prepared for bed, Beth and I discussed how all the news media were now focused on Jesus, not only in the U.S., but also around the world. From the initial descriptions of Him as the man who claimed to be Jesus or the young preacher who resembles Jesus, it now seemed all the media—radio, television, newspapers, magazine and the Internet—were simply referring to Him as Jesus. The articles and letters to the editor questioning His identify were becoming fewer and far between. This did not mean there weren't mixed thoughts being expressed about Jesus. Many of His answers on "60 Minutes" and in the newspaper interviews had sparked considerable controversy. In many ways it was similar to the heated debates waged over President George W. Bush's nominations to the U.S. Supreme Court. Jesus had many ardent admirers who were praising Him. He also had many vocal critics who were lambasting Him. But the fact remained that Jesus was not only the number one story in Ann Arbor, He was the number one story in the world.

Chapter XXXVII

Thursday mornings *USA Today's* feature story was devoted to Jesus. The story was titled "Fact or Fiction" and reviewed several of the attributes and acts associated with Jesus and classified them as fact or fiction. A few were designated as inconclusive with insufficient evidence to make a judgment.

The initial item cited the testimony of the medical personnel who'd treated Jesus following the accident on State Street. It stated, "Jesus' body bears scars that would have resulted from His torture and crucifixion as described in Biblical text." This was deemed "fact". His miraculous recovery from the severe injuries He'd sustained in the accident was also classified as "fact" based on the statements of the surgeons who'd operated on Him. Ernie Smith's transformation from a bumbling street person with severe physical and mental disabilities to an intelligent and articulate spokesperson for Jesus was also determined to be "fact". Also deemed "fact" was Jesus' fluency in over a dozen languages.

Among those determined to be "fiction" was the story of how children unable to hear or speak were now able to do so after meeting with Jesus. The article stated that while it had been verified that such a meeting had occurred with Jesus using sign language to communicate with the children, there was no evidence any of the their hearing or speaking abilities had improved. Another item classified as "fiction" was the rumor Jesus had been shot during the assassination attempt in Jerusalem.

The mysterious way in which Jesus was somehow able to make appearances at various places some distance from one another at virtually the same time or within minutes of one another was deemed "fact". The statement Jesus had not asked for or received any money from others to fund His expenses or those of His followers was regarded as "fact". As I read this I couldn't help but think of the *Ann Arbor News*' promise to ask Jesus about the source for those funds.

As I skimmed through the remainder of the article, one item in particular grabbed my attention. Classified as "fact" was the statement, "Jesus miraculously healed one of His followers who'd had severe acid burns on her face and arm." This was the first reference I'd read about regarding the attack on Ginny Roberts other than the brief article in the *Ann Arbor News*. The *USA Today* article gave her name and explained she'd been the victim in an unprovoked incident in a parking structure in Ann Arbor, Michigan in which she'd sustained other injuries as well. The article said Jesus had just addressed those injuries that would have resulted in life long scars and facial disfiguration.

The article concluded with the statement, "Jesus is who He says He is." Rather than deeming this "fact" or "fiction", survey results were printed. In the survey for the entire country 43% had agreed He was, 49% were still undecided, and 8% believed He wasn't Jesus. Survey results for the greater Ann Arbor, Michigan area were also given. In that survey, 64% believed He was Jesus, only 28% were undecided, and 8% believed he was not Jesus.

The difference in the two surveys wasn't surprising, I thought. People in Ann Arbor had been exposed to Jesus longer than those in other sections of the country. They'd been able to see and hear Him in person. Still I remembered discussing as one of the reasons Jesus might have chosen to make His initial appearance in Ann Arbor was the fact He'd be apt to find it hard to convince an audience here. The fact the Ann Arbor survey was showing a much higher percentage of people believing He was Jesus than the national survey was definitely a good sign, an indication that maybe a future U.S. survey would see an increase in the percentage for those who believed He was Jesus. I found myself smiling, though. Maybe Ann Arbor's views were reflective of the liberal thinking in this University community and how people were reacting to the answers He'd given on several controversial subjects.

I flipped to the editorial page. As I read the editorial cartoon, I immediately broke into laughter. Beth heard me and asked what I was finding so funny. Take a look yourself, I said as I handed her the paper.

The cartoon was headlined "A Boom For The Economy", with a sketch of a department store jammed with shoppers under banners carrying the message "Christmas In July". The July date on which Jesus had first appeared in Ann Arbor was in bold print at the bottom of the cartoon.

Beth was laughing, too, though very quickly her face took on a more thoughtful expression as she said, "You know Mike, this cartoon might not be as far-fetched as it first appears. Think about it. Non-Christians are probably never going to accept and celebrate Christmas and Easter. But if Jesus were to be successful in changing our world, bringing the world and all its religions together with some common shared beliefs and goals, maybe there will come a day when the world unites each year in a day of celebration. Maybe a day dedicated to God. One without any of the commercial aspects of Christmas or Easter."

"I like your suggestion of a day dedicated to God," I'd responded. "Though some would argue and I'd have to agree that every day of a person's life should be dedicated to God. And we already have a Sabbath day every week."

"That's true," Beth replied, "but I believe it would be a major mistake to have a day to just celebrate the second coming of Christ as the cartoon suggests. I think Jesus would agree the holiday would have to honor the one God He's told us about in order to get universal acceptance. Jesus is on a fast track. Look at all He's said and done in less than a month. I was going to say I hoped we lived long enough to see a day of celebration of this nature. Now I'm hesitant, I really think it could happen, maybe even in the next few years."

"Who knows?" I said. "Maybe this cartoon might be just the jump start needed to get people thinking about a worldwide religious celebration day. But Jesus has a long way to go yet. His followers are still having a problem obtaining access to China. And what is China, twenty percent of the world's population?"

"I realize that," Beth said with a smile. "But you'll have to agree it's fun to dream and envision things you never thought would happen. Maybe dream about getting involved to help make those things happen."

"I know you haven't had a chance to read this *USA Today* article yet Beth, but I think you'll be pleasantly surprised with the outcome of the surveys that asked people if they thought Jesus was truly Jesus. A high percentage here in Ann Arbor are already there in believing He is and He's only been at this for a few weeks. In another few months He may have nearly everyone convinced He's who He says He is."

Beth nodded her head before saying, "You may be right. But my worry, my biggest concern, is not whether they'll agree He's Jesus, but rather are they going to open their minds and hearts to what He has to say. Believing He's Jesus is one thing, embracing His message is another ballgame. I hope they will. I have to admit that I'm surprised with the start He's made. I just pray that's a good omen. Sometimes things that soar so quickly tend to fizzle out just as quickly. Thus far, Jesus has made things look pretty easy. I'm sure He'd be the first to agree. However, His task is not going to be an easy one."

I glanced at my watch and jumped up. "I'm scheduled to meet the gang for golf in ten minutes. I'll call and leave a message to say that I'm going to be late." I smiled at Beth, "Time flies by quickly when you're having fun. I've enjoyed this conversation. Maybe we can continue it later tonight," I leaned over and kissed her before quickly heading out the door.

Chapter XXXVIII

Saturday morning's *Ann Arbor News* and Detroit Free Press had similar headlines. Jesus had been invited to address the U.N. A special session of the United Nations General Assembly was being convened on August 8th. Jesus was scheduled to speak that morning. This news overshadowed the news that African American Church leaders in Detroit had succeeded in booking Jesus to speak that same evening at Comerica Park. The event would begin at 7:00pm. Everyone was welcome to come. Although there would be no admission charge, those making a voluntary donation of one hundred dollars per ticket or more would be able to obtain reserved seats. Proceeds from the event would be used to help fund preschool learning programs throughout southeast Michigan. The event was being titled "Together". The promoters hoped to have a broad spectrum of people attending, all races, faiths, and economic levels. Inner city residents mixing with those from the suburbs. Two of Jesus' followers, Ernie Smith and Ginny Roberts, were serving on a diverse planning committee that numbered close to fifty people. Six corporate sponsors had agreed to share all the expenses associated with the event.

Beth checked our calendars and found we'd both be free that evening. I suggested we check with the Hanson's to see if they'd like to join us. Beth took it a giant step further by suggesting we rent a small bus and invite thirty to forty friends to come with us. I made a note to check on the availability of transportation first thing Monday morning. Beth was convinced I could find something and immediately began making phone calls.

The first call was to Joy Hanson. It resulted in an agreement to share the cost of providing food and drinks for everyone, a light supper on the way there, and dessert on the way home. Both were in agreement we should only serve soft drinks, that alcoholic beverages wouldn't be appropriate. Joy and Beth also discussed who we should invite and which one would make the phone call.

While Beth was making calls, I busied myself reading the two newspapers. The *Free Press* made a practice of delivering the Sunday comics a day early. My favorite comic is "For Better Or For Worse" by Lynn Johnston. This week's strip didn't disappoint and I chuckled as I envisioned our own family dealing with the same situation the characters in the comic were encountering. It never ceased to amaze me how Johnston was able to get readers to emotionally identify with and care for the main characters, at least that was the effect on me.

I checked in the *Ann Arbor News* to see which of our own ministers would be preaching tomorrow. I realized our church was having an open meeting Sunday afternoon to discuss the implications of Jesus' return to earth. Beth and I had a conflict and regretted we couldn't go. But what I found a little surprising was how many other churches and organizations were having similar meetings. There had to be at least twenty mentioned in an article in the same section of the paper having ads for various churches. The article commented that the University and the Ann Arbor Public Schools were being criticized in some quarters for allowing their facilities to be used for religious purposes, the separation of church and state issue.

There was a letter to the editor with an update on the joint venture of Planned Parenthood and Catholic Social Services. The letter quoted statistics indicating over thirty percent of childbirths involved unwed mothers and over half of those unwed mothers fall below the poverty line. The letter also commented on the growing number of couples who were going overseas to adopt children.

Beth interrupted me with an update on her phone calls. The Cloverdales and the Strattons were definite yeses. The Strattons had asked if we'd have room for their daughter Whitney to join us and possibly her fiance, Lance, as well.

"Of course, I said yes," Beth explained, "and I also inquired how Lance's mother was doing. Mary said that's why Lance is just a maybe, that he's been spending a great deal of time with her in Columbus. Her doctors have informed the family she might only have a few months to live. Very sad.

"I was a little disappointed and surprised with the answers I received from some of the others I was able to reach. I had the impression some of them were fearful of getting involved, as if we were forming a religious sect of some kind. They didn't seem to have a conflict with the date, just very reticent about getting drawn into something they might regret. Joy experienced a similiar negative reaction from a number of people she'd reached. However, it isn't dampening our enthusiasm.

"The good news though is all those who've agreed to join us have agreed to donate the one hundred dollars per person so we can get a block of reserved seats. I'll give Joy a call and update her and discuss others we could invite."

By late afternoon Joy and Beth had received positive responses from twenty-two people including four singles. These individuals had been among the most enthused to be included and the two decided to invite several other single men and women.

As usual, Beth and Joy had some exciting ideas in mind for the food we'd enjoy on our excursion.

Chapter XXXIX

Early Monday morning I was able to pick up the latest issue of *Time* magazine. Beth was subbing at the Thrift Shop, which meant that I'd have the magazine to myself and be the first to read its interview with the Pope. The cover touted the interview with photos of Jesus and the Pope. They were separate photos, none were known to exist that pictured the two together.

The text of the interview was interspersed with several photos of the Pope. They effectively illustrated the personality of this kindly and saintly man. In one, his expression was serious and thoughtful as he was perhaps contemplating how he should answer a question he'd been asked. In another he was smiling with the tips of his fingers touching. Another showed him laughing, leaning forward and gripping the arms of the chair in which he was sitting. One showed him with a stern, angry expression of his face. The last photo showed him looking upward with a very serene look on his face.

The first question the Pope had been asked was if he truly believed the man he'd met with was indeed Jesus Christ. The Pope was quoted as having said, "I wouldn't be honest if I didn't admit I initially had my doubts as to whether He was Jesus. I can say now, however, with no lingering reservations of any kind, I truly believe He is Jesus. I think I came to that conclusion about an hour into our conversation. I assume you're aware we met for nearly six hours."

The Pope was then asked what his reaction was to Jesus reaching out to all people and all religious entities rather than just Christians. The Pope responded, "I commend Jesus for what He is attempting to accomplish, reconciling the world and establishing God's Kingdom here on Earth. Jesus tells all who are willing to listen that there is but one God. A loving God who is present in their lives and from whom they can seek guidance. A compassionate God who is there to console them in times of need. An all knowing God who prays for them. A demanding God who asks them to love themselves and their fellow human beings with all their heart and soul. A forgiving God who asks them to forgive one another. Jesus believes all people are seeking to find the God He describes. In so doing, He believes through God's love, people can be reconciled. He believes nearly all religions have some common beliefs on which a world of peace and harmony can be built. Jesus says people must change. I totally agree and hope that I and the Roman Catholic Church can be instruments to help Jesus succeed in His goal."

The following question dealt with some of Jesus' statements that challenged some of the Roman Catholic Church's basic beliefs and doctrines and asked the Pope if he believed the Church should or would change some of these long held beliefs and practices. The Pope smiled, the article stated, as he began his response. "I'll begin my answer by saying my meeting with Jesus was an awesome experience. And let me clarify the fact that at no time did Jesus seek to intimidate me. He never made me feel uncomfortable in His presence. Although as you've stated, Jesus has questioned some of the Roman Catholic Church's positions on several issues, He heaped praise on much of what the Church has done and is doing. I'd say over ninety percent of his published comments have been favorable and this was true in our private discussions as well. And I don't mean to just single out the Roman Catholic Faith, I believe He's been equally generous in

His praise for the Church of the Latter Day Saints and other Protestant Denominations .

"I also wish to remind you the Roman Catholic Church has changed in many ways over the last century and continues to change. Granted, the Church moves slowly. Some of these changes were long overdue. In answer to your question though, yes, I believe the Church should make some changes and I believe the Church will make some changes. Jesus will help us expedite many of them."

"Does your answer mean you believe your Church will change its stance on abortion, for example?" was the next question. The Pope answered, "I knew this would be one of your questions when I agreed to this interview. It's an emotionally charged issue. You may be surprised when I say this, but I think Jesus and I hold similar views in regard to abortion. I agree with Him that there are instances where abortions should be performed, should be allowed by the Church. If we are in general agreement in regard to abortions, where's the disagreement? It simply comes down to the question of who should decide when an abortion should take place. Should it be the Church? Should it be some law making governmental entity? Should it be some judicial body? Or should it be the woman who will be bearing the child? As you know, Jesus believes it should be the latter. However, even though He strongly believes women should have this choice, He hopes they will pray and seek God's guidance before making the decision.

"Sometime next month I expect to summon our Church leaders here to Rome. We'll be discussing and perhaps debating some of the questions Jesus has raised. If they are in agreement, I will ask Jesus to speak to them. Do I expect the Cardinals to be open-minded? Do I expect there will be a positive response to what Jesus is encouraging? Yes, indeed I do. As I said earlier, Jesus and I spent nearly six hours in conversation. Less than ten percent of that time involved the Roman Catholic Church's beliefs and practices. I was amazed over Jesus' knowledge. I learned a great deal from Him. Man's growing knowledge in many areas can potentially lead to a world with all haves and no have nots. How we choose to deal with the new knowledge and apply it will be a challenge. In many ways, it could be a frightening challenge, since it will raise new issues or questions for our Church to address. I'll discuss some of these at the Conclave, too. They put a different perspective on what we've been thinking are the major questions facing the Church today. They are dwarfed by the future challenges man's increased knowledge brings."

The Pope was asked if he could give a few examples of some of the other subjects Jesus and he had discussed. He was quoted as having said, "Certainly. One subject Jesus updated me on was the status of research on the conversion of salt water to fresh water. We both agreed that if an economical means could be found to accomplish this, the discovery would be one of the most beneficial to mankind in history. The thought that deserts could be turned into farmlands could mean famines could be a thing of the past. The African continent with all its immense problems could flourish. It would be a dream come true for many parts of the world. Jesus believes it will only be a matter of time before this occurs.

"We also discussed the weather. Not, of course, in terms of what the weather was outside as we were meeting, but rather in terms of man learning how to control weather. Can man learn how to minimize the effect of hurricanes and typhoons, tornadoes and severe storms, heat waves and cold waves and droughts and monsoons? We discussed the number of natural disasters that were currently occurring and Jesus assured me these were not acts of God.

"I should mention that throughout our discussions, Jesus kept reminding me that man's ability to learn and to make new discoveries and to find new cures were made possible by God. He also reminded me that man's ability to make choices was also a gift from God.

"China was another subject on which we spent considerable time. We discussed China's rigidly enforced policy of allowing only one child per family. Without this drastic measure, China would have never been able to achieve the economic growth and increased standard of living it is enjoying today. Jesus also told me of some countries where tax incentives were being given to encourage larger families. I told Jesus China's one child per family policy troubled me. He agreed it was also troubling to Him, but it was just one example of sometimes things not being all black or all white, not being totally right or totally wrong. He said that even in God's world there were sometimes grey areas.

"He explained to me the troubles His followers were experiencing in China. Though China endorsed religious freedom, there were many regulations governing and restricting religious activities. We agreed that with its vast population, the country represented an enormous opportunity, yet an enormous challenge, to introduce God into people's lives. A way would have to be found to gain access in China if God's Kingdom on Earth was to become a reality.

"We discussed recent medical discoveries, including those on the horizon, and genetics and the challenges this increased knowledge presented. The opportunities to improve people's quality of life are awesome. For example, these breakthroughs mean cystic fibrosis and other dreaded diseases could become a thing of the past. The knowledge gained in these areas of research could also extend peoples lives, adding productive years of good health and vigorous activity. But if the average person lives over one hundred years, other issues come into play. The United States and other nations are currently working to find long term solutions for industry pension plans and social security type programs. Longer lives will exacerbate this problem and make finding solutions even more difficult.

"Jesus emphasized to me that mankind is on the threshold of entering a period where engineered evolution is possible. Rather than just using technology to modify our environment, the means exist or soon will exist, to alter our minds and memories, to enhance our bodies and create children with abilities far surpassing those of their parents. For example, a technique called "gene doping" produces such muscle strength in rodents that some researchers believe the Olympics will evolve into contests between genetically altered humans. Another example is the work going on to develop a pill to enhance a person's memory. The pill would address the mental decline that occurs as one ages, as well as in dementia and Alzheimer's disease. But, what of a child using a similar pill? Would his or her SAT score be hundreds of points higher than a child not on the pill?

"We discussed the technology that enables man to currently clone plants and animals and the question of whether God's creations should be altered. The possibility of cloning human beings raises even more ethical and moral questions. Who should be deciding if and when the genes of an unborn child should be altered?

"As if these questions weren't enough to try to digest in our meeting, many more subjects were addressed. Nanotechnology, robotics, alternative sources of energy and the knowledge explosion in this computer age were all discussed. As I said earlier, Jesus' knowledge and understanding of these many subjects astounded me. He even explained to me what CVD diamonds were, artificial diamonds created by a process called chemical vapor deposition. They can be utilized in all sorts of areas from computers to manufacturing, creating enormous opportunities to enhance existing products and processes.

"You'd asked what some of the other subjects we discussed were. I'm sure you didn't expect my answer to be so lengthy. And though you might find it hard to believe, I merely scratched the surface. Our conversation was wide ranging and very informative."

The next question followed up on the Pope's last sentence. "You've said your discussions were very informative. I'm sure you had some things you wanted to inform Jesus about. Did you have the opportunity to do that?" The article stated that the Pope had smiled and hesitated for a minute, before answering the question.

"I'd thought I'd done my homework pretty well to prepare for my meeting with Jesus. I'd read and re-read in some instances the articles in the six newspapers that had the opportunity to interview Him. I also watched the tape of his interview on "60 Minutes" and reviewed every mention of Jesus in the media my staff could find. I'd prepared notes, a list of things I wanted to cover. I wanted Him to understand the basis of several of the Roman Catholic Church's beliefs and practices. I noted the scripture references to support them.

I had also prepared a list of questions for Him, some asking Him to clarify the meaning of certain scripture passages including some of the parables He'd used in His teachings and others asking how literally we should interpret some scripture as the Word of God.

"As I mentioned earlier, my meeting with Jesus was a humbling experience. As I believe you're aware, I'm regarded as somewhat of an expert with my knowledge of the world's major religions. My expertise paled when compared to His. He is indeed all knowing. Yet, at no time during our meeting was He boastful. Throughout the time we spent together He gave me the impression that He and I were both servants of God, acting as agents to carry His message of reconciling love to the world.

"As Jesus explained His mission and we discussed the challenges He'd face in bringing about God's Kingdom here on Earth, the concerns on my agenda were put in perspective. Compared to the issues He'd raised and the questions He'd asked, my list seemed insignificant and perhaps petty. I'm not suggesting the things I'd wanted to say and the questions I'd wanted to ask are no longer important to me, because they are. But Jesus had raised the level of our discussion to a much higher plane. It was not the time for me to present my list of questions. Maybe I'll have an opportunity to do so sometime in the future, with Him and also the media.

"So, to answer your question, no. I didn't get an opportunity to tell Jesus what I'd expected to, what I'd planned to do. However, I'm the one who decided it wasn't the proper time rather than Him. If you'd been privy to our discussion, I'm sure you'd understand why I was reluctant to raise those points at that time."

The Pope was then asked if he'd been disappointed or

surprised over anything Jesus had said. He answered by once again saying how awed He'd been with Jesus' vast knowledge, that he probably shouldn't have been surprised by it, but he had been. And no, nothing Jesus had said had disappointed or disillusioned him.

"Jesus is truly brilliant. His grasp of and understanding of issues is a joy to see. As I've said, nothing about Him has disappointed me with maybe one exception and that has to do with what He didn't say. In all of our lengthy discussions, He never once mentioned His resurrection and His promise of everlasting life for those who believe in Him. As you're aware that's the crux of the Christian Faith. I've spent a great deal of thought on this since our meeting. When and if I see Him again, this is the first question I'll have for Him.

"In seeking to unite all people in God's loving embrace, does He intend to leave Himself out of the equation? How can He do this when we believe He is God? We've been led to believe God the Father, Jesus Christ His Son, and the Holy Spirit are one. That His promise is God's promise. Is He now saying this isn't so? If so, I think this would be a grave mistake. One which would leave the world in turmoil rather than reconciled in peace. I intend to tell Him so. Maybe He has an answer to calm my fears and concerns. I pray that He does. However, you asked if I had been troubled by anything Jesus had said. Other than this major reservation, the answer is no."

After the series of lengthy answers it was refreshing to see several yes or no, or one sentence responses to the additional questions the Pope had been asked. For example, he'd been asked if Jesus had told him how long He'd be here on earth. The article stated the Pope had shaken his head no. He'd been asked if Jesus had demanded anything of him and he'd shaken his head again. The final question was, "Have you had an opportunity to meet any of Jesus' followers? If so, what has been your reaction to them?"

The Pope replied that yes, he had met with two of them, a man and a woman. He explained they'd been instrumental in setting up the meeting with Jesus.

"When I first learned about His followers, I was a little concerned with the fact they all came from the United States. The two whom I dealt with, however, were very fluent in German and Italian, possibly other languages as well. They were very knowledgeable about the Roman Catholic Church. The man was a Catholic. I've learned that all His followers are fluent in many languages in addition to English, particularly in the native languages of the countries to which Jesus has sent them. If the two I met are representative of the group, I have to say I believe Jesus has chosen wisely. Those two are very sincere and committed. They're also very talented, intelligent with the ability to communicate well and relate to others. I've heard the group is quite diverse. That is good, too. I've been impressed by the two I've met."

I had a noon luncheon meeting. I left a note for Beth telling her when I expected to be home. I stuck it on the cover of the magazine and left the copy on the kitchen island. My note had also said, "Think you'll find this article interesting, I certainly did. I'll be looking forward to discussing it with you."

I'd signed it with the letters, "I.L.Y.M.T.T.C.T." It was a favorite expression of ours: *I Love You More Than Tongue Can Tell.*

Chapter XXXX

The main focus of the Monday evening news and the later talk shows was the *Time Magazine* interview with the Pope. The Pope was being given generally high marks for his intellect and candor and revealing a side of his personality seldom seen by the public. There was some criticism of his failure to bring up the issues and questions he'd planned to. Reporters were saying these were probably the same issues and questions the general public and Catholics in particular, were most interested in having Jesus address. The point being made was that in a meeting, which lasted nearly six hours, the Pope was remiss in not finding time for the two to discuss the agenda he'd referred to in the interview.

Most of the reporting centered on the challenges presented by some of the topics Jesus and the Pope had discussed such as, scientists understanding of the human genome and other factors which control cellular processes in the body, the amazing pharmaceuticals which can be created using this knowledge and nanotechnology and technology in general including robotics. Several networks were already announcing their plans for "specials" to examine these and other subjects discussed by Jesus and the Pope.

One of the talk shows Beth and I watched discussed the grey areas Jesus had referred to during the discussion concerning China's one child per family policy. The panel touched on some of the "grey" areas of the "Ten Commandments". Another of the talk shows featured several pro-choice and pro-life advocates debating the abortion issue. The discussion broadened to include the subject of birth control which evolved into a heated discussion over whether U.S. dollars should be spent to furnish condoms to control the spread of AIDS in Africa.

And of course, in between the shows, Beth and I had the opportunity to discuss the *Time Magazine* interview. One thing which we both found surprising on the news was the scant mention of the Pope's concern over how Jesus was positioning Himself in delivering His One God message to the world. That had been a question that had disturbed Beth ever since Jesus had appeared on the scene. I'd been the one who argued Jesus had to maintain a low profile if He was to be successful, that the world would not be open to adopting Judeo-Christian beliefs as their own. We discussed the possibility the media was intentionally choosing not to focus on this question to avoid being accused, now or later, of jeopardizing Jesus' chance of success. Jesus was advocating change in people's lives. Could this happen with people still clinging to their separate religious beliefs, carrying on as usual, so to speak? Did Jesus believe He could succeed by adding a layer to these beliefs, one which would put people a step closer to God? A closeness which would result in changing their moral behavior to foster peace and reconciliation and create God's Kingdom on Earth?

Beth and I continued our discussion after clicking off the TV. As I was brushing my teeth, I had a thought. What if Jesus was to come up with a universal prayer that all people could identify with? Couldn't it be a means of getting all religions to understand and accept Jesus' message, see what they shared in common? The Lord's Prayer accomplished this with the many Christian denominations. As I'd climbed into bed I told Beth my thought.

She'd smiled as she nodded her head in understanding. "That's an interesting idea Mike. But my initial reaction is, what's wrong with the Lord's Prayer? Think about it, doesn't it serve the purpose? I think it encompasses the central message of all religions, what all people yearn for. Granted, it might have to be fine tuned, a few words changed to make translations into other languages easier. And of course, a decision would have to be made about whether debts, trespasses, sins or transgressions should be the wording. But isn't the Lord's Prayer applicable? Doesn't it capture in a few words Jesus' message?"

"I'm not going to argue it doesn't, I think you're probably right that it does," I replied. "But, I believe the mere fact it's called the Lord's Prayer and is so closely identified with Christianity would rule it out for what I'm suggesting. For example, for all we know the Qur'an may have a prayer which encompasses the same thoughts expressed in our Lord's Prayer, perhaps even more eloquently. I just think it has to be a new prayer, one which doesn't currently exist, one which isn't originating from one religion or another."

"And how are you suggesting that should come about?" Beth asked. "Should Jesus try to assemble all the world's top religious leaders and scholars and have them have a go at it?"

I was becoming a little defensive as I replied, "That's not as farfetched as you make it sound, Beth. But no, I think the prayer has to come from Jesus, directly from God. He could make it part of His message. You have to admit the overall response to His message has been quite favorable, thus far. A universally accepted common prayer would enhance His message."

"Don't get uptight, Mike. I hear what you're saying. But hear what I have to say, too. I'm a little uncomfortable casting aside the basic cores of my religion. Communion, the Bible, the Lord's Prayer. As much as I'm rooting for Jesus to be successful in accomplishing His goal and praying that He will be, I don't want to give up the key elements of the religion I've grown up in. I'm not ready for that and I would think millions of other Christians aren't either. This is dangerous ground."

I'd smiled at Beth and grabbed her hand. "I don't think we're really all that at odds in our thinking," I told her. "I think we're basically on the same page, the same page as Jesus, too. There are questions. Muslims, Buddhists, Hindus and others will be asking themselves the same questions you are, quite possibly more. We understand God works in mysterious ways. I've said it before and I'll repeat it again. I think we're privileged to be spectators to the unfolding of one of the greatest stories in the history of man. And I believe 'The Greatest Story Ever Told', which is the basis of our Christian beliefs, can be compatible and co-exist with this new story."

Beth squeezed my hand and whispered, "I hope you're right," before turning and switching off the light.

Chapter XXXI

Over the next few days the news media continued to highlight *Time Magazine*'s interview with the Pope. Two of the networks ran specials devoted to the subject. Newspapers were filled with stories of different peoples' reactions to the interview. The issue in which the interview had appeared had become a collectors' item. By mid-week there were no copies to be found anywhere, a complete sellout.

Two news breaking stories first appeared on the Internet and were quickly picked up and pursued by the news media. The first of these told of a second meeting between Jesus and the Pope, seemingly a quick response by Jesus to the *Time* interview. The Pope was quoted as having said, "Jesus had read about my disappointment in not having had the opportunity to ask Him the questions I had planned to. We met for about an hour and a half on Wednesday, here in the Vatican. He answered all my questions, including some I thought about after our initial meeting. His answers were very enlightening. I'm going to refrain from commenting on them until after I've met with all the Cardinals, that meeting will take place next week."

The second news story told of a filmed interview with Jesus by one of the major Arab television networks. The interview had been done by *MBC, The Middle-East Broadcast Center.* One concession Jesus had requested was for *MBC* to make the piece available to other Arab television networks without charge. *MBC* would be airing the interview a day earlier than the rest of the networks, however. The initial telecast had already occurred. Beginning tomorrow other networks would be showing the interview.

The evening news reported Jesus had made two appearances in Taiwan, speaking to audiences numbering about twenty-five thousand on both occasions. Film clips showed very enthusiastic crowds. Interviews with people who had been present to hear Him speak were mostly positive. In addition to addressing the two crowds, Jesus was said to have met with a group of government and religious leaders. As I'd watched this news segment, I'd wondered whether His appearance in Taiwan would help or hinder Jesus' and His followers' attempt to gain entry into China.

The evening news also reported the response to Jesus' interview on Arab television had been lukewarm at best. One reporter said it was definitely not Jesus' finest hour. Far from it in fact in that what had been promoted as an hour-long interview, had turned out to be less than twenty minutes. The best that could be said for Jesus was that He spoke fluently in Arabic and seemed to speak with some knowledge about the Qur'an and different Islamic sects. It was reported that His answers to several questions hadn't really addressed them, giving the impression He didn't have answers or was attempting to dodge the question. The reporter said Jesus wasn't helped by the interviewer, who expressed virtually no reaction to His answers. There was no sign the two had established any rapport what so ever.

I was shaking my head, saddened to learn about the negative reactions to the interview. It was, to my knowledge, the first setback for Jesus since His arrival in Ann Arbor. When Beth returned from attending a meeting of her Alumni Association, I reported the highlights of the two stories to her.

"I think it was a mistake for Him to go to Taiwan before China," Beth said. "He should be aware of the extreme tensions that exist between those two countries. I think one of His followers should have warned Him of the political implications of going to Taiwan first. It will just add to the difficulty of His gaining access to China. As far as the interview on Arab TV, from what you've said, I think the interview may have been edited to present Jesus in an unfavorable light. You said the program was originally planned to be an hour long. How long did it turn out to be, less than twenty minutes? I don't know what Jesus and His followers can do about it now, though. The damage has already been done and they'll just have to find a way to counteract it, I guess. I always thought the Arab countries and the Muslim communities would probably represent the greatest challenge for Jesus. The fact He's Jewish gives Him another hurdle to face to begin with even though the Islamic religion always acknowledged Jesus with respect."

I'd nodded in agreement with Beth's thoughts, wondering why it hadn't dawned on me earlier the possibility that the interview had been edited in a way to portray Jesus in a negative light. The damage wasn't over yet, either. Many other Arab networks and others throughout the world would soon be airing this same segment previously shown on *MBC*. With that thought in mind, I changed subjects, asking Beth how her meeting had gone.

Chapter XXXII

What a change a day can make. The lead story on the Internet and on the Thursday morning television news shows dealt with the new developments in the *MBC* Jesus interview. The producer, director and interviewer had all come forward charging the interview with Jesus had been edited in a way that totally altered the interview. The three had threatened to resign. To its credit, the *Middle East Broadcast Center* had immediately begun an investigation. It had reported a single individual had been responsible for the editing that resulted in presenting Jesus in an unfavorable light. The man had been fired and *MBC* was currently airing the full hour-long unedited interview. The network had also contacted those stations and networks to which it had previously sent the edited version with an explanation of what had happened and an apology. They were being supplied with the unedited version, which *MBC* was currently airing.

The reaction of nearly all those who had seen the full interview was a night and day difference from what the reaction had been to the edited clip. Commentators said viewers were describing the interview in glowing terms, saying Jesus and His message of peace and reconciliation had come across well. Jesus was being praised for His sincerity and forthright answers, earning high marks for His knowledge of Islam and His fluency in the Arabic language.

Rather than just airing the unedited interview with Jesus, the other stations and networks were planning to show viewers both the edited and unedited clips. Viewers could see for themselves how editing had been used to change the context of the program. Following these Arab networks' lead, other networks throughout the world were requesting both versions from *MBC*. While its agreement with Jesus provided that *MBC* would provide tapes of its interview with Him to other Arab networks without charge, nothing had been mentioned about other markets. As a result, commentators were saying, what had been an embarrassing incident for *MBC* was now turning into a financial windfall. For example, in the U.S., *Fox News* had paid a substantial sum for exclusive broadcasting rights. The network was already running promos announcing it would be showing both versions of the interview beginning at 9:30pm Eastern Standard Time. Similar arrangements were being negotiated in other parts of the world. What had started out as an interview which would have probably only been seen in the Arab world had suddenly become an event the entire world would be seeing. Fox had said it would be using English subtitles so its viewers would understand all the questions and Jesus' answers. Broadcasters in other countries would no doubt be doing the same, using subtitles in the native language of the country.

One of the commentators had mentioned *MBC* had been predicting that close to 5% of the Arab population would be seeing its interview with Jesus. Due to the editing incident and the huge amount of publicity surrounding it, *MBC* was now saying this percentage might soar to over 50% in the Arab world. The attempt, by supposedly one individual, to discredit Jesus had clearly backfired. Because of his actions, millions more people in the Mid-East would now be tuning in to view the interview. Millions more throughout the world would also be seeing and hearing Jesus. And if the commentators were correct, seeing and hearing Him in a very favorable light.

Beth and I were ecstatic over this new development. We'd both gone to bed last night somewhat disheartened, saddened to learn that Jesus had stumbled in His initial attempt to communicate to the Muslim world. And now we were learning that the script had changed, rather than a set back and a misstep, Jesus would now be getting His message out to far more people than had been initially envisioned.

"What a turn of events!" I exclaimed to Beth. "It's hard to believe what's happened. And you saw it coming. You immediately thought the interview might have been edited, that it had been done in such a way that viewing it would turn people off, rather than inspiring them. I have to hand it to you, Beth."

"Hold up a minute," Beth interrupted, raising her palms and smiling, "I may have had a correct hunch in thinking the interview had been drastically edited, but not in my wildest dreams would I have envisioned this outcome. Maybe a lucky break for Jesus, but I'd go a step further and call it miraculous. He keeps amazing me and I think this tops the list. You keep saying God works in mysterious ways, Mike. I think He has in this instance."

I nodded and joked, "Like to join me in watching *Fox News* at 9:30 tonight?"

Chapter XXXXIII

The *Ann Arbor News* featured the story of *MBC*'s interview of Jesus on its front page. Most of the details were familiar to me from the television reports I'd seen earlier. However, the news article also gave a brief synopsis of the interview that *Fox* would be broadcasting. It included some of the questions Jesus had been asked and a summarization of some of His answers. Jesus' vast knowledge of Islam clearly showed in His answers. He quoted from the Qur'an in many instances. One question and answer I found extremely informative related to Jihad, a term I'd associated with terrorism in recent years. Jesus gave Jihad a fresh, new definition in His answer, referring to it as the struggles man encounters in life, struggles with the spirit and religion rather than a challenge or command to destroy or subjugate all opposing faiths and non-Muslims. This new context removed the evil and threat I knew many associated with the term. Jesus also made clear in one of His answers that He was not simply coming to the Arab World with good intentions, with pleasing words and thoughts. By acts and deeds, He said He would be showing people of all faiths how God's Kingdom On Earth could come about. The *News* article made readers more anxious than ever to watch *Fox News* that evening.

There was also an article reporting Jesus had succeeded in arranging a meeting with key government officials in China. Though the actual date for the meeting was unknown, Jesus' followers were quoted as saying China's acquiescence to Jesus' request for such a meeting was a major accomplishment from which they were certain positive actions would flow. I remember Beth and I having thought the timing of Jesus' visit to Taiwan was a mistake, maybe that wasn't true after all.

We'd gone out for dinner and I'd turned on the radio during the drive home. There was some good news. The Detroit Tigers were leading the New York Yankees by a score of 5 to 3 heading into the bottom of the 5th. There was also a story concerning Jesus' robe. While in Rome, it had been sent out for overnight cleaning. The company doing the work was uncertain about whether to launder or dry-clean the garment. Fearful of damaging the robe, a small swatch of material had been taken from the hem to test whether dry-cleaning chemicals would damage the fabric. An enterprising employee had later taken the swatch to be tested to determine the age of the garment. The results of this testing had been released today. They showed the material to be at least 2,000 years old.

I glanced over at Beth. She raised her eyebrows as she said, "Maybe that will get a few more people into believing Jesus is who He says He is."

"It no doubt will," I replied. "But I imagine we'll have some controversy over this, too. People questioning the testing procedure and the results. Others suggesting the age of the fabric is just part of a well planned scheme to get people to believe He's Jesus."

"I think you're probably right, Mike. And the sad thing about that is that rather than focusing on His message and the reason He's returned to the world, attention will be centered on whether He's truly Jesus."

As we drove into our driveway we noticed our neighbor's

garage door was up with the light on. There was a ladder standing in the middle of the garage.

"I think there's someone lying on the garage floor next to the ladder," Beth exclaimed. "Maybe its Ralph, maybe he fell."

Our neighbor, Ralph, was a widower and in his late-seventies. He was a great neighbor to have, often giving me advice on household repairs and maintenance and frequently doing the work himself to show me how.

I immediately stopped the car and Beth and I hopped out and ran over to his garage. Sure enough, Ralph was stretched out on the floor, bleeding profusely from a wound on his head. It appeared the accident had occurred moments before our arrival. Ralph was conscious, telling us he may have broken his arm. Beth had gone into his house and grabbed several dish towels, which we wrapped around his head. He was strongly opposed to us calling 911 to get an EMS vehicle to take him into Emergency. I told him we could drive him if he felt he could stand. As he did, he told us we should take him in his car. He didn't want to get his blood on our seats. I drove him in his car and Beth followed in ours. The plan was to get him to the hospital and then call his son who lived nearby.

Fortunately, Ralph's injuries were not severe, although the loss of blood did require a blood transfusion. Several stitches were required for his head wound and indeed, he'd broken his arm. We'd been unable to reach Ralph's son. We were later to find he and his wife had been at a friend's house watching the interview with Jesus on the *Fox Channel*. Beth and I were able to see a portion of the interview in the waiting room while the doctors were tending to Ralph's injuries. We were told Ralph would be kept overnight, possibly even an additional night as well. Ralph was very concerned about how he was inconveniencing us and told us we should just leave him. However, we kept him company until I'd reached his son shortly after midnight.

We turned the radio on as we were driving home. There were discussions taking place on nearly every station about the interview with Jesus. Preliminary surveys were calling it the most watched *Fox News* program ever and *Fox* was being praised for showing both the edited and unedited versions of the interview. There seemed to be general agreement that Jesus had come across well. I mentioned to Beth that I'd go out and get a copy of *USA Today* in the morning, suggesting it would probably have a pretty thorough coverage of the interview. Although, we were grateful we'd been able to come to Ralph's aid, we were disappointed in not having been able to see the interview. Beth suggested *Fox* might be showing it again because of the great interest and we'd be able to see it after all.

As we were preparing for bed, Beth reminded me we were going to have dinner at the Cloverdales tomorrow evening and had told the Hansons we'd be picking them up shortly after 6:00pm.

Chapter XXXIV

I'd been right in assuming the *USA Today* would have a feature story on the interview of Jesus, in fact there were two. One story was devoted to the heavily edited and abbreviated version, showing how segments had been omitted and remaining segments pieced together to give an entirely different picture of Jesus and the interview than the one conveyed in the unedited version. It was a very detailed analysis, graphically illustrating the influence and power an editor can wield in shaping a news story.

The feature article was virtually a recap of the full interview, providing the interviewer's questions along with Jesus' answers. Beth and I were both fascinated by the article which covered a broad range of issues. In one of His answers Jesus even touched on the possibility of Arab nations joining together in a similar fashion to what had already been done in Europe. He'd also suggested in another answer that the Mid-East could soon face a major challenge as alternatives to oil were perfected and implemented. I mention these two points to show that the interview was not confined to religious and moral issues alone.

The article concluded with several paragraphs describing reactions to the interview. They were generally very favorable, in the Arab world as well as throughout the world, by various government and religious leaders and the general populace. The most sensitive subject Jesus had raised was in regard to women's rights. Several people were quoted as having said the Arab world wasn't quite ready to place women on an equal par with men, even though the vast majority of them believed it would happen in a generation or two. But on the subject of education, the need for people to change their moral behavior and Jesus' challenge for people to accept, forgive and love one another, there appeared to be near unanimous support. Though I was pleased to learn this, I couldn't help but think that individuals involved in extremist organizations and militant factions, which seemed to abound in the Arab world, probably hadn't been heard from yet.

Beth and Joy had done their best to try to convince Jerry and me to wear our "Why Ann Arbor??" T-shirts to the Cloverdales. Fortunately, Jerry had sided with me in electing not to. We were all in good spirits during the drive across town to Tom's and Kristi's home.

One of the joys about Joy was the fact she always seemed to be able to come up with some juicy tidbit of news whenever we were together. Today was not an exception. She'd had an opportunity to meet Ginny Roberts, the follower of Jesus who'd been attacked while being accused of having an affair with Him.

"She's a lovely person," Joy explained. "Very charming and engaging. I was very impressed by her, what she had to say and how she said it. She spoke at our Farm and Garden Club meeting. And after her talk I had an opportunity to personally chat with her for a few minutes. She's a very intelligent young lady. And describing her as beautiful is maybe an understatement; she's gorgeous. I could easily understand how Jesus could be attracted to her, any man would be."

Joy had paused after this last statement. Beth and I were

waiting to hear what she'd say next.

"Ok Joy," Beth finally said, "what aren't you telling us? Do you know something more about her relationship with Jesus?"

"No!" Joy quickly responded. "Honest, I don't. I shouldn't of even made that last remark. That's how rumors get started, isn't it? I apologize. I just thought you'd like to hear that I'd met her and my reaction, that's all. Let's change the subject. I know who'll be joining us for dinner at the Cloverdales, maybe you do, too. It should be a fun evening."

Beth replied that we knew the Strattons and Babcocks would be joining us, but not who the others would be. Joy grinned, pleased she could divulge some insider information to us. She said fourteen people had been invited, that Kristi would be having two tables of eight. She went on to tell us who the other guests would be. Though the names were familiar, most were strangers to Beth and me.

Nicholas and Kathryn Rumalto would be there. Nick was a professor in the Political Science department. Kat was very involved with several non-profits and was currently serving on the UMS board. Paul and Joan Ulrich would also be there. Paul was a fairly well known local attorney in general practice. Joan was a past-president of the Junior League and involved with the Ann Arbor Area Community Foundation. The other two were both single. Jean Hernandez had recently retired from heading up Ann Arbor Hospice. Joy believed she was a widow, but wasn't sure. Jim Nixon was a well known and very popular professor in U of M's LS&A School in the Religious Studies department. He'd been a speaker a few years ago at my Rotary Club. He'd given a very dynamic and entertaining talk on the subject of major religious observances by various faiths. Joy was right; it should prove to be a very interesting and fun filled evening.

Jerry asked Beth and me if we'd seen the story about the dating tests done on Jesus' robe. We acknowledged we had. Joy raised the question of whether Jesus should continue to wear the robe and sandals or should He now be switching to more conventional attire. Jerry and the two of us agreed that continuing to wear His biblical garb made sense by setting the tone for His numerous meetings and speeches. Joy said her opinion was the same as ours, but that she thought it was an interesting question to ask. Beth teased her, suggesting she should ask it again this evening.

We were the next to last group to arrive at the Cloverdales, the Babcocks came a few minutes later. Following all the introductions, Kristi suggested we all go out on the patio for cocktails. Tom had his bar set up out there. I'd pitched in to help him. Beth and Joy told Tom we'd expected him to be wearing the "Why Ann Arbor?" T-shirt. He'd laughed, asking them if they were aware of how many Kristi had purchased for him. Both had grinned and nodded as Beth explained she'd been with Kristi when she'd bought them. She went on to tell him how she and Joy had tried to talk Jerry and me into wearing ours tonight. Tom said we'd be surprised over how many times he'd had occasion to wear one of his.

"I'll have to say they've really been a conversation opener, getting the ball rolling in terms of getting people to voice their opinions about Jesus. They've stimulated some interesting discussions. I think Kristi has all my shirts in the laundry as a matter of fact. Unlike the two of you," Tom continued, gesturing at Beth and Joy, "she suggested I not wear one tonight. I think she was afraid if I did, the evening would be monopolized in talk about Jesus. I told her it would be a miracle if we didn't get around to discussing Jesus sometime this evening, even if I didn't' wear one."

I replied I thought that would be a safe bet, commenting on how much the media was focusing on Jesus. Tom agreed, laughing as he'd compared the coverage to that of O.J. Simpson's, Michael Jackson's and Clinton's trials, all combined.

The Strattons brought everyone up to date on their daughter's wedding plans, or lack of wedding plans I should say. Whitney's fiance's mother's precarious health was still keeping them from firming up a date. Mary said the couple was continuing to tease her about eloping. She hoped they were truly speaking in jest.

The stock market had soared over the past few days with the Dow up over 300 points. Everyone was asking Brad for his explanation. "Believe it or not," he'd said, "I think Jesus has something to do with it."

Kat Rumalto was enthusiastically telling us about the fall program for the University Musical Society and advising everyone to get their ticket orders in soon as they anticipated many of the performances would be sold out.

Next week's bus trip into Detroit to hear Jesus speak at Comerica Park was also discussed. Three of those present who hadn't been approached earlier signed on, Jean Hernandez and the Ulrichs.

Jim Nixon, who'd been intriguing us with stories about some of the humorous things that had happened in his classes, raised his arms and asked for everyone's attention.

"If all of you are willing, I'd like to conduct a little informal survey," he said. "I'd like to see how this group matches up to some of the surveys that have been done concerning the man claiming to be Jesus. You're going to have four options. One, you believe He's truly Jesus. Two, while still not sure, you're thinking He might be. Three, you're very doubtful He's Jesus. And four, you still haven't formed an opinion. Do you all understand the four options? Any questions? If not, why don't you go first Tom. How would you classify yourself?"

"Oh, I'm for sure a number one. I have to say though, when He first appeared, I was probably one of the most skeptical people in Ann Arbor. I can't say there was any one thing that turned me into a true believer. Looking back, I guess it was a gradual process. But I'm firmly convinced He's who He says He is. There's no doubt in my mind now."

"Who wants to go next?" Jim asked. Tory Babcock was hesitating as she raised her hand. "I'm not really volunteering," she said. "I don't know what the rest of you think, but I don't believe this is the time to be doing this. And it's not that I'm reluctant about telling everyone I'm probably a two. As most of you know, Brad and I are Catholics. The recent interview with the Pope did a lot to change our thinking. I should really say my thinking. I think Brad would say he's a number one and probably was even before the Pope's interview. But I'm concerned about putting people on the spot in a social setting. Someone who classifies him or herself as a three or four is apt to be harassed all evening."

Jim Nixon attempted to interrupt Tory, but she held up her hand to signal she wasn't quite finished. "I'm sure your intentions weren't to embarrass anyone Jim. And I don't' want to suggest discussions about Jesus should be off limits this evening. He is, after all, the main topic on nearly everyone's mind. I'm just suggesting maybe we could go about it in a better way. Isn't the question of whether one believes Jesus will succeed in His mission far more important than whether one believes He is truly Jesus?"

As Tory was speaking, Kristi had come out onto the patio again with another tray of hors d'oeuvres. She quickly set the tray down and began to applaud. "Bravo Tory!" she exclaimed. "You're saying exactly what I'd been tempted to say. And as the hostess I think I have a few prerogatives. Let's stop the quiz, Jim. But how about you leading us in a discussion on the question Tory suggests. I think you're the most knowledgeable one here to do it. What's your personal opinion? Do you think Jesus has any chance of bringing about God's Kingdom here on Earth?"

Jim was smiling as he replied, "I was hoping we might get into a lively discussion or two this evening. And I guess we are. I apologize if anyone felt as if I was trying to put them on the spot or embarrass them with my questions. It was definitely not my intention, Tory. And I wasn't envisioning myself being put on the spot as you've done with your question Kristi. But I'm game if you all want to listen to my opinion."

"I think everyone's eager to hear what you have to say Jim," Tom said. "But what's our schedule Kristi? You realize Jim's used to giving hour long lectures to his students."

Amid the laughter, Kristi explained we still had about half an hour before she planned on serving dinner. She suggested that Tom freshen up everyone's drink before Jim began and once again I pitched in to help him.

Jim began by saying the subject was one of the first things he had on his agenda to discuss with his students when they returned in another month. And no, he said chuckling, he wouldn't be taking up the full half hour giving us his opinion.

"When I first heard this man speak, and let's refer to Him as Jesus, I was very impressed. I'm still impressed for that matter. And I was truly awed that evening at Hill Auditorium when He identified who He was and outlined the reason for His return, the challenge He'd laid out for Himself, the mission God had given Him. But what did I think His chances for success were? Zilch! In my mind it was an impossible undertaking, in my mind I was comparing it to a Don Quixote like venture."

Jim paused and took a sip of his cocktail before continuing. Glancing around I could tell he certainly had everyone's attention.

"Has my opinion changed during the past few weeks as I've seen Him in action? Yes, it definitely has. But on a scale of one to a hundred, I believe He's only moved up to somewhere between five and ten. A five to ten percent chance of attaining His goal of reconciling the world under One God, establishing God's Kingdom here on Earth.

"There's no question Jesus has accomplished some amazing things in a very short time. Big and small. The instant rapport He's established with the Pope is a major accomplishment. Getting His message out to the Arab world is another. And here in Ann Arbor, are you all aware that over three thousand more of us are involved as volunteers for nonprofit agencies than before His arrival. Agencies, which were pleading for volunteers, are now forced to send those interested in volunteering elsewhere. Just a little thing, but multiply the effects of this happening in thousands of other communities around the world—it could have an amazing effect globally.

"We believe God is all knowing, that Jesus is all knowing. But I've found myself questioning whether They're aware of the immense animosity and the deep level of distrust that currently exists between people. And the extent of the conflicting beliefs dividing them. I still believe Jesus faces a huge challenge.

"I applaud Him for attempting to calm down the dialogue on controversial subjects such as abortion, birth control, creation, stem cell research, homosexuality, gene alteration, and a myriad of others. I applaud Him for saying that among the many blessings God has showered on mankind is an individual's ability to make choices. I applaud Him for saying men and women must change, that they need to turn to God for guidance, that they need to truly love and forgive one another, that they need to be good stewards and take good care of the world God has given them, and that they should use their collective God given talents to establish God's Kingdom here on Earth.

"And though I've never heard Jesus make the claim or even suggest that the goal He's laid out for Himself and mankind will be easy to achieve, I sense He's confident people can change and that reaching His goal is possible with God's help and guidance."

Jim paused again and I was thinking he was probably picturing us as his students, soaking up everything he was saying, captivated by his every word. He'd concluded by saying, "I hope and pray that Jesus knows what He's doing. I still believe His chance for failure is far, far greater, than His chance for success. But, I also believe that He might not envision His success to come in my lifetime, in our lifetimes. I will say that in the last few weeks, I've never been so fervent in my uttering of the Lord's Prayer. And there you have it. Kristi asked me to give you my opinion and I have. I'm open to questions, maybe some of you might have some comments. We still have about ten minutes before dinner, right Kristi?"

Kristi nodded. She smiled as she thanked Jim, suggesting we should all give him a round of applause. With her lead, we all enthusiastically did.

"I know that Jim's is a hard act to follow," Tom said. "But we still have a few minutes, and of course we can carry on this conversation during dinner. Anyone want to volunteer to go next?"

I was pleased and not surprised when Beth raised her hand. She indicated what she was about to say was a comment and then a question for Jim.

"I may be wrong, but I think that evening when Jesus introduced His followers at Hill Auditorium, He said something about having asked them for a six month commitment," Beth began. "If I'm right, this suggests to me that Jesus foresees something occurring by the first of the year or shortly thereafter, rather than sometime in the distant future. But that's not my question for you, Jim.

"In the discussions Mike and I've been having, he's suggested Jesus should come up with a universal prayer that all people could embrace. I agreed with him, but I questioned why the Lord's Prayer wouldn't be suitable. In my mind it incorporates most of the key points in Jesus' message. When you mentioned the Lord's Prayer a few minutes ago Jim, I thought about the discussion Mike and I had. I guess my question to you is actually two fold. First, do you agree with Mike that a universal prayer could play an important role in uniting the world in its worship of God? And if so, do you believe the Lord's Prayer could fulfill this need?"

"Those are interesting questions Beth," Jim replied. "And Mike, my compliments to you for coming up with the suggestion. Yes, I believe a prayer of some sort to reinforce Jesus' message is a great idea. I'd be very surprised if Jesus hasn't thought of it, wrestled with the wording and the best timing for presenting it. And no, even though as you suggest Beth the Lord's Prayer might cover the essentials of His message, I don't think it would stand a chance of being universally accepted. It's too closely identified with Christianity, even in its title. But I believe it does place Jesus in a quandary. Any new prayer would be compared to that prayer. Especially if it's a prayer introduced by Him. Am I suggesting God alone would have to originate it similar to the delivery of the Ten Commandments? Perhaps that is the best answer. But who would God choose to communicate through, if not Jesus? We believe, and often say, all things are possible through God. I believe Jesus will find a way to come up with the type of prayer Mike suggests. How and when is anybody's guess."

As Jim concluded, Kristi moved to the center of the group and started to speak. Tom had a horrified expression on his face and began waving his arms to stop her. "Don't worry Tom, I'm not going to say anything to embarrass you or jeopardize what you're intending to do. I'm not saying your idea isn't an original one, Mike. But Tom's had some of the same thoughts you've had. He's authored a suggested prayer he's planning on delivering to Jesus through one of His followers. He's pledged me to keep it confidential and I intend to as far as its contents. He was concerned that Jesus in His answer as to why He came to Ann Arbor was accused of plagiarizing, giving many of the same reasons Tom wrote about in his letter to the *Ann*

Tom. He's not doing it for any glory or acclaim. It just comes from the heart and I thought you all should know."

Tom was blushing as several of us spoke up, congratulating and thanking him for what he was doing. I'd found myself smiling. Less than a month ago if I'd been asked to classify Tom's religious beliefs, I would have said he was probably an agnostic. And now he appeared to be a giant step ahead of me in his religious convictions.

Kristi announced dinner was now being served and we all found our places.

Chapter XXXXV

My seatmates for dinner were Jean Hernandes, Mary Stratton, Kathryn Rumalto, Kristi Cloverdale, Jerry Hanson, Paul Ulrich, and Brad Babcock. It was a good group. The conversation was lively, it was surprising how many times we were engaged in laughter. So much so that Tom was prompted to come out from the room in which the others were seated to ask us what was so funny.

The food was delicious and we all kept complimenting Kristi. Several of us went back for seconds. It wasn't until we were having dessert that we got back on the subject of Jesus. Brad initiated it by saying the question of where Jesus was getting the funding to finance Himself and His followers still hadn't been answered.

"Someone or some group has to be contributing big bucks," he said. "Just the cost of His followers' travels has to cost a bundle. I know I'd feel a lot more comfortable about Him if I knew the source of His money.

"A friend of mine was teasing me the other day. He knows I'm a died in the wool Catholic. He suggested that the Catholic Church might be financing Him, that it certainly had ample resources to do so. I laughed it off telling him it was more likely Planned Parenthood. However, the more I've thought about it, the suggestion of the Catholic Church being involved doesn't sound as ridiculous as it first seemed. You're all aware many of my faith would like to see some changes. That's particularly true here in the U.S. It now appears Jesus might be the catalyst to spark some of those changes.

I'm sure most of you are familiar with what the Pope had to say about his meetings with Jesus. The Cardinals are going to be meeting next week in Rome. Maybe there's some truth to the thought that the Church or some faction in the Church is financing Him. Who knows?"

Paul Ulrich was the first one to respond to Brad. He explained that when Brad first mentioned the possibility of the Catholic Church being involved he'd started to laugh.

"But like you, Brad, now I'm not so sure that's as crazy as it first seemed to me. I learned yesterday that a case which was on a fast track to get to the Supreme Court has now been put on hold. It's that New Jersey case you may have read about. A challenge to Roe vs. Wade and abortion rights. Right to Life Groups had been financing it. The scuttlebutt is that if the Catholic Church was to alter its anti-abortion stance, the case would become a moot issue. I myself, don't believe we'll be seeing the Catholic Church changing its position anytime soon. But as you've said Brad, there's going to be that meeting of the Cardinals next week in Rome. Who knows for sure what will occur there?"

Others jumped in offering their opinions and comments. I stayed out of the discussion. The general conclusion was the meeting in Rome might bring some surprises, but no one was willing to bet on the fact the Catholic Church was the financing arm behind Jesus.

Jean Hernandes led us into another subject. She'd said she was intrigued by what Jesus had been saying, that the God He was describing was the God she wanted to have to glorify and worship. "I have to confess that some of the images of God portrayed in the Old Testament in particular, made me feel uncomfortable at times.

I don't know if that's good or bad.

"But the point I wanted to raise is my concern over the media's focus on the Roman Catholic Church and Catholics' reactions to some of the views expressed by Jesus. I think they're being unfairly singled out. Many other faiths are also being challenged by what Jesus has been saying. For example, mega-churches currently represent the fastest growing segments of Protestant denominations. In general, they appear to be characterized by their more fundamentalist beliefs compared to other main line Protestant churches, their literal interpretation of the Bible. I believe some of the things Jesus has been saying run counter to this conviction, counter to the sincere beliefs of many of Christianity's most fervent advocates. He's said, for example, that God is not responsible for everything that happens in the world. I don't know most of your religious affiliations, but if I were a Southern Baptist or a member of one of those other fundamentalist congregations, I think I'd believe Jesus was turning my world upside down, threatening my core beliefs. And I'd be asking Him if this was what God really wanted Him to be doing, the reason for His Second Coming. I realize I've been rambling, but I hope you understand the point I'm trying to make. The beliefs of many millions, in addition to Catholics, are being challenged by Jesus."

Kat Rumalto was the first to respond to Jean's comment. She began by saying she thought all of us understood what Jean was saying, complimenting her for clearly making her point.

"But I think we all have to remember that Jesus is taking His message to the entire world," Kat continued. "If He was just attempting to establish God's Kingdom On Earth here in the good old U.S.A, I think His approach would be different. Here we have over

250 million Christians, over 80% of our population. If you lumped Jews, Muslims and believers in other faiths together, the total would be less than 11 million. I think we have to understand the need for Jesus to refine His message if He's to succeed in His goal of making God's Kingdom On Earth a reality."

As Kat was speaking, I thought of some of the conversations I'd had with Beth along this same line. I'd chimed in, telling Kat I agreed with her. "And even here in this country there are probably nearly 30 million people who currently profess no religion. And I think the percentage of those involved in no religion is even higher in many other countries where Christianity is the dominant faith, France, for example. Jesus has to find a way to get His message across to them, too. A message which will turn them into living lives to glorify God. Loving and respecting themselves, their fellow man and God. It's an enormous challenge as Jim said earlier."

"A huge challenge," Mary Stratton said, "But I think the way in which people are gathering to worship today will be helpful to Jesus. Remember when if you knew a person's nationality you could pretty well guess their religion. Germans were usually Lutherans, those of English heritage were usually Episcopalians, the Scotch were Presbyterians, the Irish and the Italians were Catholics and so on. That's not so much true today. The growing mega-churches, Jean referred to earlier, usually don't even have a traditional denomination in their name. And even though Jesus is saying people are free to make choices in how they choose to honor and worship God and that they therefore, can continue on in their respective faiths, I believe more than ever people are open to an ecumenical message. I think this is why Jesus hasn't prompted more criticism."

"Have you considered that people might still be in a state of shell shock?" Jerry Hanson said, laughing. "I think they're still pondering over how Jesus is going to affect them as individuals or as a congregation if they're in one. What needs to change?"

The conversation continued for nearly another hour before Brad glanced at his watch and exclaimed it was past 11:00pm. All of us were surprised it was so late, the time had flown by quickly.

Chapter XXXXVI

During our drive home Jerry and I filled our wives in on some of the discussion at our table and they did the same for us. Jim Nixon's observations had dominated the discussion at their table.

"It wasn't because he was seeking to hold center stage and monopolize the conversation," Joy explained. "It's just that he's so knowledgeable about faiths other than Christianity, we flooded him with questions. I learned a lot. How about you, Beth?"

"I agree. It was a fascinating discussion," Beth replied. "Do you know, for example, that Hinduism is thought to be the oldest religion in the world? That it's the only major religion in the world not identified by a founder."

"And that 80% of the population in India identify themselves as Hindus," Joy added. "And as a Hindu you're free to believe in one deity, one God, or multiple deities, or not even in any God at all."

"What about reincarnation?" Jerry asked. "Isn't that one of the basic concepts of Hinduism?"

"Yes, it is," Joy said. "Jim explained the Law of Karma where one is reborn to a higher level of existence based on their moral behavior in a previous state of existence. But there's no single creed or doctrine. The caste system originated out of Hinduism."

"And the Hindu religion continues to evolve," Beth said. "It was as recent as the 1950s that India passed laws banning individuals from treating others as Untouchables for example."

I said I'd also always associated Buddhists with India and asked if Jim had said anything about them.

"Oh yes," Joy responded, "they're still a major factor, India has such a huge population. That religion focuses on one establishing peace of mind, an inner peace. Buddha means "Awakened One", according to Jim. An awakening from the sleep of ignorance, seeking perfection in their lives. Various sources explain the steps an adherent needs to take to achieve this inner peace.

"What Jim was trying to do for us was to layout some of the problems facing Jesus in the non-Christian world. He did a good job of it, too; everyone was really involved. Nick and Joan asked some very thought provoking questions. And Tom amazed everyone with his ability to contribute quotes from memory and not just Biblical ones. He's well versed on Judaism, Islam and Hinduism as well. We had a very congenial group. The closest we came to an argument, and it wasn't much of one, was when someone suggested we speculate on the outcome of next week's conclave in Rome. Tory would have none of that, arguing that we shouldn't be attempting to place ourselves in the mindsets of the Pope and Cardinals, that to do so would be sacrilegious."

I commented that it was surprising how the discussions at the two tables could be so different even though we were both conversing on basically the same subject. The others agreed with me. During the remainder of the drive, Beth and Joy discussed arrangements for next Tuesday's bus trip into Detroit.

Chapter XXXXVII

The Saturday morning papers featured the story on the special meeting the Pope had called for at the Vatican. There were profiles on the Cardinals who would be attending from the United States. There was also a story on the investigation underway in Israel. The five under arrest were expected to plead guilty. They were now thought to have been the only ones to have been involved in the assassination attempt on Jesus. All were sticking to the same story, that the act had been a botched attempt to smear the Palestinians. There'd been no desire to harm Jesus or any of His followers. The shooter was supposed to have fired a shot over Jesus' head and escape in the panic and confusion, which the shot was expected to provoke. It was thought the security personnel guarding Jesus would refrain from shooting back at the would be assassin because of fear of killing or injuring innocent people he'd hide among. The five seemed to be full of remorse and saddened their actions had resulted in the death of David Epstein.

It seemed apparent Israel wanted to get this matter wrapped up as quickly as possible and not have to deal with a highly publicized trial. There was even speculation that after the five pleaded guilty, they might be turned over to the Palestinian authorities for sentencing. While this struck me as a farfetched idea as I first read it, the more I thought about it, the more it seemed that it would be a smart move on the part of Israel. Any plea bargains or sentences doled out by Israel were bound to be second guessed, regardless of what they were. The five might even have a better chance for receiving shorter sentences from the Palestinians than the ones Israel might feel were necessary to counter any thought it condoned the incident. The move also could be viewed as an attempt at reconciliation by Israel. The risk I guess was that the Palestinians might determine capital punishment was warranted or draconian prison terms.

Later as I was discussing the article with Beth and telling her why I thought Israel might consider turning the five over to the Palestinians for sentencing, she came up with an interesting suggestion.

"I think it would be wonderful if the Palestinians were to come forward and suggest that in lieu of prison sentences, Israel mandated the five to do something constructive like building or repairing homes of Palestinians for two or three years. If they didn't comply, they'd go to jail."

I smiled. "That's an excellent idea, Beth. Israel could just do that on its own, too, without a suggestion from the Palestinians. I think you should e-mail someone, maybe phone Rabbi Winkleman. He'd advise you who you should contact. What you're suggesting could turn a negative for Israel into a big positive."

"I think I will," Beth said. "It's Saturday though, Rabbi Winkleman will be involved with services. I think I'll call our Congressman. Let him take some credit for the suggestion if he thinks it's a good one."

Beth immediately got a phone call through to our Congressman's office. Though he wasn't in, the assistant to whom she'd spoken was very enthusiastic over the idea and assured Beth she'd get word to him within the next few hours. She promised Beth that she or the Congressman would get back to her.

As Beth was making the call I'd spotted one more article of interest in the *Free Press*. Martha Seidman was reported to be making arrangements for Jesus' speech at the U.N. next week, the morning before His coming to speak at Comerica Park. Martha Seidman was David Epstein's sister. The article said she'd be heading to the Mid-East following Jesus' appearance at the U.N.

The remainder of the morning passed by rather quickly. We phoned all four of our children to get an update on how they and their families were doing. Things appeared to be going well for all of them. Our grandchildren would be busy in a slew of activities over the weekend, it exhausted the two of us in just hearing their schedule of events. All were interested to learn of our plans to be heading into Detroit to hear Jesus. That led into some interesting discussions. Our offspring were not yet as convinced as Beth and I were that the preacher was truly Jesus, but they were getting there. From the time of my initial encounter with Jesus at the Farmer's Market, we'd kept them informed of all the happenings in Ann Arbor.

I paid a few bills while Beth was doing the wash. We were due to meet the Strattons for golf at 1:30pm. We'd made arrangements with them at the Cloverdales last night. We'd also be staying on for dinner.

Chapter XXXXVIII

The weather was ideal for a day on the golf course. We hadn't had much rain in the past few days and as a result our balls were rolling a little farther than usual.

Later as we were having cocktails Mary announced she had some major news for us. Whitney had phoned them that morning saying she and Lance wanted to set a wedding date for sometime in November. She explained she hadn't mentioned something earlier because she hadn't been sure how much she should be telling us.

"You know Whitney and it shouldn't surprise you to hear she did contact Ernie Smith and Ginny Roberts to discuss the possibility of Jesus officiating at her wedding. They informed her that it wouldn't be likely, that there'd already been numerous invitations for Him to participate in funerals, baptisms, weddings and family celebrations which had been turned down. He was hesitant about accepting any, knowing He'd then be swamped by more requests. The uncertainties in His busy schedule makes it difficult for Him to commit to a date. As you've probably read or heard, He's often made spontaneous appearances at various events. Ernie and Ginny did say they'd speak to Him, however, and get back with her. And they did, Ernie Smith phoned her last night."

"And the answer was no," Rob said. "Jesus couldn't guarantee He'd be available regardless of the date."

"But they've decided on a November date, does that have something to do with Lance's mother's prognosis?" Beth asked.

"Yes and no," Mary replied, clearly hesitant about going into further details. "Nothing's really changed in that respect. But in addition to telling Whitney Jesus had declined her invitation, Ernie also said Jesus was advising her to have the wedding before the 1st of the year. He told her Lance's mother would be making a dramatic recovery in the next month or so, but that it would only be temporary."

"The strange thing about this is that our daughter had never even mentioned anything about Lance's mother in her previous conversation with Mr. Smith or Miss Roberts," Rob said. "How they or Jesus knew about her is a mystery."

"Now you know the full story," Mary added. "You can understand why I was reluctant to explain why Whitney and Lance were picking a November date. You've been dear friends for a very long time. I hope you'll keep what we've told you to yourselves. We assured Whitney we wouldn't tell anyone about this. We've already broken that promise in telling you."

We'd both told Mary and Rob not to worry, assuring them we'd keep this discussion a secret. Sensing they were still a little uncomfortable about having confided in us, I'd attempted to change the subject. I asked if they'd heard about some of the positive things happening in Ann Arbor since Jesus' arrival, the fact that over three hundred people, including several UofM students, had signed up for the Peace Corps in the past couple weeks. There had been a rejuvenation of the Peace Corps in recent days. The fact that John F. Kennedy had presented the idea for it right here in Ann Arbor, on the steps of the Michigan Union, heightened local interest in this rejuvenation. Mary replied that they had, Whitney had told them about it.

"She also told us about a rumor on campus you might be interested in. I know she's told you about other rumors, I don't think she'd be offended if I told you the latest one. You've probably read that Jesus has visited Iran a couple times in recent weeks. The rumor is that another meeting will be taking place there in a few days. What makes this planned meeting so unique is that a sizeable number of Israeli religious and government leaders will be accompanying Jesus to the meeting. The fact that it wasn't that long ago the President of Iran was advocating the destruction of Israel is what makes this so exciting. If Jesus can truly bring about peace and reconciliation in that area of the world, He should be able to do it anywhere. Rumor has it that six UofM students have been invited to the meeting. Martha Seidman, the sister of David Epstein, who was the young man who was killed during the assassination attempt on Jesus, is the one who contacted the students. I think you're aware she's signed on to be a follower of Jesus."

Beth and I both nodded. I asked if the students were all Jewish. Mary shook her head, saying Whitney had told them at least two were and that at least two were Iranians, five men and one woman. Beth commented about what a great opportunity it would be for the students, an exciting educational experience and a possible chance of witnessing history being made.

We had wine with our meal and made two toasts, one to Whitney and Lance and their upcoming marriage, the other to Jesus and His success.

Chapter XXXXIX

The Sunday papers mainly featured stories on what would be occurring over the course of the next week; the meeting of the Cardinals in Rome, the appearance of Jesus at the U.N. on Tuesday morning and the event at Comerica Park on Tuesday evening. All the tickets for the latter event had already been spoken for. Over ten thousand of the attendees had made the one hundred dollar donation for early childhood learning programs, I couldn't find any mention about the upcoming meeting by Jesus in Iran.

There was one letter of interest among the Letters to the Editor in the *Ann Arbor News*. The letter was critical of Jesus for spending so much of his time in the world's troubled spots. The writer lamented the fact squeaky wheels seemed to always draw more attention than they warranted and commented on the fact Jesus was thought to have been in South America only once since He'd begun His travels. The writer also suggested Australia and New Zealand were due a visit by Jesus.

I smiled as I read the letter in that I'd just finished reading a short article about Jesus' visit to Northern Ireland. The article had stated Jesus had accomplished a great deal during His two day visit. One outgrowth from His visit was the start-up of a new church which was meeting and holding services in a building located on the dividing line separating the Catholic and Protestant areas in the city of Belfast.

It was being staffed by two Catholic Priests and two Protestant Clergy and was welcoming Catholics and Protestants in joint worship. It had been named God's Church.

Northern Ireland definitely qualified as one of the minor trouble spots the letter writer had been referring to. But though it might be minor, it appeared as if Jesus' success had been major. He'd brought hope that reconciliation and peace could occur in an area torn by conflict over many generations. I hoped that Jesus and His followers wouldn't see the letter and He'd continue to seek out areas, small or not, where He could make an immediate impact for good.

Beth and I watched the recap of Jesus' appearance before the U.N. as we had our lunch on Tuesday. Other than a few pickets and people criticizing the decision of having a religious leader addressing the world body, the coverage of Jesus' appearance at the U.N. was very favorable. His speech had encompassed an hour with an additional half hour of questions. He'd been given a rousing round of applause at the end. Delegates interviewed on the news we watched were unanimous in their praise of Jesus, they called His remarks very inspirational. Some described His talk as a wake-up call, coming at a time when the U.N. was being heavily criticized in many quarters. He encouraged the delegates to put their petty differences and jealousies aside and work together for a better world. One delegate interviewed said, "He restored our confidence into believing we can truly accomplish the great things the U.N. was designed to do. The level of enthusiasm among all the delegates following His appearance was a joy to behold. He wasn't critical of anything the U.N. had done in the past or the past actions of any countries. Everything He said was positive, pointing to the future."

The U.S. Representative to the U.N. was equally lavish in his praise saying he now had renewed hope for the organization. He announced he'd be pressing his government to pay up its past due assessments as quickly as possible.

The bus ride into Detroit was enjoyable. We had nearly a full load, thirty seven people. Joy and Beth received rave reviews on the goodies they'd prepared for the trip. Jesus' appearance before the U.N. was one of the main topics of conversation. Jerry led the group in a couple of songs, old time favorites such as "For Me and My Gal". The highlight was a chorus of "Tell Me Why". Jerry passed out a song sheet with a change in the lyrics and said the new version was dedicated to Tom Cloverdale. The revised lyrics asked the question "Tell Me Why He Chose A Square, Tell Me Why He Came There".

The weather was beautiful, a grand evening for sitting outside. We were all in our seats by about 7:15pm. They were good seats, too. A few rows behind what was normally third base. A small stage had been set up in the middle of the field. At 7:25pm about twenty people took their seats on the stage. They represented the planning committee for the event. One of the most well known preachers in Detroit approached the microphone and introduced himself and then each of the people on stage with him. He'd asked the crowd to withhold its applause until all were introduced. Following the ovation, he'd announced how much money the event had raised. This was greeted by another round of applause. The preacher then introduced Jesus. To the delight of all, Jesus jogged in from the bullpen. As He waved to the crowd which was standing and applauding, He'd nearly tripped on his robe. The crowd laughed as He reached down and lifted the hem of the robe to prevent His tripping again. As He went up the stairs and approached the lectern, the audience quieted. In fact, there was close to complete silence as He started to speak. The preacher who'd introduced Him had used a microphone, but Jesus gently pushed it aside. Similar to our experience in the UofM Stadium, you could clearly hear every word He said.

He began by thanking the organizers. He'd then thanked everyone present for coming, using about six languages to express His appreciation. On the bus ride over someone had mentioned Jesus had circulated through the audience following His appearance at the U.N., greeting delegates in their native languages. I continued to be awed by the fact Jesus could communicate in so many languages. However, except for these initial welcomes, His speech was in English.

To say He'd held the crowd spellbound for the next hour and a half would almost be an understatement. The crowd appeared to absorb every word, responding at appropriate times with laughter, tears or applause. Early on He raised the question of affirmative action. As He'd done in other instances, He began His answer by asking the audience a series of questions. He then said that rather than looking at legislative bodies or the courts for answers, we should all look to ourselves. He said God in His commandment instructing us to love one another was asking each of us to take affirmative action. He said God was directing each of us to give of our time, talents and resources to help the less fortunate among us. He provided vivid descriptions and examples of who some of those less fortunate in our own communities and country were. Those with physical and mental handicaps, those who were economically and/or educationally drug and alcohol addiction, and those who found themselves trapped in an abusive marriage or an abusive home environment. He'd said the less fortunate were of all ages and not confined to any one race.

He'd then gone on to describe some of those who were less fortunate in other parts of the world. He'd quoted some of the remarks He'd made before the U.N earlier in the day and praised the organization for its affirmative actions. He'd also praised the U.S. and its government leaders for taking the lead in providing money, technology, and knowledge to many of those nations in Africa with dire problems. And He also acknowledged and commended the fact this aid was moving in the direction of providing more than just food and medicine, but also the tools, technology, education and financing to enable people to help themselves.

Jesus had then turned to the subject of discrimination. He'd said God does not discriminate, that His love knows no boundaries. God was always present for His children regardless of their sex, race, or socioeconomic status. He acknowledged that there was sometimes a fine line between discrimination and affirmative action. He then gave a parable. As He spoke I couldn't help but think of the parable of the Prodigal Son. There was some similarity to the message that it often is the least deserving child in a family or the least deserving individuals in a society who are in most need of a parent's or a community's love, attention, help and forgiveness. He said God rejoiced when one or more people went out of their way to assist a stranger, conveying His love through their actions. God demanded more than good intentions from us He said. Affirmative actions without discrimination appeared to be Jesus' theme.

But His main message was still His challenge for people to

actions without discrimination appeared to be Jesus' theme.

But His main message was still His challenge for people to change to truly establish God's Kingdom On Earth. His message was upbeat as He'd asked people to imagine what that could mean for the city of Detroit. I failed to mention earlier that approximately two-thirds of the attendees were African Americans and probably most of those were residents of Detroit. Glancing around, I could see they were being inspired by Jesus' message. There was only one time when Jesus was at all critical and I couldn't help but think He was addressing this group. In stressing that God was a forgiving God, He'd said God demands that we forgive one another. He said that a person or group of people who believed they were owed something by society or government because they'd been sinned against in the past were not listening to God. He said people were motivated to help others by God's love and their love for their fellow human beings, not by accusations designed to make them feel guilty and require them to compensate for their or their ancestors past sins.

Jesus ended His talk by quoting from a letter which had appeared in the *Detroit Free Press*. It was written by a woman who lived in the suburbs. She'd recently visited the Detroit Institute of the Arts to see a special exhibit it was having. She'd been delighted and surprised by the reception she'd received. She said the staff and volunteers couldn't have been more gracious, caring or kind. They made her day a very special one. She concluded her letter by saying how wonderful it would be if whenever and wherever she visited in Detroit, she'd experience the same warm and friendly welcome she received at the Art Institute.

Jesus concluded by telling the crowd that could happen, that they and others could make it happen with God's blessing and God's guidance. As the crowd stood and enthusiastically applauded, Jesus went around the stage, embracing each member of the organizing committee. And then, as the audience collectively seemed to gasp, Jesus suddenly vanished. I'd never read or heard of Him ever doing something of that nature in the past. I glanced over at Beth who was also wide-eyed. I was convinced that in Jesus we were witnessing the most important happening in world history unfolding. What a privilege! I bowed my head in prayer, praying Jesus would be successful.

Chapter L

On the bus ride back to Ann Arbor, the conversation was quite subdued. I think all of us were in awe, the others probably having the same thoughts or feelings I'd been having. God and Jesus were out to change the world and we were present to watch it happen, challenged to change ourselves.

Paul and Joan Ulrich were sitting across the aisle from Beth and me. Joan commented to us how impressed they'd been with Jesus. She explained it was their first exposure to Him, they hadn't seen Him in the UofM stadium or at Hill Auditorium.

"I'm just hoping the media doesn't play up those comments of His that seemed to be directed to the African American Community. His message was so positive otherwise. Besides, I don't fully agree with what was said and I doubt if I'm alone in my thinking. African Americans have had their civil rights violated for years. I think they have a legitimate grievance, a reason to ask for favored treatment in regard to college admissions, employment opportunities and so on. Yes, probably they should forgive those who've wronged them over the past few centuries. But this is about how they were mistreated, not the guilty parties. I think they have a valid reason for believing the current plight of many African Americans is directly related to the opportunities they were denied. It maybe is reverse discrimination, but I don't see how we can place them in the position of asking for charitable handouts when their grievances are so real."

"I agree with you, Joan, in respect to hoping the media doesn't blow that part of His message out of proportion," Beth replied. "They were only a handful of sentences in what was it, an hour and a half long speech? In some of His previous statements Jesus has emphasized the importance of diversity. I'm surprised He didn't today. That's the basis for UofM's admission policies, modified affirmative action which the Supreme Court blessed. I think Jesus would, too. And I believe what Jesus was trying to emphasize today was the need for people to come together to address problems and inequities and indicating that becomes more difficult when a group comes in with a chip on its shoulder."

"You may be right, Beth," Joan said. "And thank you for explaining that Jesus stressed the need for diversity in other instances. As I said previously, Paul and I were truly enthralled by Jesus and what He had to say. It was only that one portion of the speech that was unsettling to me. And rather than the media blowing it out of proportion, its probably just me."

Joan was smiling as she finished her statement. Paul smiled as well as he thanked us for having invited them to join us. "It's truly been a fabulous day, seeing and hearing Jesus, the food, the company and even the singing," Paul said. "I notice no one's asked Jerry to lead us in a few more songs. It would seem inappropriate after this awesome experience. The other night Jim was asking us to classify ourselves as to what we believed about this man who was calling himself Jesus. I'd say after today I'm definitely a 'one' and I believe anyone who was there today would answer the same. Thank you again for encouraging us to come."

It was a little past ten-thirty when our bus pulled into the parking lot bordering Pioneer High School. We'd boarded the bus there and left our cars parked in the lot. Joy and Beth were being thanked and complimented by everyone. A few joked that we'd have to do this again sometime soon. Tom told me I should look into the possibility of chartering a plane next time as it appeared Jesus would be spending the bulk of His time overseas. I couldn't tell if he was teasing me or not.

As Beth and I were preparing for bed I clicked on the TV I was interested in seeing what the news commentators were saying about tonight's event. Maybe we'd find our group pictured. I'd noticed several cameras panning the crowd as Jesus was speaking.

The main story being highlighted wasn't about Jesus' appearance in Comerica Park, however. There had been a bomb scare on an international flight. The plane had been on its way to Rome from New York City and had been diverted to Ireland. There had been a phone call warning a bomb was on the aircraft. A bomb squad, which boarded the plane after the passengers had disembarked using emergency chutes, had indeed found a bomb. Officials were calling it a miracle that the bomb hadn't detonated during the flight. Among the passengers on the flight were seven or eight Cardinals on their way to the conclave at the Vatican. After stating viewers would be kept updated on this story, coverage turned to the speech by Jesus at Comerica Park.

The highlight of this coverage was footage of Jesus vanishing after embracing members of the event's organizing committee. The clip was rerun several times. The newscaster kept repeating no one thus far, had been able to come up with an explanation as to how Jesus had accomplished that feat. The newscaster also reported Jesus had spoken without the use of a microphone and yet everyone in the huge crowd had appeared to hear him clearly. I was a little disappointed not to see more coverage on the content of Jesus' speech, instead focusing on His mysterious disappearance and His being easily heard by the huge crowd. There was only a sentence or two about what He'd said. The reporter stated Jesus had firmly come out in favor of affirmative action. As the reporter turned to the story of Jesus' appearance at the U.N., I switched channels. The new channel was highlighting Jesus' speech. This reporter was saying Jesus had built a strong case against discrimination in any form. I found myself shaking my head. Viewers of the two channels would get totally different pictures of what Jesus had said. I hoped tomorrow's newspapers would do a better job of fully reporting what He'd actually said.

The newscaster was now introducing a reporter on the scene at the airport to which the plane with a bomb aboard had been diverted. He was interviewing one of the men who'd removed the explosive device from the aircraft. The man gave a detailed description of the device. It was still a mystery as to how it had gotten on the plane and who was responsible.

Chapter LI

I was pleased to see the *Detroit Free Press* had published the full text of Jesus' speech in its Wednesday edition. However, the focus of the story on the Comerica Park Event was Jesus' disappearing act. There were two photos on the front page. One showed Jesus thanking and embracing the members of the event's organizing committee following His speech. The photo next to it showed the same scene minus Jesus. There were wide-eyed expressions on the faces of those on the stage.

I was pleased when I reached the editorial page, however, to see the main editorial dealt with the "Together" theme of the Comerica Park Event rather than Jesus' miraculous vanishing act. It was upbeat, suggesting Jesus' speech could be the spark to fuel a new beginning for the city of Detroit. That it could lead the citizens of Detroit and people from all over the state of Michigan to join together to find and finance solutions to address the many problems facing the city. The editorial had concluded by saying, "Hopefully, the widely held belief that Detroit is a lost cause will change. Can Detroit become a place where people want to visit, want to work, want to live? We believe it can. The road map laid out by Jesus can get us there."

Over the course of the morning there were several calls from people who'd been on the bus trip with us, once again thanking us for having included them and telling us what an enjoyable evening it had been. With several medical appointments, numerous meetings and baby sitting chores, the next few days passed by quickly. The investigation dealing with the explosive device found on the plane was still ongoing. No answers to the many questions surrounding the incident had been found. The meeting of Roman Catholic Church leaders at the Vatican was underway, shrouded in secrecy. The individuals involved in the assassination attempt on Jesus had pleaded guilty. They were to be sentenced in two weeks. Beth had still not heard back from our Congressman concerning her suggestion. Saturday morning's newspapers had articles about a meeting Jesus had attended in Iran. I'd been looking for mention of the meeting ever since the Strattons had told us about the rumor which had been circulating around the UofM campus. The articles stated that in addition to Iranian government officials and religious leaders, several Israeli government and religious leaders had also attended the meeting. There were few details as to what had been discussed. However, those in attendance were being quoted as saying the meeting had been productive and a good beginning. A decision had been made to have a follow up meeting in three weeks. The location had yet to be decided. There was no mention of the UofM students who supposedly had been invited to attend the meeting.

There was also a story reporting Jesus had been invited to speak to the group of Cardinals currently meeting at the Vatican. His appearance was scheduled for Monday morning. Even though the time difference would give newspapers the opportunity to report in their Monday morning editions how Jesus had been received and what He said, the fact that everything was being kept so secret about the meetings thus far, probably meant they wouldn't have much to report.

The *Ann Arbor News* had an article giving an update on Jesus' followers. They were being given an enthusiastic reception in nearly every locale they'd visited. Thousands of people were showing up to hear them. The article mentioned that initial meetings were underway in China, Burma, North Korea, Indonesia and Argentina to establish ground-rules for the followers in those countries, nations which had, thus far, been reluctant to giving them full access to their citizens. One of the most interesting things in the story was the statement saying at the end of the month Jesus' followers would be returning to Ann Arbor to meet with Jesus. Beth and I had been thinking we'd perhaps seen the last of Jesus in person at Comerica park, maybe that wasn't true. Hopefully, His return to Ann Arbor wouldn't be limited to meeting with His followers, that there'd be a public appearance of some kind.

There were at least half a dozen letters to the editor in the *Ann Arbor News* which had seemingly been prompted by Jesus' speech at Comerica Park. Only one was negative, alleging Detroit was a disaster zone. "The state shouldn't be pouring money in to solve problems which Detroiters brought on themselves. They dug the hole they're in, let them dig themselves out of the mess. It's a war zone down there. We should hope the Detroit River overflows and washes the place away."

I was turned off by the anger and bitterness reflected in the letter. Rather than feeling Detroit was a lost cause, I felt the letter writer was the problem and was probably not alone in his thinking, there were no doubt many others with similar thoughts. How do you turn them around, how do you get everyone pulling together, I asked myself? People's prejudices presented an awesome challenge.

I felt much better after reading some of the other letters. None really minimized Detroit's problems or the huge obstacles faced in solving them. However, they were all positive, most making suggestions as to how best to help Detroiters. One letter writer had heaped praise on Michigan citizens for their generosity in coming to the aid of the victims of recent natural disasters. Not only with their dollars, but in many instances with their time and talents as well. The writer also praised the hundreds of churches in Michigan who were involved in Mission Trips to Mexico, Haiti, the Philippines, and other spots all over the world. The letter continued saying, "We need to remind ourselves we have neighbors right here in Michigan which also require our help. I'm not only referring to the city of Detroit, communities such as Flint, Saginaw and Benton Harbor are also filled with people who need our help. Earlier this week, Jesus reminded thousands of people at Comerica Park of God's command to love our neighbors and to demonstrate that love by affirmative acts. God expects us to step forward with our time, talents and dollars to alleviate the pain and suffering of others. The pain and suffering might be the result of drugs, the result of being unable to find work, the result of not knowing where your next meal is coming from or a host of other reasons. There are many avenues through which we can individually and collectively make a difference in peoples lives. Get involved! Now!"

Another letter writer made the suggestion that a percentage of the dollars raised by Washtenaw United Way, possibly 10%, be allocated to less affluent communities in Michigan. One proposed a program, similar to World War II's Marshall Plan, to help Detroit, financed by charitable gifts. One letter writer referred to the intellectual brain power the University of Michigan could call on to help find solutions to address the city of Detroit's problems. The writer urged the University to set up "Think Tanks", diverse groups charged with the responsibility of coming up with recommendations to address specific problems.

My favorite of the letters was titled "Hands Off Or Hands On". That writer made a strong case for people becoming involved in coming to the aid of Detroit in a "hands on" fashion, not just with their dollars or other contributions such as food, clothing, books or toys. The writer then painted a dire picture of what might be the result if people were to simply shrug their shoulders and take a hands off approach to Detroit's problems. This scenario was frightening, yet in many ways this is what had been happening. A reader of the letter could really only come up with one answer, a "Hands On" approach was required. The letter writer ended with the statement, "We're running out of time, it's now or never."

Beth and I served communion on Sunday morning. The sermon was an especially good one. I couldn't help but think our pastor had been in the crowd at Comerica Park to hear Jesus. Sometimes a sermon left one sitting back and counting their blessings, God's blessings. Not that this sermon didn't, but it was also a call to action message. A call to action for us as individuals, a call to action for us as a congregation. His sermon didn't leave us thinking whether we should be involved, it left everyone thinking how best they could be involved. It was a wonderful feeling. I wondered if a similar message was being heard in other Ann Arbor churches, in churches throughout the state. If so, the spirit of goodwill which would be launched would be awesome. Jesus had clearly sparked this. I couldn't help but think and feel God was guiding things.

Chapter LII

Monday morning's *USA Today* ran a front page story on Jesus' meeting at the Vatican. The article reported Jesus had addressed the group for close to an hour followed by another hour in which He answered questions. The news media had been camped outside for the past few days with little to report. They'd attempted to question Jesus as He departed from the Vatican following His appearance, but He'd declined to answer questions. The article said He'd been smiling as He waved from the limo as it was driving off.

The article went on to report the news media was taken by surprise when less than an hour later the Pope came out to meet with them. The Pope told them Jesus had been warmly received by the Cardinals. He'd also explained the group had been unanimous in its vote to extend an invitation to Jesus to speak to them. The Pope then gave the media another surprise by announcing he'd made the decision to adjourn the meeting. He'd quickly added that he was going to have the Cardinals reconvene in thirty days. Over that period, He explained everyone would have the opportunity to reflect on what Jesus had said and to prayfully consider what their response should be. He'd said the Cardinals were in agreement with his decision. The third surprise came when the Pope said he'd allow a few minutes for questions. This was almost unprecedented.

The first question, the article stated, concerned what Jesus had said to the group. The Pope explained the content was much the same as what Jesus had covered in His previous private conversations with him. "There were no real surprises. My previous interview in *Time Magazine* covered much of what we discussed then."

The next question dealt with what questions the Cardinals had asked. The article reported the Pope had smiled before beginning his answer. He was quoted as having said, "Similar to what I had done in preparation for my initial meeting with Jesus, several Cardinals had made notes in advance in hopes they'd have an opportunity to direct questions to Jesus. They had the relevant passages of scripture at hand to reinforce their questions. And they were excellent questions, I was very proud of my Cardinals. They covered a broad range of subjects: Salvation, The Holy Trinity, His prophesied Second Coming, Heaven, Hell and many more. Rather than me going into detail as to how He answered these questions, I think it would probably be best if Jesus were to personally give you His answers at a later time. I believe He has plans to do this, to answer everyone's questions while He's with us."

The article stated that the Pope's final sentence had prompted one reporter to ask if Jesus had told them how long He'd be here on Earth? The article said that the Pope had shaken his head and explained that the lack of an answer wasn't because the question hadn't been asked, it had been. Again the Pope was quoted as having said, "Jesus told us He didn't know the answer to that question, that it was in God's hands."

There was then a question as to whether Jesus had been asked questions about some of the subjects where His previously reported statements regarding them appeared to be in conflict with current Roman Catholic doctrine and practices. The questioner had followed up her question with examples: married priests, women in the priesthood, abortion, homosexuals, creation and literal acceptance of the Bible as the Word of God.

The article said the Pope had replied these subjects hadn't been touched on during the questioning. He was quoted as having said, "Jesus covered most of these subjects in his opening remarks. I don't know if what he said satisfied everyone. We'll know better when we reconvene in another month."

"Do you expect the Church to adopt changes when you reconvene?" was the next question. The Pope was quoted as having said, "Perhaps. I think it would be premature for me to say yes. As I've said previously, the reason I called for this thirty day break was to give everyone an opportunity to mull over what's been said and discussed over the past few days including today. I not only did it for the Cardinals benefit, but for mine as well."

The article reported the Pope had then graciously thanked the media, saying he hoped to see many of them again next month.

Beth had turned on the TV as we were having breakfast. The morning shows all had extensive coverage of the Pope's meeting with the news media. As we watched film clips, I couldn't help but think the Pope seemed to be enjoying himself. Though he still projected the humbleness and saintliness which had made him so loved and admired, he also seemed to be reflecting a new persona. In the past when I'd seen him appear on television, I thought he looked as if he was carrying the world on his shoulders. His facial expression had been one of concern. Today, however, he appeared to be much younger. He seemed to have renewed vigor. There was a glow about him, a look of excitement and joy in his eyes.

I mentioned this to Beth. She agreed the Pope seemed to

be speaking with far greater confidence and enthusiasm than she'd observed in the past. She joked, saying she thought Jesus was having a positive influence on everyone and that I was an example of this as well as the Pope. She told me as of late she thought I'd been standing taller, having much more energy and sharper than I ever was. I'd laughed and taken Beth in my arms, whispering in her ear that I thought she was becoming sexier by the day.

Chapter LIII

Kat Rumalto phoned the following morning and asked if we'd be able to join them to go to Ann Arbor's Comedy Showcase on Thursday evening. She explained a colleague of Nick's had seen the comedian who'd be appearing when he performed at a club in Chicago a month or so ago. Nick says his friend is still raving about the guy, Kat said. I checked with Beth who informed me our calendar was free and that she was game. I told Kat we'd be delighted to join them and suggested we meet before the performance for dinner at Seva, a vegetarian restaurant next to the Comedy Showcase. She said that sounded fine to her; they'd meet us there at 7:00pm. However, that evening Kat had called again and left a voice mail telling us she'd checked with Nick and he'd prefer the Real Seafood if that was all right with us. Beth called her back and said Real Seafood would be fine, that it was one of her favorite restaurants in Ann Arbor.

Thursday morning's *Detroit Free Press* had a story about a group out of Traverse City who'd be heading down to Detroit over the weekend for a mission trip. Nearly 125 volunteers would be involved in a caravan of approximately 30 vehicles. The article stated that this was only the most recent, but probably the largest such group to be coming to Detroit in recent days. Many other suburban churches had already arranged mission trips to Detroit. The article went on to explain some of the work the groups were accomplishing, ranging from things as simple as serving as reading and math tutors to the tearing down and building of houses.

I knew our church had already sent one group into Detroit and that Beth and I had signed up to go with a second group. In addition to this outpouring from churches, many ideas were flowing out of Lansing as to how best to help Detroit. Some of them involved dollars, others didn't. It was amazing to see how fast things were happening due to the simple message Jesus had delivered just over a week ago.

Beth and I found a place to park on 4th avenue. It is amazing how much easier it seemed to be to find a parking place when the University isn't in session. It was a lovely summer evening. As we headed toward Real Seafood we were able to observe the many patrons seated outside the restaurants lining Main Street, enjoying their cocktails and food. Ann Arbor was fortunate to have such a vibrant downtown. I thought of downtown Detroit which became a ghost town in the evening in many areas, wondering if it would ever be able to emulate Ann Arbor's success. A2 was buzzing, many of the stores were still open for business. Beth had joked maybe this was another reason Jesus had chosen to come to Ann Arbor.

The Rumalto's had arrived just ahead of us and were already seated. Beth and I stopped a minute to chat with friends as we headed to the table. We'd enjoyed getting to know Kat and Nick a little better at the Cloverdales. We knew of them previously, but hadn't known them well. Nick was frequently being interviewed by the news media, especially around election time. During our conversation at dinner we had the opportunity to get to know them better. They were a delightful couple, perhaps a dozen or so years younger than Beth and me. Their oldest child, a daughter, was in her second year at Michigan

State and loving it. Two, a son and a daughter, were at Huron High. The youngest, a boy, was at Tappan Middle School where two of our children had gone. I gathered during our conversation that the two were probably middle of the road in their politics, similar to Beth and me.

We arrived at the Comedy Showcase a few minutes before 9:00pm. The vast majority of the audience was considerably younger than the four of us. As a matter of fact, we'd attracted a few stares as we'd headed to our seats. Glancing around at the audience, I wasn't surprised in not seeing anyone I recognized.

The comedian attracted laughter as he came out onto the stage. He was dressed to resemble Jesus, a flowing white robe, sandals, long hair, a beard and a cord around his waist. He was of average height and appeared to be in his mid-thirties, not too different in age or build from Jesus.

He'd started out with a few quick one-liners, which were very topical and quite funny. It took me a minute before I'd realized it was a take off on "Why Ann Arbor?", the reasons Jesus had chosen to come to Ann Arbor. The crowd loved it. They'd come to laugh and were enjoying his jabs at the UofM and Ann Arbor. When he'd said the UofM might not have the prettiest coeds in the Big Ten, but they certainly had more tattoos and piercings than the coeds at the other ten schools combined, he'd drawn his biggest laugh. Partially because of the way he'd raised his eyebrows and enunciated when he'd said "the other ten". With the addition of Penn State, the Big Ten was now comprised of eleven universities instead of ten.

He'd then said he was calling this portion of his act "Questions you wanted to ask Jesus, but were afraid to ask." As he glanced around the audience he'd asked "Do I wear underwear under this robe?" He'd spun around as he bent over and lifted the robe to show the very baggy yellow undershorts he was wearing with a "Go Blue" on the seat and block M's on the yellow fabric. The crowd howled and the four of us laughed as well and joined in the applause.

"What's my favorite wine?" the comedian asked. "Actually I avoid the stuff. Remember all the wine in biblical times was before we had bottled water." He interrupted the laughter adding, "But a dry martini with olives, that's another story.

"Am I still a virgin? Well I think you'd agree I got screwed by Judas, Pontius Pilate, too. But you're probably curious to know what my relationship with Mary Magdalene was. I assure you, it was strictly 'play tonic'. No, I'm not mispronouncing the word. Playing around with Mary was always a refreshing tonic for me."

It was clear the audience was in tune with the comedian, gales of laughter followed each of his answers. I had the feeling he might be pushing the limits of decency a little too much at times, though. Jesus wasn't a politician to be lampooned.

He'd asked if anyone in the audience had a question for Jesus. A coed seated a few seats down from ours, wearing a "War Is Not The Answer" T-shirt, shouted out, "Are you against war?" Another sitting farther back in the audience yelled, "Are you pro-choice?"

The comedian paused for a moment before asking if there happened to be any World War II veterans in the audience. The crowd laughed. As I mentioned earlier, the four of us were probably the oldest ones there. Looking and pointing at me he said, "You probably come the closest to qualifying sir." The Rumalto's and Beth joined in the laughter as I chuckled, too.

The comedian was no longer smiling as he said, "Remember, this is supposed to be a comedy show. You're asking me to get serious with those two questions. I know you weren't around young lady when Hitler was on a rampage in Europe and there were rumors of death camps. But I'm personally glad you weren't wearing that T-shirt back then. You wouldn't have been alone however, in not wanting F.D.R. to get us involved in World War II. Millions of people were opposed to it, including Henry Ford and Charles Lindberg. But in hindsight, does anyone now believe we shouldn't have entered the war to stop Hitler?

"Hindsight is a wonderful thing. It will enable us to determine if the U.S. was right to send its military forces into the mid-east. But the benefit of hindsight comes after the fact. We don't have crystal balls to see the outcomes of our acts. I agree with you young lady that war is seldom an answer. But sometimes it is."

The comedian continued saying he'd heard someone ask where he stood on choice. "If a woman was informed her baby would be born blind and without hands or feet, would anyone want to deny her the right to terminate her pregnancy?

"That's an easy question to answer. However, questions regarding pregnancy and conception can become very complex. But tonight I've come here to entertain you. It's not the time to focus on those questions and answers. If you'll allow me about a five minute break while I change, I'll be back with my regular routine."

During this short break I'd asked Nick if the comedian's Jesus skit had come as a surprise or had his colleague told him about it. Nick replied it had come as a total surprise, that his colleague had seen the comedian a couple of months ago, weeks before Jesus had arrived on the scene.

Kat joked that we apparently couldn't go anywhere these days without getting into the subject of Jesus. Beth smiled and nodded, taking a minute to inform Kat and Nick that she and I were joining a group from our church this weekend for a mission trip into Detroit. She admitted if not for Jesus, we'd probably been hesitant about going.

The comedian returned to the stage, dressed now in blue jeans, a sport shirt, docksiders and minus the beard and long hair. He was a handsome young man, very appealing with his smile and engaging personality. His material in this second phase of his performance was hilarious. From portraying himself as a grade school teacher to a parent dealing with teenagers, his humor was right on. I was somewhat surprised by the absence of profanity during his performance and found it refreshing. The last time Beth and I had been to the Comedy Showcase we'd been offended by the overuse of four letter words. This absence hadn't prevented him from fully engaging the exuberant and youthful crowd, however. There was virtually non-stop laughter throughout the remainder of the evening.

The young man ended his performance with dramatic flair. As he'd thanked everyone for attending he'd been unbuttoning his shirt. In a move, which reminded me of pictures of "Superman" emerging from a phone booth, he flipped the shirt off to reveal the "Why Ann Arbor?" T-shirt he was wearing. The only thing missing was a trumpet fanfare. Laughing, he'd suggested we should all be wearing one of those T-shirts. "You should all be celebrating and touting the fact Jesus picked Ann Arbor for His return," he'd said. "It could have just as easily been Bethlehem again. But it was right here in Ann Arbor where Jesus began His quest to change the world."

The comedian's expression had turned serious and there had been a dramatic pause. The audience had quieted, waiting to hear what he'd say next.

"I want to suggest to each of you that you now have something to prove, a unique opportunity to show the world Jesus didn't make a mistake in choosing Ann Arbor for His debut. Can each of you find the courage and strength to lead your lives governed by God's love and your love for others? I pray that you will. God bless you!"

I'd found myself floored by the sudden turn of events and I could sense that Beth, the Rumalto's and the rest of the audience were too. Moments ago we'd been sharing belly laughs. Now we were somber, reflecting on the challenge this comedian had thrown out to us. It was an evening I'd long remember.

Chapter LIV

The media continued to be focused on Jesus. Over the past few weeks his picture had appeared on the cover of nearly every major news magazine. All the networks had run several "Special Reports" concerning Jesus and His followers. There were daily stories in the newspapers. He was the main topic of conversation on the radio talk shows.

An article in Friday morning's *Detroit Free Press* told of a book which was being published soon, titled "All About Jesus". The article speculated that many similar books would soon be forthcoming. The article also reported that sales of Bibles and other religious works had quadrupled over the past month at Crossroads, Nicola's Books, Borders' stores, and Barnes and Nobles.

In sharp contrast, another article updated the story on the suit that had been filed to have the motto "In God We Trust" removed from all currency. Although generating an abundance of discussion, the article quoted several sources that were all in agreement in predicting the legal action would go nowhere.

One letter to the editor was titled "The Bible According To Jesus". The letter writer had taken several recent statements of Jesus and shown how they were in direct conflict with passages in the Bible. In some instances, the author of the letter had showed how the statements were at odds with verses in the New Testament which were attributed to Jesus. He alleged the differences weren't a matter of interpretation, but a question of opposing views of thought. The writer said he was confused and asked the question, "What should I be telling my parishioners, men and women who have faithfully sought God's direction for their lives for many years? Do I tell them the Bible should no longer be revered as 'The Word of God'? Should I explain it was written in ancient times and is no longer able to provide the answers to the complex questions facing today's enlightened generation? I think not. Though I trust in God and have accepted Jesus Christ as my Lord and Savior, I'm troubled. I still find myself questioning whether this man who calls himself Jesus is truly Christ. Many now firmly believe He is. I'm praying to God for answers to my questions."

The letter was signed by Dr. Ray T. White, Pastor of the Church of The Living God. I couldn't help but identify with the quandary this preacher was in. I think that there were many more religious leaders and other people asking themselves the same questions. As Beth and I had so frequently discussed, it seemed that nearly everyone was very reluctant to express their doubts the way Dr. White had. We attributed it to their not wanting to negatively influence this man's mission in any way if He were truly Jesus Christ, not wanting to later regret they hadn't welcomed His return. I couldn't help but think, however, that if Jesus had been able to successfully address the Pope's many questions, and it appeared He had, He could answer Dr. White's as well. Still I was pleased Dr. White had written the letter, he'd raised some valid and timely questions.

The *Ann Arbor News* ran a front page story reporting Jesus and His followers would be returning to Ann Arbor for two days at month's end. What pleased me most was the news Jesus would be speaking again at the "Big House", a week before UofM's football opener. There was going to be a fifty dollar per person charge with reserved seating throughout the stadium. All proceeds were to go to the "Together, Let's Save Detroit Fund". His appearance was to be televised and therefore, in the opinion of the event's organizers, eliminating the need for allowing anyone free admission. The chair of the organizing committee was quoted as saying she hoped the stadium would be packed, carrying on the tradition of one hundred thousand plus crowds. The event was scheduled to start at 4p.m. Concession stands would not open until after the program, though there would be free bottled water before hand. Television stations were agreeing to air Jesus' talk free of commercials. It was expected He'd speak for an hour to an hour and a half.

I relayed to Beth the good news, that we'd have the opportunity to see and hear Jesus once again. She immediately suggested we should try to see if we could get a block of seats and have the same group we went with to Comerica park sitting together. I dialed the phone number given in the article. I was put on hold for nearly twenty minutes. After a rather lengthy discussion, I was able to book a block of fifty seats. Beth and I felt certain more of our friends would like to join us in addition to those who'd been on the bus. I guaranteed payment with a credit card, but explained people would be sending in their own checks because the cost would be tax deductible. They would be noting payment was for seats with "The Why Ann Arbor? Bunch". The woman I'd spoken to told me she'd been amazed over how many people had already called in for tickets.

Beth phoned Joy and explained what we'd done. She was thrilled. The two of them discussed the names of people they'd call and which of them would phone them. When Beth told her about people noting on their checks that they were for seats with "The Why Ann Arbor? Bunch", Joy suggested they try to get as many of the group as possible to wear a "Why Ann Arbor?" T-shirt.

Chapter LV

Beth and I arrived in the church parking lot shortly before 8a.m. on Saturday. We'd driven our mini van, advising the couple who were heading up the trip we'd have room for five more people to join us for the drive into Detroit. I'd loaded the van with rakes, shovels, lawn bags, trash bags, gloves and other gear. We'd been briefed that we'd be cleaning up a number of vacant lots with the help of some local residents. Although, I'd been disappointed we weren't going to be doing something more meaningful when I'd first learned this, Beth and I couldn't have been more pleased on how the day turned out.

Our group of twenty-three church members had been met by over fifty local residents. They were of all ages. From a boy and a girl of about ten years of age to a couple in their seventies. Most were in their late teens or early twenties. We'd immediately gone to work. Except for a lunch break featuring a delicious array of food and soft drinks provided by the local residents, we'd worked steadily until close to 7:00pm. We cleaned up well over one hundred lots and filled three times that number of lawn and trash bags. Beth had to leave to purchase more of the bags following our lunch break. The fact she had to drive nearly five miles to do it merely dramatized the problems Detroit faced.

We were extremely proud of the work we'd accomplished. There was a night and day difference in the appearance of the neighborhood from when we'd arrived. But the highlight and real reward had come from the opportunity to mix with the local residents. They were so enthusiastic and so appreciative of our efforts. There were tears in many eyes when we'd said our goodbyes. We'd assured them this wouldn't be a one time thing, we'd go back and get other members of our church involved, too.

One nifty outcome was our group's agreement to come up with the funds to provide the cost of two years of tuition at community colleges for three of the youngsters who we'd worked with and gotten to know fairly well during the course of the day. They were neat kids and the fact we might be providing them the keys to unlock doors of opportunity in their lives was very heartwarming. In relation to the immense needs, our impact was very minor. Still, I think all of us felt a great deal of satisfaction over what we'd accomplished. Being able to work side by side with the residents of the area as we listened to their stories was without question the most rewarding part of it.

Frankly, I'd been a little concerned prior to venturing into Detroit. I'd expected we'd encounter some animosity and possibly be swamped by people begging for a handout. But there'd been none of that. We'd been so warmly received, so graciously treated. Local residents hadn't shown up to merely see what we were doing, they'd jumped in to do their share of the work and then some.

In church the next day, the couple who'd headed up our mission trip had the opportunity to address the congregation. They did an excellent job of explaining what had taken place in Detroit and of encouraging others to sign up for future trips, proposing that our church should have several.

To our surprise, the *Detroit Free Press* had an article about our group in its Sunday edition. There were several photos accompanying it. A shot of people working, before and after photos of the areas in which they'd been working and a photo of everyone having lunch. We could spot Beth in the corner of one of them. Though we'd noticed someone taking pictures, Beth and I had just assumed it was one of the local residents. We'd had no idea there was going to be an article. And it was an excellent one which hopefully would encourage other churches or groups to get involved in similar visits.

Chapter LVI

    Tuesday's evening news was focused on the unique sentence handed out to the five Israelis who'd participated in the assassination attempt on Jesus. The group had been given two year suspended sentences. Rather than being sent to prison, the five had agreed to work in Palestine for the next two years. They'd be directed by Palestinians and involved with projects chosen by the Palestinians. The commentator speculated that many of those projects would probably require strenuous manual labor. He went on to say that the five had recruited nearly thirty former members of the militant group in which they'd been involved to join them on a volunteer basis, to spend one to two days a week working on the projects along side them.

    Reporters on the scene interviewed Israeli and Palestinian authorities. They both said Israel had approached Palestinian leaders with the idea a few days ago. Following rather lengthy discussions, the two sides agreed this unique sentence could be an important step in improving relations between the two countries.

    The news commentator ended the news story by saying, "Not only have Palestinian authorities enthusiastically endorsed these unique sentences, they have also pledged to try to involve members from groups such as Hamas in volunteering to work alongside those volunteers coming over from Israel."

"I think you had a hand in that," I said looking over at Beth. "I'm surprised our congressman or his staff never got back to you."

"I hope my suggestion had something to do with prompting this," Beth said. "But regardless, I'm just pleased something like this was bought into by the two sides. And the fact other members of that Israeli militant group seemed to have changed their thinking, deciding to involve themselves in a positive way, is quite a breakthrough. I'm happy."

Beth then clicked her fingers and said, "I just remembered I'd forgotten to tell you Joy called earlier today. She's gotten her twenty-five people. And she had the same luck as I did, everyone she contacted said yes. A little different from when we were trying to fill up that bus. Now let's hope there aren't any foul ups, that everyone mails their checks in and gets the right tickets. It'll be interesting to find out where we'll be sitting."

"I'm sorry," I replied. "We received ours in today's mail. I should have told you. They're great seats, thirty rows up on the press box side of the field and near the fifty."

"Perfect," Beth replied. "And Joy also told me at least six people plus Jerry will be wearing the 'Why Ann Arbor?' T-shirt."

I grinned and replied, "That's great! I was worried I might be the only one. But you know, after hearing that comedian the other night I have an entirely different attitude about wearing it. It'll be fun."

"Don't forget, you have a dental appointment tomorrow morning," Beth reminded me.

"I won't. And don't forget I have a 'Y' board meeting tomorrow, too. I probably won't be home until 6:30pm or so."

"That's fine, we'll just be having leftovers," Beth replied.

I'd been glancing at the newscast as we talked. Jesus continued to dominate the news. In the past twenty-four hours He'd appeared in the Philippines, Japan, Korea, and Seattle, Washington. He was drawing crowds and receiving favorable media coverage wherever he went. Jesus' whirlwind pace was mind-boggling. That was true for His followers as well. It was good they were all heading back to Ann Arbor in another week. Hopefully, they'd have some time to relax and unwind.

Chapter LVII

Beth received a Fed-Ex package on Thursday. It contained a letter from our Congressman. He apologized for not being in contact earlier and explained Israel had requested that everything regarding the sentencing be kept a secret until the Palestinians were in complete agreement. He wrote, "I'm sure you're now aware of the details of the unique sentencing arrangement, the news media has done a thorough job of reporting them. I believe your suggestion played a major role in this outcome. The President and the Secretary of State were told of your input. I wish to convey their thanks and appreciation as well as my own for what you did. Your 'thinking outside the box' was instrumental in leading the two parties to implement something which I believe could have historic implications."

The final paragraph of the letter stated, "You will probably be receiving a phone call in the next few days from the Israeli Ambassador expressing his nation's gratitude for your contribution. I doubt if you'll receive anything in writing. I believe the Israelis want to take full credit for coming up with the idea." The letter ended with him thanking her once again.

Beth had read the letter first and then handed it to me. I was beaming as I finished reading it. I wrapped my arms around her as I told her how proud I was of her, telling her she deserved a hug.

Later, as we were having dinner, we discussed how one person could make a difference in the world, one idea. And of course, that led us on to discussing the difference Jesus was making in the world.

"I wonder if Jim Nixon has changed his thinking," Beth said. "Increased the odds of Jesus being successful in His mission."

"I would have to think so," I replied. "It's amazing the impact Jesus has made in such a relatively short time. Look at the difference right here in Ann Arbor. Literally, thousands more are volunteering their services to the community in various ways. In many cases, people who'd just been sitting on the sidelines prior to Jesus' arrival. You can sense the change in attitudes and behavior. And look what's happening in Detroit."

"I know," Beth said. "Tonight's newspaper had a story about the many projects being proposed for Detroit, several are already underway. And from what we've read, what's happening here is also happening in many other areas of the country and the world. Just like our involvement in Detroit on Saturday, a small step maybe, but combined with those of others—"

I grinned as I interrupted her saying, "—a giant step for mankind."

Beth laughed, "Thanks for that little touch of humor, Mike. I probably needed that. Maybe I've been getting a little too carried away by all that's been happening. A little too serious. Maybe you're guilty of that, too. I can't help but think things have been going a little too easily for Jesus. There are bound to be some setbacks, some disappointments. I hope He's ready for them and won't lose His sense of humor. That's been one of the things that's surprised and impressed me the most about Him. The fact He does have a sense of humor and doesn't appear to be taking Himself too seriously. He's so gracious with everyone, so compassionate. You don't get the sense you're being lectured to."

"And those are probably some of the reasons He's met with such success," I suggested. "He isn't trying to intimidate people or place Himself on a pedestal. He's selling His message as opposed to Himself.

"I believe you're right. Early on you were the one who suggested He'd have to do that if He was going to be successful. That religions other than Christianity wouldn't buy into His message if it meant they'd have to worship Him along with God. I was reluctant about that as you know. But now after seeing and hearing Him and watching Him in action these past few weeks, I'm more understanding of His need to build up God at the expense of Himself."

Chapter LVIII

The Sunday papers reported that over fifty thousand tickets had already been sold for Jesus' appearance at the University of Michigan Stadium. In my head I tried to calculate what that represented in terms of dollars. Was I right, over two and a half million dollars? The event organizers had to be ecstatic. And there was still time to sell more tickets.

The *Detroit Free Press* had a two page photo spread on the Traverse City Group who'd come down to Detroit. With the help of many local residents, they'd fixed up and painted over one dozen homes. Some of the homes involved major repairs. But among the group were three plumbers, four electricians, six carpenters, two masons and four painters. Even after receiving substantial discounts, the group had spent nearly twenty thousand dollars for paint and materials.

The accompanying article also reported that the group was planning on attending various church services on Sunday morning. A number of the volunteers and local residents had been interviewed for the article. Their comments ranged from, "I never anticipated this would be so much fun", "They fed us like you wouldn't believe", "We're already planning for our next trip down here", to "They've been like angels from Heaven", "God bless them for all they're doing", "It's amazing what so many hands can accomplish".

The article also mentioned the many other volunteer groups at work in the city, the numerous "Habitat For Humanity" projects underway and the dollars pouring into the "Together, Let's Save Detroit Fund" from all over the state of Michigan.

The *Ann Arbor News* had two Letters To The Editor that caught my eye. One was titled "Right To Be Born Is Sacred". Letters such as this used to appear fairly frequently. However, I couldn't recall having seen one recently, not since Jesus has clarified His position in regard to abortion. Jesus said a woman has the right to choose to terminate her pregnancy. At the same time, He'd emphasized this decision was not to be made in haste, but only after much reflection and prayer. In my mind, His position was far from encouraging abortions. I also believed He'd been instrumental in the forming of a joint venture by Planned Parenthood and Catholic Social Services to enable women to go to full term and place their babies for adoption. It had been very successful, thus far, and many other communities were attempting to emulate it.

The letter writer was attacking Liberals, asking how the same ones who were promoting higher minimum wages, universal health care and fair housing and condemning capital punishment and war could support the killing of an unborn child. He stated the unborn child would never have the opportunity to benefit from the higher wages, better health care and nicer housing. He alleged these Liberals were allowing the greatest genocide in the history of the world to continue. The man's anger and frustration were clearly apparent as he'd rambled on in the letter.

I couldn't help but think many of the people he was so harshly criticizing simply believed as Jesus did. They weren't pro-abortion, they were just supportive of a woman's right to terminate her pregnancy.

I recalled the discussions Beth and I had after reading about what Jesus had said about a woman's right to make a choice. He'd said God had given men and women the ability to make choices in their lives. Not just in this one instance, Jesus had said people's lives were filled with choices. The choice to decide how they wished to worship and honor God, for example. Jesus had said that with God's guidance individuals would hopefully make right choices, decisions which would be pleasing to God. Jesus had even gone so far as to say one of the choices a person had was whether or not to believe in God.

Beth and I had hoped Jesus would be able to get everyone to agree that personal beliefs regarding abortion, birth control and family planning should not be the major issues dividing the nation. There were so many other pressing issues which required discussion and debate. We'd even joked about what Democrats and Republicans would do if they no longer had the emotionally charged issue of abortion on which to base their respective party's fund raising efforts. It truly seemed to be the number one motivator for people's political contributions.

The letter was evidence of the fact he hadn't been able to get everyone to accept his thinking. I glanced at the letter again as a thought passed through my mind. Had it been written by some right-wing Republican in an attempt to get liberals embracing his beliefs? Maybe it was just a religious individual expressing his or her views. I smiled, thinking probably not. Then I had an unsettling thought. What instead of everyone agreeing with Jesus, the reverse happened. Everyone coming together to totally ban abortions?

The second letter which drew my attention was titled "Science and Religion Shouldn't Be Bedfellows." The letter began by stating Galileo had been imprisoned for alleging the earth was not the center of the universe, a view which ran counter to church doctrine. The letter writer stated that science is based on fact and proof and religion on myths and beliefs some people hope are true. He then referenced the two schools of thought on "Darwin's theory of evolution" and the theory of "Intelligent Design" before concluding while the two may coexist, it is not wise to mix them.

My initial thought was the writer's probably an atheist or at least an agnostic. But then I thought about how Jesus had responded when asked about the story of creation in the Book of Genesis. His answer was not at odds with the conclusion of the letter writer. Of course, Jesus has made it clear that God is real, not a myth as the letter writer suggested. And Jesus has also said God plays an important role in man's scientific discoveries by having endowed man with the intelligence and ingenuity to make them. It was clear to me the letter writer was one of those who'd chosen not to be a believer in God.

Thus far, somewhat to my surprise, Jesus seemed to have provoked little controversy. But the two letters indicated to me that He was far from home free. He still had major challenges ahead of Him, here in Ann Arbor as well as abroad. There was still some selling to do.

Chapter LIX

Over the next few days, I continued to be awed by the number of appearances Jesus was making throughout the world. Rather than easing up and allowing Him a little time to catch His breath, His demanding schedule seemed to be accelerating. On Monday evening He'd been the main speaker at an Anti-Defamation League dinner in New York City. The following day He'd addressed a crowd of thousands in Beijing, China.

The media coverage for both of these events was extensive. At the dinner in New York it was reported He'd been generous in His praise for those involved in the work of the organization, saying their actions in fighting discrimination were a reflection of God's love and His commandment to love one another. He said there was no room for discrimination of any kind in God's world and also reminded them that in doing good to combat evil, they should remember to love their enemies.

The media reported Jesus had used much of His speech to comment on the role and importance of diversity among people. After telling the audience God's love encompassed the world and every single human being, He said each individual is unique. The *Free Press* had quoted Jesus as then having said, "In the same way people have different preferences when it comes to foods, music, customs, colors, clothes, cars, television programs, books, hobbies, and life styles, they also differ in their thinking, politics and opinions. Though united in our belief in God and our desire to reflect God's love in our daily lives, we differ in many ways. In God's Kingdom here on Earth, God knows there will still be arguments and disagreements over what should be done and how it should be done. God doesn't view the diversity of people and their ideas and talents as a negative, but rather one of the joys and beauties to be found in His world."

The newspaper accounts reported Jesus had spoken for nearly an hour and frequently used humor and parables in His talk. His audience had been very attentive and responsive. He'd been given an enthusiastic ovation.

The *Free Press* article had concluded with a quote from one of the rabbis who'd been in the audience. "Jesus is very impressive. He's very intelligent, very charming. He's giving the world much to think about including those of us of the Jewish faith."

It seemed as if Jesus was being warmly received by Jews in the Middle East. However, to my knowledge this was the first occasion in which He addressed a predominately Jewish audience in the United States. I couldn't recall having read much about the U.S. Jewish reaction to Jesus. It appeared as if the response to Him and His message had been positive and genuine in New York. That was good.

The articles reporting on Jesus' appearance in China were equally interesting. The mere fact He'd been given permission to speak to a large gathering there was impressive in itself. China monitored religious activities quite closely.

The articles stated the main thread of His talk there was the message to love God with all your heart, all your soul and all your mind and to love your neighbor as yourself. During His talk He also used several parables the audience could readily relate to. The articles stated Jesus had spoken in Chinese and seemed to have been clearly understood by the audience.

Rather than the enthusiastic reception which Jesus often was given, the articles stated the Chinese audience had been far more subdued, treating Jesus with reverence rather than applause. The articles said Jesus had spoken about the separation of church and state. As I read the quotes from this portion of His speech, I couldn't help but think His comments were equally applicable here in the U.S. Jesus and His followers were quoted as having said they were hoping this was only the first of many occasions where Jesus would have the opportunity to address groups in China. The initial plan had called for Jesus' speech to be televised. However, at the last minute that decision had been reversed.

Beth and I switched on the TV as we were climbing into bed. We were glad we had. A special news story was breaking. The commentator was saying Jesus might be experiencing some health problems. Two film clips were shown several times. Both showed Jesus stumbling as He was coming down steps, in one sequence as He emerged from an airplane and in the other as He was leaving a stage. In both clips you saw the pained look on His face as He'd slowly struggled to His feet. The sharp contrast compared to when He'd tripped coming out of the bullpen at Comerica Park was apparent. On the latter occasion, He'd turned a potentially embarrassing incident into a positive one as He'd quickly righted Himself and lifted the hem of His robe, smiling and waving to the crowd as He jogged to the stage. The crowd had loved it and had laughed along with Him.

Beth asked if I remembered when Gerald Ford had been President and been caught on film stumbling on several occasions. I replied

I certainly did. How could I forget the news media's unrelenting coverage? The embarrassing incidents became fodder for the late night shows, for jokes in their opening monologues. Saturday Night Live made imitations of his pratfalls standard fare for weeks on end. Some even alleged this portrait of a bumbling Gerald Ford did as much damage to his re-election attempt as his pardon of former President Nixon.

The commentators reported Jesus had been forced to cancel several appearances. Beth and I wondered if He'd have to cancel his stadium appearance on Saturday.

"I can't say I'm that surprised," Beth had said. "His schedule has to have been exhausting. Hopefully, a day or two of rest will help. I hope it's because He's just getting worn down and nothing more serious."

"Me, too," I replied. "But I guess I've been picturing Jesus as being sort of invincible, not vulnerable to the same ills as a normal human being. Maybe that's not true."

Chapter LX

Wednesday's *Ann Arbor News* reported Jesus' appearance on Saturday would go forward as scheduled. Ginny Roberts and Ernie Smith were quoted in the article. They said Jesus would be arriving in Ann Arbor on Thursday and be having meetings with His followers all day Friday and Saturday morning prior to speaking on Saturday afternoon. In response to the question on the status of Jesus' health, they said He was now much better after taking a few days off from His strenuous schedule. The article reported over 75,000 tickets had been sold for the Saturday event.

There was a commentary by Jim Nixon on the editorial page. It was titled "Jesus' Message In Four Letter Words". The piece began with the listing of the words: real, love, give, good, and pray. Jim had then written, "Jesus' message is simple and clear. Jesus tells us God is <u>Real</u>, not an imaginary creation of man. A caring and forgiving God who loves us, an all knowing God who will always be there for us. Our <u>Love</u> of God and our <u>Love</u> of our neighbors requires us to lead lives and make choices that will be pleasing to God. In the giving of ourselves we will come to realize it is more blessed to <u>Give</u> than to receive. In the <u>Good</u> that we do, we are able to combat evil. In turning to God as we <u>Pray</u>, asking for guidance, we will be able to establish God's Kingdom here on Earth.

"Though Jesus' message is simple and clear, God demands much from us," Jim's commentary continued. "Loving our enemies is not easy. Truly forgiving others is difficult. Living perfect lives is an immense challenge. However, Jesus tells us that with God's help, all things are possible. With God's presence in our lives, we can make His Kingdom on earth a reality. There is no room for hate and envy in God's world. Jesus also tells us God is understanding and forgiving, that God is there to comfort and console us when we err in our ways. We can't begin to count all God's blessings. God demands our best, God deserves our best."

Jim concluded by saying he'd had doubts about whether Jesus would be successful in getting the world to hear His message, doubts over whether the world would embrace His message. "But Jesus has been erasing those doubts," Jim wrote. "I pray for Him to succeed and I ask everyone who reads this to pray for Him, too."

I was very moved by Jim's commentary. I wondered if he'd also submitted it to other newspapers and publications. I hoped so. I wanted everyone to read it. I thought he'd done a beautiful and concise job of summarizing Jesus' message. After Beth had the opportunity to read it, she'd suggested I scan it into our computer and e-mail it to all our friends. I did. The positive response and thank-yous returned from our e-mail were mind-boggling. It was apparent others reactions to what Jim had written had been similar to mine.

Later in the evening, I tried to call Jim to compliment him. His line was busy for nearly an hour before I'd been finally able to get through to him. I probably went a little overboard in praising him, explaining how I'd e-mailed his piece to all our friends and quoting some of their responses. I suggested he should e-mail his commentary to other papers and magazines and named a few I thought he should include. He very much appreciated my call, explaining though it wasn't the first he'd received, it was by far the most flattering. He'd thanked me for my suggestion to send the letter to other publications, saying he'd only sent it to the *Ann Arbor News*.

Thursday night Beth and I tuned in to a few minutes of the "Tonight Show" with Jay Leno. Much to our surprise, one of his featured guests was the comedian we'd seen last week at the Comedy Showcase. Jay had him do some of the Jesus routine we'd seen. He was a little more polished than I'd remembered. He'd also added a few new jokes.

Chapter LXI

There was a surprising photo of Jesus in Friday morning's *Free Press*. He was wearing a sport shirt with a blue blazer rather than the white robe we'd grown accustomed to seeing Him in. His beard was gone and His hair had been cut, now resembling what used to be referred to as a Princeton cut. However, His smile was as warm as ever.

My first thought was He looked to be a twin of the young man we'd seen at the Comedy Showcase. Except for Jesus' slightly darker complexion, their features were close to identical. The photo had been taken in front of the Campus Inn. The accompanying article reported Jesus had come out to speak to the nearly two-dozen media people gathered in front of the Campus Inn. They were present to cover the meetings Jesus would be having there with his followers.

The article stated Jesus had graciously asked them to leave. He'd explained the meetings with His followers were to be held with no media coverage or interviews until the close of the meetings. Jesus informed them He'd be making a statement following their lunch on Saturday. There would also be ample time for questions. He'd said He and His followers would look forward to seeing them back at 1:15pm on Saturday.

I'd immediately shown Beth the photo. Her eyebrows had arched in surprise. "He certainly is handsome," Beth commented. "But why do you think He's chosen to make a change now? Everyone seemed to be accepting Him so well the way He was, probably because it was the way they'd imagined Jesus would look and dress. Remember the conversations we had? All of us agreed He should continue wearing the robe and sandals."

"And for good reasons," I'd said. "I still remember the first time I saw Him at the Farmers Market. His robe was the first thing that caught my eye. Such a bright white, it almost gleamed. It made Him stand out as someone special. In the *Free Press* photo He looks like a normal guy. I think it's a mistake to change His attire and shave His beard and cut His hair. Now when people see Him in a crowd, some will be asking which one is Jesus. Before, there was no doubt."

"I think maybe you've just answered the question of why He's done it," Beth replied. "He probably wants people to focus on His message rather than on Him. You're the one who first suggested He'd have to do that in order to be successful in getting non-Christians to embrace His message."

"I remember saying that," I'd said. "And you're probably right in your thoughts as to why He's done it. Even so, I think it's a mistake."

Beth had smiled as she'd replied I was entitled to my opinion. "But I've just thought of another reason why Jesus may have decided it was time to alter His appearance. It might have something to do with His health. Maybe He's wanting people to see His human side and realize He's subject to the same frailties they are."

"That's an interesting thought," I'd replied. "It'll be fun to see if He goes back to wearing the robe tomorrow when He speaks in the Stadium. He might."

"And He might don a false beard and a wig, too," Beth said as she giggled. "But I doubt it."

Later in the evening we turned on the TV and watched the news. One of the lead stories concerned the possible invitation Jesus might be receiving to address a joint session of Congress. There was still considerable controversy over the issue with questions being raised regarding the separation of church and state.

Another story focused on the growth of the video game industry. The commentator stated it was now larger than the motion picture industry. Many universities were now offering degrees in video game design. It's hard to keep up with all the changes going on in the world, I'd thought as I watched. The pace of changes has certainly accelerated since I was a kid. Children have their hands full these days dealing with them.

A third story dealt with the fragmenting taking place in the world's major religions. The thrust of the story was that Jesus faced a challenge in trying to reverse this trend in His attempt to unite people with their common beliefs. The commentator went on to give examples of the broad divisions in the Christian, Muslim, and Jewish faiths that Jesus was addressing.

Chapter LXII

As Beth and I were waiting on Saturday afternoon for the Hansons to pick us up to go the stadium, we had the TV on. We were watching highlights of Jesus' statement to the news media regarding the meetings He'd been having with His followers and the question and answer session that followed. The format was an unusual one. Jesus and His followers had just finished having lunch together. They were all seated on one side of a long table. Several yards away in front of the table, reporters and camera crews faced them. Jesus had spoken while still seated at the middle of the table.

The commentator reported Jesus had spoken approximately ten minutes, giving details of the ambitious plans He and His followers had laid out for themselves for the next few months. Their itineraries would be taking them all over the world, to over 160 different countries with plans to speak to over 10 million people. He was hopeful television and media coverage would get His message delivered to many millions more.

As the commentator was speaking, the TV screen showed Jesus and His followers seated at the table. I recognized many of the faces, from time to time photos of them had appeared in the media. However, other than at Hill Auditorium, this was the first time I'd seen the entire group assembled with Jesus.

Highlights of the question and answer portion of the briefing were now being shown. Not surprisingly, most of the questions were directed to Jesus. But on several occasions, one of His followers would answer the question. The camera would zoom in on the reporter asking the question and then zoom in on the individual, usually Jesus, responding to it. From time to time the entire group at the table would be shown. At other times as the question was being answered, the camera would pan the group, sharing close-ups of Jesus and His followers. All of them were dressed in fairly casual attire. Jesus, along with the majority of the men, was wearing a sport shirt and a blazer, looking much the same as He had in the photos taken in front of the Campus Inn that had been in yesterday's newspapers.

"I think you're right," Beth said. "Jesus probably shouldn't have changed His dress and appearance. Can you envision how this scene would look if He hadn't and if His followers were wearing robes, too? Wouldn't it remind you of paintings of the "Last Supper"? A reenactment?"

I'd smiled as I nodded my head in agreement. A reporter who I recognized as being on the staff of the *Ann Arbor News* was now directing a question to Jesus. As he was asking where Jesus was getting the money to finance His mission, I couldn't help but recall the newspaper's pledge to get the answer to this question.

Jesus had smiled before beginning His answer, explaining the answer would probably disappoint those who'd been speculating on the source of the funds. He explained He'd brought ample funds with Him initially. Then He went on to say, "Shortly after my arrival here in Ann Arbor I visited Glacier Hills. One of the women I'd spoken to while I was there contacted me a few days later. She was in her eighties. Though her mind was still very sharp, she had some serious health problems. She was also a very wealthy woman. She said she knew My mission would be an expensive one and wanted to give Me the funding to finance it. I told her that I had no need for it, that God had provided Me with ample resources. She begged, however, that I accept her offer so she could play a role in bringing about God's Kingdom on Earth. Her only request was that she remain anonymous, that during her lifetime no one was to know of her involvement. This kind and saintly woman passed away earlier this week. She had been the source of much of our funding and will continue to be. She made provisions in her will for it to continue."

Beth and I had glanced at one another. We knew the woman Jesus was referring to, we'd attended her funeral a few days ago. Her husband had founded a high tech company in Ann Arbor and sold it a few years ago for a huge sum. She and he had been stalwarts in Ann Arbor for many worthwhile endeavors.

"That's a sweet story," Beth commented. "It ends one of the mysteries, by answering one of the questions people have been asking."

"And just think of the legacy she's leaving," I replied. "They say people's good works live on long after their deaths, it's certainly true in this case. God bless her. She's in Heaven now."

"The Hanson's are here," Beth said. "I think they just pulled in our driveway."

As we were heading out the door, Beth had leaned over and whispered in my ear. "Have I told you I think you look cute in that T-shirt?" I smiled and kissed her, hoping I wouldn't be the only one wearing one.

Chapter LXIII

Jerry was wearing his "Why Ann Arbor?" T-shirt, too. I could tell by the expression on his face he was relieved to see me also wearing mine. Joy immediately asked us if we'd been watching the news coverage of Jesus and His followers. We acknowledged we had been and explained we'd still been following it as they'd arrived to pick us up. Joy asked our opinions about Jesus changing His garb and appearance. She and Jerry agreed with our thoughts, they were also not thrilled about the change. We spent the remainder of our drive discussing some of the highlights of the coverage, Jesus' explanation of where His funding was coming from.

The weather was ideal, partially cloudy and in the high seventies. Beth asked Joy and Jerry if they were still game to stay on after Jesus spoke and get our dinner from the concession stands. They assured us they were. Joy suggested it would also give us an opportunity to hear other people's reaction to Jesus' speech.

We were in our seats about twenty minutes before the event was scheduled to begin. We were surprised to find we were among the last of our group to arrive. Nearly a dozen in our group, in addition to Jerry and me, were wearing their "Why Ann Arbor?" T-shirts, including two or three of the women. I could also see a smattering of the shirts in the huge crowd. It appeared to me there were less than ten thousand empty seats and people were still arriving.

Right to the minute, Jesus, trailed by His followers, filed out of the tunnel entrance across the field. They were greeted with laughter and applause. They were all wearing "Why Ann Arbor?" T-shirts. I glanced over at the Cloverdales who were sitting a few seats down from us. They were both beaming, but I could also see tears in their eyes. Beth had nudged me and said she wasn't sure about this, that Jesus looked more like a rock star than the Messiah. Though maybe true, there was no doubt He had a commanding presence. There was a personal magnetism about Him. There was no doubt as to who was the leader of the group climbing the stairs onto the small stage.

The Mayor of Detroit was the first one to come to the microphone. His voice was filled with emotion as he expressed the heartfelt gratitude of the City of Detroit for the attendees contributions to the "Together, Let's Save Detroit Fund". He also thanked those in the audience who'd volunteered to come into Detroit in recent days, telling them they were definitely making a difference. "There's a whole new attitude," he said. "And now it is my great pleasure to introduce the one responsible for this change. Ladies and gentlemen, meet and greet Jesus Christ, Superstar!"

The reaction of the crowd was spontaneous with everyone rising to their feet with thunderous applause for several minutes. Jesus stepped to the front of the stage and raised His arms to quiet the crowd. Similar to the last time He'd spoken in the Stadium, He was using no microphone. He smiled in joy as He began speaking, a radiant, angelic smile.

"With all this enthusiasm maybe we'll have to perform a wave or two before we're through here today." The crowd laughed, a wave or two at football games had become a UofM tradition in recent years. Around the Stadium the fans would raise their arms in sequence by section. Alternating between lifting them normally, hurriedly or in slow motion added to the fun.

After thanking the mayor and the chairs of the event, Jesus proceeded to introduce His followers. He did it by pairs, explaining where each of the teams would be over the next few months. He revealed the region of the world the team was assigned to and the countries and major cities in which they'd arranged to address crowds such as the one assembled today. He also detailed His own schedule, naming several groups and individuals with whom He'd be meeting. One couldn't help but be impressed by the ambitious plans He described. His mission wasn't going to fail because of lack of effort.

He said one of their objectives was to recruit additional followers. Each team had a goal to add six more members to the team over the course of the next two months. He explained this would be done by invitation. However, He emphasized that everyone was welcomed, encouraged and needed to be involved in other ways for His mission to change the world and establish God's Kingdom On Earth to succeed.

Jesus then thanked everyone who'd come today, joking about those He'd spotted wearing the same T-shirt He was. He also expressed His appreciation to the residents of the greater Ann Arbor area who'd so warmly received Him and praised them for their positive response to His message. "Your collective good deeds are setting an example for the rest of the world. Your striving to bring about changes in attitude and behavior is making an impact far beyond Washtenaw County. Am I pleased I chose Ann Arbor as the site for my initial appearance? You bet I am!"

Jesus continued by once again outlining the reasons God

had directed Him to return to earth at this particular time. He said God was distressed to see religion being used to split people into warring factions rather than being used to bring them together. He said that rather than people uniting in their worship and honoring of God, their conflicting beliefs were having the opposite effect. They were polarizing people and separating people from the love of God. Many people were becoming disillusioned and drawing away from God. He said this was not just happening between the major faiths, but also within them. He cited the U.S. as an example of where this was occurring. He said a predominantly Christian country is daily becoming more divided. Hatred and anger are surfacing and diminishing people's love, understanding and compassion for others.

Jesus stated He hadn't returned to point fingers at who or what was to blame for the growing predicament the world faced. "I'm here to tell you God is real," He said. "I'm here to tell you God loves us all and asks each of us to love Him and to show our love for Him in how we treat others. Not just those who attend the same place of worship we do, not just those who are members of the same race we are, not just those who've experienced the same educational benefits and economic opportunities we've had, not just those with the same opinions, but rather everyone, even our enemies. I'm here to tell you there is time to change, for individuals to change, for the world to change. I'm here to tell you God's Kingdom On Earth can still become a reality. But only if we all agree to listen to God and act as God would have us act. Only then can love over shadow evil and make this happen.

"Groups often times refer to themselves as God fearing people.

I tell you God is not to be feared. The loving and compassionate God I've told you about is a God of mercy, a forgiving God, an all knowing and all powerful God through whom all things are possible. I've also told you God is not responsible for everything that happens in His world. Evil things do happen, whether they are acts of nature or actions of evil men and women. Man is capable of doing evil, making bad choices which not only effect their lives, but sadly the lives of others as well. But I tell you that with God's help and guidance, evil can be overcome.

"I've come to convince you a world at peace with sufficient food, shelter and health care for everyone can become a reality. I never claimed this would be easy. But together, embraced by God's love, and by embracing others in love, people can create such a world."

Seeming to realize how thought provoking His comments had been and the sober mood the crowd shared, Jesus smiled again and injected a touch of humor into His remarks. "Wouldn't it be wonderful if God could merely with a click of His fingers establish His Kingdom On Earth? Why shouldn't He? What, and deprive all of you, and others, of the joy and reward that will come from having played a role in bringing this about? God doesn't envision a world filled with gloom and despair. He wants the world to be filled with joy and laughter. The giggles of children, the fun of Santa Claus and the Easter Bunny, the awe of making a wish upon a star, the thrill of a roller coaster ride and the excitement of having a new puppy or kitten are all parts of God's world. We're all God's children and He has blessed each of us with the roller coaster ride life provides us, the highs and lows, the joys and sorrows. God wants to remind us we can have fun serving Him, that we shouldn't take ourselves too seriously in the process, and that life sometimes plays tricks on us. He just asks us to put our God given talents to good use and find true joy and happiness in the process."

Jesus then went on to say He'd been criticized for having said there were some gray areas in the scriptures of all religions. As He had on other occasions, He referenced some of these areas. In some instances He also made use of the approach He utilized previously in answering questions, asking the crowd a series of questions. They led the crowd into reaching the conclusion He was seeking. He said although God wanted everyone's lives to be governed by absolute moral values, God realized there were instances when that proved difficult, telling the truth, for example. Retaining His sense of humor He asked, "How do you answer to your wife if she asks you whether you think she's getting too fat? How do you respond to your mother-in-law when she asks if you enjoyed her cooking? How do you answer the young child who asks if there is a doggie heaven? What do you say when an author asks for your reaction after reading his or her book?"

Jesus then switched to another subject. He said God's commandments did not require that people would no longer have differences of opinion or would no longer debate and discuss their different views. Far from it, He said. God only asked that people engage in these dialogues with mutual respect for one another. Their love of God and their fellow men should be the overriding principles to govern them.

Jesus then focused on several of the controversial issues people were currently wrestling with or would soon have the need to. He elaborated on one in particular, euthanasia or assisted suicide.

He spelled out some of the arguments on both sides of the issue, acknowledging that in several European countries, the question now wasn't whether it should be legalized, but the boundaries for governing when it should be allowed.

Jesus then said He hadn't returned to the world to provide answers to all these complex questions. And that even though He said He previously may have suggested what some of those answers should be, He confessed, this was not what God had sent Him to do. "I've been sent and have come to deliver a message of hope. A hope that you will heed My message. A hope that each of you will turn to God in prayer. A hope that each of you will lead lives and make choices that will be pleasing to God. A hope that each of you will play an instrumental and vital role in bringing about God's Kingdom On Earth.

"In closing today, I want you all to join me in singing a song which reflects the message I've brought you. You'll see the lyrics are on the two scoreboards."

I glanced up. Sure enough, the lyrics for "Let There Be Peace On Earth" now appeared on the scoreboards at each end of the stadium. The musical intro was now being played over the Stadium's public address system. Following it, a joyful Jesus began to lead the crowd in singing. *"Let there be peace on earth and let it begin with me. Let there be peace on earth, the peace that was meant to be."*

As we sang, I could feel my eyes watering. It was a very emotional experience. Glancing around, I could tell the entire audience was enthralled. Everyone appeared to be singing. Beth had grabbed my hand and nodded to me to take the hand of the person next to me. I saw this was being done throughout the stadium. Warmth and love seemed to radiate through the crowd. As the song concluded, Jesus spoke again.

"This then is my message. And though I'll bid farewell to you now, please know God is always with you. Now and forever more. Amen."

The crowd was silent for a few moments before breaking into applause. Jesus raised His arms and turned a few times with a look and smile that seemed to give everyone in the audience the sensation He was focusing directly on them. He then left the stage and followed by the others, exited through the tunnel. The applause continued until He'd disappeared from view.

Chapter LXIV

The Hansons and Beth and I passed the word around that the four of us were planning on staying around for another half hour or so to get something to eat from one of the food concession stands and chat about what Jesus had said. Most everyone in our group said they'd like to join us.

The crowd was in a jubilant mood as we filed up the steps and out of the stadium, buzzing in conversation. Joy and Beth were once again being thanked for orchestrating our group's sitting together. To a person, everyone seemed delighted to have been present to see and hear Jesus. Several were referring to it as a historical occasion, one we'd all long remember.

As Beth and I were waiting in line at a stand featuring gyro sandwiches, Whitney Stratton and her fiance, Lance, passed by. They'd come with her parents and although they'd been sitting with our group, we hadn't had an opportunity to speak to them. They stopped and we immediately asked how their wedding plans were going. They told us they were falling nicely into place. They had the church reserved and arrangements for the rehearsal dinner and reception completed.

"You're going to be invited," Whitney said. "It's going to be a much smaller affair than mother initially wanted, but we both want you there. You'll have a chance to meet Lance's parents and sister. And I think you'll love the band, they'll be playing lots of oldies and we'll be having some group dancing, too. You won't need earplugs until toward the end of the evening."

I asked if I should be getting my request in for a dance with her now. "Don't commit yourself just yet, Whitney," Beth said laughing. "Best to wait. Sometimes Mike is Mr. Lightfoot and other times I need toe protectors. I'll advise you that evening as to how he's doing."

I frowned as I joined in the laughter. "She's exaggerating of course," I said. "I'm far from being lightfooted, but I love to dance and Beth and I still do a pretty mean swing. I promise not to step on your toes, Whitney."

I asked if they wanted us to buy a couple of the sandwiches for them as an early wedding present, but Whitney said Lance's mouth was watering for some barbecued ribs and they'd pass.

The gyro sandwiches were a good choice, they were delicious and just hit the spot. We sat along the fence next to Kat and Nick Rumalto as we ate them.

"Didn't you think Jesus looked like a dead ringer today for that comedian we saw at Comedy Showcase?" Kat asked. We both agreed and said that had been one of the first thoughts we had when we first saw him today.

As I glanced at the crowd nearby it appeared as if news of some kind was circulating. People had surprised and concerned looks on their faces. Nick had noticed what was occurring, too. He stood and said he'd try to discover what was up. He headed towards two nearby couples who were speaking to one another. After a minute or so of conversation with them he quickly came back to report to us what he'd learned.

"It appears Jesus collapsed in the tunnel as He was leaving," Nick explained. "No one's quite sure about His condition. They say He lost consciousness. He was removed on a stretcher and loaded into an EMS vehicle. He's been taken to Emergency at UofM Hospital. People are saying it didn't appear to have been a heart attack or a stroke."

"Oh, no!" Beth exclaimed. "I hope it's not serious, maybe just exhaustion. He appeared so healthy as He spoke today, energized by the crowd."

"I hope it's nothing major too," Kat said. "I probably shouldn't say anything, but I had an ominous feeling today as He ended His speech, bidding us all farewell. I was thinking it was going to be the last time we were going to have the opportunity to see Him in the flesh."

The mood of the people around us had clearly changed. People were now clustered together in small groups, speaking in hushed tones. I spotted tears in some of their eyes. The news had clearly shocked everyone including me. Probably for much the same reason. Moments ago as He was speaking and challenging the crowd, I'd viewed Him as a larger than life persona, invincible and not subject to the same maladies as mortals. Perhaps as Beth had suggested, his ailment was something minor brought on by fatigue and stress. I suggested to Beth that we round up the Hansons and head home. We'd be able to get an update on Jesus' condition on the television news. I was certain it would be the major story on every station along with a recap and analysis of His speech.

Chapter LXV

We turned on the TV as soon as we were home. Jesus was still in a coma. Witnesses to His collapse reported He hadn't struck His head. To the contrary, those nearest Him had caught Him as He was falling and eased His body down to the floor of the tunnel. There was no suggestion He'd been struck or shoved.

Doctors who'd examined Him earlier in the week, when He'd been hospitalized for a short time following His previous stumbles, were being interviewed. They said Jesus had to be suffering from enormous pain as the result of the near fatal injuries He'd sustained when the car had crashed into Him a month or so ago. They reported He'd been given a couple shots of a painkiller during His recent stay in the hospital. Yes, they said, surgery to address the problems had been discussed at that time. It had been ruled out as being too risky, with no assurances the complex surgery would alleviate the pain.

There were many rumors afloat. One suggested He'd been struck by a poison dart, another assassination attempt. There was no evidence anything of that nature had occurred. Another rumor suggested Jesus was heavily into drugs to treat His pain and had had a drug seizure of some nature. This had also been determined to be false, there was no evidence that other than the pain shots taken during His recent hospital stay, Jesus was taking medication of any kind.

A group of several thousand people had made the lengthy walk from the UofM Stadium over to the UofM Hospital. Ernie Smith had come out to speak to them. He advised them to disperse and go home and keep Jesus in their prayers.

During our church service the following morning there was a special prayer for Jesus. In the coffee hour following the service, Jesus was the main topic of conversation. It appeared over half of those present had been in the Stadium to hear Him speak. All the comments Beth and I heard were favorable. Most seemed to have been truly inspired by what He said. The only negative was some people grousing over why Jesus had altered His appearance. I think most of those in our congregation would have preferred He hadn't.

Beth and I frequently turned on the TV during the remainder of the day and also on Monday. There were no new developments, Jesus was still in a coma and doctors, thus far, had been unable to come up with an explanation for why. None of them were making any predictions as to how long He might remain in the coma.

Tuesday's *Ann Arbor News* reported nearly all of Jesus' followers would be leaving town on Wednesday to scatter to all parts of the world. Numerous commitments to meet and speak to various groups had been made and the followers had all agreed they should be honored. Only Ernie Smith and Ginny Roberts were staying behind. Ernie had become the main spokesperson for updates on Jesus' condition.

The television news on Wednesday reported medical experts from all over the world were congregating in Ann Arbor. The group of surgeons who'd performed the operation on Jesus following His accident were suggesting those previous injuries were likely the cause for His remaining unconscious. They believed His body had shut down in response to the severe pain He was suffering. They also quoted what Jesus had told them prior to the previous operations, telling them God was with Him and to go ahead with the high-risk procedures. They were advocating surgery as soon as possible.

Friday morning's *Free Press* reported Jesus would be operated on later that morning. Medical experts from throughout the world were in agreement the surgery should be done. A number of them would be joining the team of surgeons who'd operated on Him previously. The article quoted several sources who were saying the surgery held no guarantees and could easily result in Jesus' death.

Beth and I had both read the article. "I guess I'm not surprised they're going ahead with the surgery," Beth said. "Everything that's been reported pointed to the fact they probably would be. But I'm struggling with the probability Jesus could die. I'm not ready for that. That would be devastating."

I'd nodded in agreement. "I guess it's in God's hands," I'd said. "We've been praying a lot lately. I think we should again."

Beth and I turned on the TV as we were having lunch. We left it on for the remainder of the afternoon. Other than the fact the surgery was underway, there was no news as to what was occurring. We both tried to occupy our minds with various household chores.

It was nearly 3:30pm when programming was interrupted for a special news bulletin. Tears were evident in the newscaster's eyes as he stated in a choked voice, "Jesus Christ died this afternoon during surgery. The time was exactly 3:00pm. We hope to have further details in the next few minutes."

Chapter LXVI

Beth and I sat in silence for several minutes. "We were praying for a miracle," Beth finally said. "I guess it wasn't to be. I'm having trouble understanding what's happened, I can't believe He's actually dead."

I'd nodded, all kinds of thoughts and questions were swirling through my head. Was this God's doing? What did it mean for Jesus' quest to establish God's Kingdom here on Earth? Would there be a funeral, a memorial service of some kind? If so, where? What about a burial?

Several of the surgeons who'd been involved were now being interviewed as we continued to watch the TV screen. Their looks of disappointment and defeat were obvious. All were saying they'd realized going into the surgery that it was risky, yet all had been optimistic. Several said they could sense God's presence guiding them. They had thoroughly discussed what had to be done prior to the actual surgery. There'd been no surprises, all had felt things were going as well as could be expected. Though they'd realized the risk of death was high, they'd been shocked when Jesus died. He'd never regained consciousness.

A short time later, Ernie Smith and Ginny Roberts had come out of the hospital to address the media. She'd spoken for both of them. She said they were confident Jesus was now in Heaven and reunited with God. All of Jesus' followers had already been informed and would be returning to Ann Arbor as soon as possible. The arrangements for a viewing and funeral service were still being worked out and Mr. Smith and she would hopefully be able to provide them the details tomorrow morning. In response to questions, she'd replied that there'd been no decision yet as to where Jesus might be buried. And no, Jesus had not said anything to His followers to indicate His death was imminent or to prepare them for that possibility. She reminded the reporter who'd asked the question how enthusiastic Jesus had been as He detailed His travel plans and those of His followers when He'd spoken in the UofM Stadium.

The final two questions took us by surprise. The second was a follow up to the first one. One of the reporters asked Miss Roberts if she or Mr. Smith saw any significance in the fact Jesus' death had occurred on a Friday and exactly at 3:00pm? Ernie Smith's face had reddened in anger as the question was being asked. Miss Roberts was calm and composed as she pointed out that there are distinct differences between the two deaths occurring on a Friday — the first death, that Christians celebrate as "Good Friday", occurs in the spring, not in the fall. The same reporter then asked if they thought Jesus might be resurrected in the next couple days? Miss Roberts repeated the statements she'd made earlier, they were confident Jesus was now in Heaven and reunited with His Father.

I'd asked Beth if she'd noticed Ernie Smith's reaction as those last two questions were being asked? She'd replied she had. "He was clearly upset. I thought the questions were ones that probably many people are asking. I don't understand what prompted Ernie's angry reaction. Maybe there's something more behind the questions that we haven't been privy to."

And there was. A half hour later a group of three or four pickets appeared on the screen. The reporter said they'd suddenly appeared outside the UofM hospital less than an hour after Jesus had died. Their signs proclaimed this man people were calling Jesus was a fraud, that a conspiracy was underway. The spokesperson of the group was quoted as having alleged the man pretending to be Jesus, his followers and the medical establishment were all engaged in a plot to deceive the public. He claimed the man's death had been staged, the timing pre-arranged. He said plans to also stage a resurrection were in the works, that the man hadn't died. I could now understand why Ernie had been so upset. They were wild, absurd charges. I was a little surprised the channel we were watching was even giving the story airtime. Talk about a conspiracy. How had the men mobilized so soon after Jesus' death, equipped with fairly professional looking picket signs? Something was amiss here. Had they just been lucky in banking Jesus would die during the surgery? Had they prepared in advance in case he died? The high risk associated with the surgery had been well publicized. But what was motivating these men? What did they hope to gain from this? A moment in the spotlight, a few minutes of fame? As the camera panned in on the faces of the four men and their signs, all I could think of was evil did exist in the world.

Beth was also turned off by scene. "That's so gross and the timing's so tragic. Millions of people are mourning Jesus' death without the need to have to deal with something like this."

I told Beth I agreed and suggested our right of free speech in this country also meant we had to tolerate an incident such as this occurring from time to time. "It stirs up my anger though. If someone was asking for volunteers to come forward to cart these folks out of town, I'd be inclined to sign up. Love thine enemies. Those men are really testing that commandment. Just imagine the quandary Ernie and the rest of Jesus' followers face in deciding how best to confront these people."

"I suppose it's best to just try to ignore them," Beth said. "Hope that when they find nobody's paying any attention to them they'll pack up and leave. I hope that'll be the case. If they continue what they're doing and attempt to maybe picket Jesus' funeral too, I would almost bet they'll be violence of some kind. This is such an emotional time."

The reporter was moving on to another story. He was announcing the President had just ordered flags to be flown at half-mast. Not unexpectedly, he was already being criticized in some quarters for ignoring the separation of church and state doctrine.

There was also an announcement that tomorrow afternoon's Michigan vs. Notre Dame football game was being postponed. The reporter didn't indicate which school had initiated the cancellation. It was only the second time I could ever remember this being done. It had also happened following the assassination of John F. Kennedy. This proved to be only the first of several reports announcing college and professional teams were canceling their events. Many Governors were also following the President's lead and ordering flags to be flown at half mast.

Beth and I had a quiet dinner as we continued watching the news coverage, frequently switching channels in the process. There was much speculation going on over the funeral arrangements. The students were now back in town. A group of them were proposing an open casket viewing on the UofM Diag, a location which was easily accessible by all students. The same group was suggesting that following a short service there, Jesus' casket be transported to Forest Hill Cemetery at the corner of Observatory and Hill for burial next to Fielding H. Yost and Fritz Crisler, two UofM legends. Other suggestions included flying the casket to Jerusalem and having a memorial service and burial there. Others suggested the Vatican be the site for this to occur. Beth and I could only imagine how Jesus' followers were probably being besieged, so many people wanting to offer their advice. There was no doubt in our minds, however, that whatever location was decided on, there'd be dignitaries from all over the world in attendance.

As we were going to bed, we still had the television on. On one of the talk shows the rampant rumors that had been circulating were being discussed. According to one rumor there had been a Judas among Jesus' followers. He or she had embedded a deadly slow acting poison in Jesus' lunch. The poison had triggered Jesus' later collapse and coma. It was virtually undetectable. Another rumor alleged one of the surgeons had been drinking heavily prior to performing a critical piece of the surgery on Jesus. He'd accidentally severed a major artery. This had led to Jesus' death. The other surgeons had agreed to keep this a secret to protect the reputation of their esteemed colleague and to also avoid being criticized for allowing him to participate in the surgery while knowing he was intoxicated.

"Had enough?" I'd asked Beth, the TV control in my hand.

"I guess so," she replied. "My head's swimming. I can't help but compare today with the day J.F.K. was assassinated. How they said everyone sat glued to their TV sets for days. How they said there were so many false rumors."

I'd smiled, "I know," I said. "I was one of those watching the TV, listening to the rumors. I guess it's just another example of the difference in our ages."

Beth had a twinkle in her eye as he leaned over and kissed me. "I love older men," she whispered.

Chapter LXVII

Beth and I switched on the TV as we were having breakfast the following morning. A press conference at which Ernie Smith had given details of the funeral arrangements for Jesus was just ending. Plans called for an open casket viewing in Crisler Arena beginning at 3pm this afternoon. The Arena would be open until midnight and then reopen again at 7am Sunday. The viewing and paying homage would continue until 2:30pm. The funeral service would also be held in Crisler Arena, scheduled to begin at 3:00pm. It was expected to end around 4:30pm. There had been no decision yet on a burial site.

The announcer also reported Mr. Smith had identified some of those individuals who'd be speaking at the funeral service. They would be a very diverse group. The Pope would be there, the Dalai Lama, the Secretary General from the U.N., a woman from India who was said to be following in the footsteps of Mother Teresa, the religious leader from Iran, a widely respected Hindu leader, a South Korean who headed the Presbyterian Church there, and the first woman to serve as a head of state on the African Continent. Also in attendance, would be the minister who'd actually be conducting the service. He was from the Congregational Church in Ann Arbor. The announcer reported Mr. Smith had explained there were four churches very close to the Campus Inn in Ann Arbor where the followers of Jesus had frequently attended church services; a Baptist Church, a Methodist Church, a Catholic Church and the Congregational Church. The followers had voted to invite the Congregational Minister.

Mr. Smith had said over seventy individuals had asked for the opportunity to speak at the service. He'd said the followers had a great deal of difficulty in determining who should be selected. In asking for guidance from God and Jesus, Mr. Smith said the group was confident it had made wise choices. In response to questions, Mr. Smith declined to reveal the identities of those who'd asked to be considered but were not chosen. The reporter said that Mr. Smith had smiled as he'd spoken and commented some of the names would be very surprising to them. He'd explained the followers had utilized tele-conferencing for their deliberations to accommodate those followers who had not yet made their way back to Ann Arbor. He'd also declined to answer the question as to whether or not the eight selected had been among the seventy who'd asked to be considered. As to the question of when Mr. Smith expected a decision to be made in regard to a burial place, he'd said he was hopeful he'd have an announcement later today or tomorrow morning. He did indicate the service would be televised.

Beth and I both agreed we wanted to go to Crisler Arena for the viewing, "Let's go this afternoon," Beth suggested. "That'll give us an opportunity to inquire if there's going to be any reserved seating available for the funeral service. I'm worried there won't be enough room for everyone who wants to attend."

"I think you're right," I'd replied. "Of course, we can always watch it on TV. We'd probably get a better picture and understanding of what's happening than if we were there. Still it's a historic moment. I'd be game to go a couple hours early to assure us of getting a seat if you are."

The phone had rung as I was talking. I could tell by Beth's

side of the conversation it was Joy Hanson. They'd be picking us up tomorrow at 12:30pm to attend the funeral. We'd be picking them up at 4:00pm today to go to the viewing and then out to dinner.

Chapter LXVIII

There were close to a thousand people in line outside Crisler Arena as we arrived. There were a number of volunteers directing the crowd. The young man who'd guided us indicated we'd have about an hour and a half wait. It was another beautiful day and we all agreed we should wait. We discussed perhaps having an early dinner and coming back later, but there was no assurance the line would be any shorter then, possibly even longer.

I recognized one of the ushers from our church directing the crowd. He also spotted us and came over to chat. I introduced Bill Autin to the Hansons. He asked us if we were aware tomorrow's funeral service was going to be moved to the Stadium. We told him we weren't and explained how the four of us had planned to come a couple hours early tomorrow in order to get seats. He'd told us that might not be a bad idea anyway, he'd heard people thought they'd be having to close the gates and turn people away. "It's supposed to be another beautiful day," Bill said, "at least that's what's being predicted. And the Ann Arbor Symphony Orchestra will be performing starting at 2:00pm."

Beth asked if he knew if there'd be any reserved seating and if so how you'd go about reserving seats. Bill replied he'd been told a block of 5000 seats had been set aside for Jesus' followers. "It's basically for the large number of international guests who are expected and the many religious and government leaders. Probably those who'd put in a request to speak at the service and weren't selected will be invited to sit there too. The followers are the ones in charge of the seat assignments. It's really a V.I.P. section, but they're very hesitant to refer to it by that term in that everyone was treated as a V.I.P. by Jesus. Unless you have an inside track with one of the followers, I'd just advise you to get there early, probably one thirty at the latest."

We thanked Bill for the info. We were surprised over how quickly the line was moving, we'd advanced nearly 100 feet in the short time we'd been conversing with Bill. The four of us discussed whether we should be phoning for a dinner reservation. With the students back in town in addition to the many visitors who'd be arriving for tomorrow's service, the restaurants on a Saturday night were apt to be very crowded. We decided to wait to call until we were closer to the head of the line in that we still had no idea of how long we'd be.

Jerry commented it was good we'd arrived when we had as he pointed to the large number of people now in line behind us. There appeared to be another 500 or so of them. I'd nudged Beth as we were passing one of the large trash receptacles a few minutes later. Picket signs similar to the ones we'd seen the four men carrying outside the UofM Hospital on TV had been jammed into it. Not in a way to display the signs, far from it. The signs were torn and several of the wooden sticks on which they'd been hoisted were broken in half. "Those men must have shown up here," I suggested to her. "Looks as if they were stripped of their signs. I wonder if they were roughed up, maybe injured."

One of the volunteers directing people was not far from us and

I motioned to him to come over. I pointed to the trash container and asked if he could clue us in about what had happened. The man told us though he hadn't been present, he had been briefed. According to what he'd been told the four men carrying picket signs had been confronted by a huge muscular man carrying a couple baseball bats. "He told the men they had ten minutes to clear out and if they chose not to, he guaranteed they'd have every bone in their bodies broken. Everyone waiting in line would have a crack at them, he threatened." We shuddered as we envisioned what must have happened. The man continued describing what he'd been told. "The men initially argued they were just exercising their right of free speech and that they'd summon the police to protect them. But then a couple, quickly joined by others, formed a wall between the four men and the man who was threatening them. They said this wasn't the way Jesus would have wanted the situation handled. The group who'd intervened conversed with the four men for a few minutes. Then, to the surprise and relief of everyone, the men ripped up the signs and stuffed them into that trash container. I don't know what the men had been told, what prompted the action. There's a rumor circulating that the men had been approached and offered ten thousand dollars to picket at the hospital, here at Crisler and at the funeral tomorrow, twenty-five hundred a piece. They supposedly never met the man who engaged them, just a phone conversation. They were told where to pick up the signs along with half the money in cash. They'd be mailed the remainder of the money after they'd performed their assignment. That's all I really know. Oh yes, one other thing. I was told the four men had joined the group in line who'd spoken to them along with the man who'd confronted them. It was nearly an hour ago, they're probably inside Crisler by now."

We all thanked the man for his explanation, expressing our relief that things had turned out the way they had with no one being seriously injured. After he left, the four of us speculated over what must had been said to the four men to alter their behavior so quickly. None of us could really come up with an answer.

Just after six o'clock we began to file into the entry tunnel leading into Crisler Arena. The crowd quieted down as we entered the complex. An impressive, yet simple, sight greeted us. Jesus' open casket was in the middle of the floor with close to a hundred floral arrangements surrounding it. They ranged from white lily arrangements to colorful fall bouquets, from exotic flowers to simple lily of the valley blossoms. There were also several photos on easels. Most of them I recognized from having seen them in recent weeks in newspapers and magazines. One however, I'd never recalled seeing and it took me by surprise. Jesus was pictured sitting on a huge tree stump. There were nearly twenty small animals gathered around his feet and a few small birds flying over him. One was perched on His shoulder. All of the photos, I noticed, pictured Jesus in His biblical garb with His beard and long hair. I didn't see any showing Him after His recent change in appearance.

Jesus was dressed in His white robe. The purity of the color appeared to cast a glow. Some people stopped to kneel and pray as they filed past the casket. Others gazed upward as they voiced a prayer. Jesus appeared so serene. His hands were clasped at His waist. Many of us had tears in our eyes.

During our drive to the restaurant, we commented on the diversity of the crowd who'd come to Crisler. There'd been a number of small children with their parents. Some of the elderly were in wheel chairs or using walkers. Over a third of the crowd appeared to be of college age. All nationalities seemed to be represented. There was a heavy concentration of blacks. Everyone was well groomed with most of the men wearing coats and ties as Jerry and I were.

We couldn't help but notice in the restaurant and on the streets as we were walking there, the solemn mood. Though people were still outgoing and friendly, the noise level was much lower than normal.

Chapter LXIX

The Sunday morning papers were filled with stories and photos of yesterday's viewing at Crisler Arena. Over 20,000 people were said to have viewed Jesus. The building had remained open until nearly 2:00am to accommodate the crowd. There was an aerial shot in the *Ann Arbor News* showing the lines of people weaving around the outside of the Arena and a half dozen or so photos of people waiting in line.

There were also several photos from inside the building, an awesome one showing Jesus in the open casket was in full color. There were front page stories in both the *News* and the *Free Press* about the plans for today's memorial service. Both featured photos of those who would be speaking at the service with brief biographical sketches. I was surprised to see Martha Seidman would be a speaker. She'd taken her brother's place as one of Jesus' followers after her brother had been killed during the assassination attempt on Jesus.

The articles advised people to arrive early in order to be assured of seating. They noted that at 2:00pm, an hour before the service was scheduled to begin, the Ann Arbor Symphony Orchestra would be performing.

An article in the *Ann Arbor News* reported the followers of Jesus were giving $500,000 to the University of Michigan to cover the expenses involved in the use of its facilities and personnel and for making free parking available on its properties. A like amount was being given to the City of Ann Arbor to cover the extra expenses it would incur in handling traffic and security. I thought as I read the article, what a smart move that was by His followers. It would hopefully dilute any criticism and minimize questions as to who was footing the bill for this event.

There was just a short article titled "Confrontation Avoided", that mentioned the four men who'd carried the picket signs outside the UofM Hospital and Crisler Arena. I was relieved to see the *News* hadn't played up the story or run a photo showing the signs. The article stated that after a brief conversation with some of the people waiting in line to see Jesus, the men destroyed their signs and joined in the viewing of Jesus. The men had told the *Ann Arbor News* they regretted what they'd done and wished to apologize to all those they'd offended. They'd declined to answer additional questions.

As Beth and I were having an early lunch we turned on the TV. The reporter was just announcing the University of Michigan had received a communication earlier this morning warning there was a bomb inside the Stadium. The reporter said a search of the Stadium was currently underway and bomb demolition experts were now on the scene. The reporter attempted to down play the news by saying it was not uncommon to receive a warning of this nature before a major event. He also compared what was happening to a warning, prior to takeoff, that a bomb was aboard an airplane. "After the aircraft has been thoroughly searched, it becomes one of the safest flights in the sky," the reporter said. "And after the search of the UofM Stadium, it will probably be one of the safest places to be in America this afternoon."

As the reporter was speaking I was thinking how major an event Jesus' memorial service was going to be. The entire world would be watching on TV, probably hundreds of millions of people. If some terrorist group was trying to draw attention to itself, they couldn't hope for a larger audience. The Stadium could be searched, but what about the more than one hundred thousand people who'd be gathered there? People were being advised that similar to football games, no containers of any kind would be permitted inside the Stadium. And with the warm weather, the danger of someone smuggling some type of device in under a bulky jacket or sweater was lessened. But still, I knew I'd have my eyes peeled for anything looking suspicious.

Beth must have been having some of the same thoughts I was. "Can you imagine what a catastrophe it would be, Mike, if someone did set off a bomb at the service today? What a tragedy! What an ending to Jesus' mission! All of His followers will be there. Many of the world's leaders. Talk about a grand finale, that would be it. What a scary thought!"

"I've been having some of those same thoughts," I replied. "I guess we can only hope and pray that they just remain thoughts and nothing occurs. But you're right, it's scary to think about the consequences if something like that were to happen."

Beth glanced at the clock and reminded me the Hansons were due to pick us up in about ten or fifteen minutes. She suggested we take our binoculars, maybe a pair for each of us. I'd nodded in agreement and went to get them.

Chapter LXX

As we were climbing into the car Joy asked if we'd heard about the bomb scare. We told her we'd just learned about it. Jerry asked if we had any reservations about being in the Stadium today and we told him we didn't. We assured them we were still looking forward to being there.

Joy told us today's *New York Times* had a feature story on Ernie Smith. "It's very complimentary, he's had quite a life," she'd said. "He gives Jesus full credit for changing his life. The article speculates Ernie might be a likely candidate to lead Jesus' followers if they decide to continue on without Jesus."

Beth asked Joy to save the article for us to read. She told the Hansons Ernie had impressed us and he might be the logical choice for a leader in that he seemed to have handled the role of spokesperson for the group extremely well.

"Want to hear some of the latest rumors?" Joy asked. "They might alter your opinions about him though." I'd smiled, Joy always seemed to be the one to come up with the latest scuttlebutt. We told her to go ahead and clue us in.

"Jesus' surgery was originally planned for Saturday morning. At Ernie Smith's prodding it was advanced to Friday. That's not all. He's said to be the one who picked out Jesus' casket. There's a rumor it's equipped with a lever to enable it to be opened from the inside. And here's the one that tops them all. The reason Ernie has yet to announce where Jesus will be buried is because His resurrection will be staged today at the close of the service."

Joy smiled as she observed my shocked expression. My initial thought was recalling Ernie's angry reaction when the reporter had asked Ginny Roberts questions about the timing of Jesus' death and His possible resurrection. My second thought was about the pickets and their allegations, which I'd thought to be ridiculous at the time. Maybe they weren't so farfetched after all.

Beth quickly responded to Joy's comments, however. "Let's get all the facts out," she'd said. "First, the reason Ernie Smith wanted to get the surgery switched to Friday was because more staff would be on duty that day as opposed to Saturday, available in case they were needed. Second, the manufacturer of the casket Ernie chose for Jesus has traditionally equipped its top of the line model with a means for opening it from the inside. I read they've done it for nearly a hundred years. The story is that a century ago a wealthy man had requested the feature, probably concerned that his heirs might bury him alive. There was nothing devious about the choice of the casket or switching the time for the surgery.

"And, as far as your rumor about His resurrection today, I heard it, too. There was concern Jesus' followers might remove His body at Crisler before the casket was closed. Or open it and remove it as the casket was being transported to the Stadium. I believe His followers heard of the rumors. I think Ernie was the one who made arrangements for the news media and some local preachers to observe the closing of the casket and to accompany it as it's being moved to the Stadium. It doesn't sound to me he's part of any deception or staging."

I looked at Beth in surprise. I couldn't help but admire her knowledge concerning the rumors. At the same time I was a little disappointed she hadn't taken the time to discuss these things with me. Beth finished up by saying this last rumor had a thick cloud of smoke suddenly appearing at the close of the service and blanketing the casket from view. As the smoke cleared the crowd would see an open empty casket. They'd be unaware Jesus' body had been removed earlier by His followers and that one of them had opened the lid of the casket.

Joy did not seem at all offended by Beth having blown holes in her rumors. "I was just wanting you to know what people were saying," Joy said. "I'm aware of everything you've said Beth. I just wanted to stir up things a little before, as Paul Harvey would say, telling you the 'rest of the story'."

I told Joy she'd succeeded in getting me concerned and worked up, but I was glad Beth had been prepared to deal with the rumors.

Chapter LXXI

The traffic was already quite heavy as we approached the Stadium. Jerry and I decided to drop Joy and Beth off before trying to find a place to park. We told them to try to get seats near where our group had been sitting the previous week and we'd find them. There was still a long line outside Crisler Arena with people waiting to view Jesus. We noticed volunteers now instructing people the line was being closed. Though there was still nearly an hour and a half before the scheduled viewing would end, Jerry and I expressed our doubts over whether everyone currently in the long line would be able to view Jesus' open casket before it was moved into the stadium.

We finally found a parking place about half a mile from the Stadium. It was another lovely day though, and we didn't mind the walk. We were surprised to find the stands were already half filled. We had no trouble finding Joy and Beth who'd found seats a couple sections over from where we'd been seated before. They spotted us first and had stood and waved.

There was a rather large platform in the center of the field with chairs already in place for the Ann Arbor Symphony Orchestra and another approximately thirty chairs in front of them. There were already a few floral arrangements in front of those chairs where we assumed Jesus' casket would be placed. As had been done previously, people were being given free bottles of water on the concourse surrounding the Stadium. The ushers had also provided us with programs as we entered the Stadium.

As I'd sat down next to Beth she'd leaned over and said she thought I'd find the prayer at the close of the service particularly interesting. She showed me her program and pointed to where the prayer appeared. Martha Seidman's name was printed to the right of it, evidently indicating she'd be the one leading the crowd in the prayer. I read the prayer.

"Our God, we come in reverence to honor and praise You. Thank You for Your love for us. Help us to share Your love with one another. Guide us in making the right choices in our lives. Give us the strength and courage to act as You would have us act. Empower us to establish Your Kingdom On Earth; a world where all are reconciled and at peace. We ask this of You with our hearts, minds and souls. Amen."

I reread it again before turning to Beth and asking what she thought about it. "I guess it pretty well sums up what Jesus has been saying," she replied. "Remember you suggested Jesus would have to come up with some sort of universal prayer other than the Lord's Prayer which everyone could accept and embrace. Do you think this is the prayer He came up with or do you think maybe it's the work of Martha Seidman? Her interpretation of a prayer Jesus would have authored?"

"That's a good question," I said. "I'd be surprised if she doesn't address it before asking the crowd to join in the prayer."

"You're probably right," Beth replied. "I'm sure you've noticed there's no mention of heaven. No mention of forgiveness. No mention of delivering us from evil."

I smiled as I told her I had. "I get the impression you still prefer the Lord's Prayer."

"Don't you?" Beth asked. "I know you've kept reminding me Jesus wasn't asking people to change the ways they'd chosen to honor and worship God, just adding another dimension. But are you still thinking we can keep the Lord's Prayer and also adopt this one, too?"

"I guess I am," I answered. "Maybe not this exact prayer. I agree it could probably stand a little refinement. I know forgiveness was a point Jesus emphasized. Maybe over time it could be polished up a little. If it's Martha Seidman's doing, I'm sure she'll be the first one to suggest that."

Joy tapped Beth on the shoulder and said she was sorry to interrupt our conversation but wondered if she and Jerry could borrow our binoculars for a few minutes. "I think I've spotted several celebrities coming into the reserved section," she said. "We want to take a closer look."

Over the next few minutes, Joy and Jerry rattled off the names of several people they were recognizing and there were a slew of them. Prominent people from all walks of life. Movie stars, politicians, religious leaders, rock stars and other entertainers, star athletes, foreign dignitaries, business leaders, news commentators, college presidents. It was an amazing mix of celebrities. The stadium was nearly filled and there was still over an hour before the service was to begin.

A short while later as members of the orchestra were filing into their seats, an announcement was made over the public address system. Everyone was being asked to move in toward the center of the rows they were sitting in so more people could be accommodated along the aisles. There was no doubt in my mind that today's crowd was going to break the all time attendance record.

As the Ann Arbor Symphony Orchestra was introduced, there was a round of applause. The conductor approached the microphone and thanked the crowd. He then asked, out of respect and in honor of the occasion, for the crowd to refrain from any further applause for the remainder of the afternoon. "There are several people who will be speaking today, all of whom are very deserving of your applause," he said. "However, we ask for your cooperation. Please no applause. Now if you'll please switch off your cell phones and lean back and relax and hopefully enjoy this musical prelude to today's service."

I had to smile. We were so squeezed into our seats, relaxing wouldn't be easy. But we were in for a treat. The concert was wonderful; I couldn't imagine how their choice of music could have been improved on. Following one selection, which was a medley of middle-eastern tunes, there was a smattering of applause. The conductor stepped up to the microphone again with a smile on his face and simply said, "Thank you, but remember that is a no, no."

The time passed very quickly. It seemed as if the orchestra had only begun as Jesus' casket appeared, being carried by His followers out of the tunnel on the opposite side of the field. It was placed on the stage along with several more floral arrangements. A few moments later a procession of men and women emerged from the tunnel and proceeded to the platform stage. All were seated as the orchestra played its final number, "Let There Be Peace On Earth." Thoughts flooded my mind, remembering that last day we'd seen Jesus alive.

Bob Littleton, the Congregational Minister, stepped to the microphone and asked us to bow our heads in prayer. The prayer was rather brief, but very meaningful in its message. It was a prayer of thanks to God for having sent Jesus to be with us. It thanked God for being present with us not only today, but every moment of everyday from now through eternity. The prayer acknowledged it was a time of great joy and great sorrow, great joy from having been blessed by Jesus' visit, great sorrow because the visit had been so short. It referred to the message Jesus had brought, a message of love and hope. It asked God to give us all the strength and courage to change and rededicate our lives to establish His Kingdom On Earth. It concluded by asking God to dry our tears, calm our fears and inspire us to emulate the example Jesus Christ had shown us.

Following the prayer, the Pope was introduced as the first speaker. My initial thought was this was a mistake, that he should have been the final speaker. The others on the program were certain to be intimidated by having to follow him. But as the Pope spoke, I found I couldn't have been more wrong. In a wonderful humble way he was able to set the tone for the service. His description of the times he'd spent with Jesus brought tears and smiles. He praised Jesus for His humility and sincerity and acknowledged how much he'd learned from Him in the short time they'd been together. "Because of Him, I know I've changed," he said. "Because of Him, I'm sure my church will change. Because of Him, hopefully all of you will change. God bless you all."

The Pope was followed by Sister Maria. She told of taking a break from her labors in India to meet Jesus. She smiled as she explained she'd been reluctant about leaving what she was doing for even a couple days to journey and meet with Him. "I felt a burden with the pressing needs of the men, women and children I was attempting to help. Their needs were so great, I hesitated to desert them for even a day. Jesus thanked me for all my efforts on behalf of others. But then as He clasped my hands, He said that rather than being troubled and discouraged, I should find joy and happiness in what I was doing. His touch seemed to send a current through me. I felt re-energized and more at peace than I'd been for some time, I thank Jesus for making me better at what I do. His love radiated through me and now I'm able to pass it on to others."

The Secretary General of the United Nations also praised Jesus, saying He'd inspired him to set higher goals for himself and the U.N. "Mother Maria has explained how Jesus re-energized her. I can't begin to tell you how he changed those of us at the U.N. by giving us new hope and direction. There hasn't been a single day since I met with Him and He spoke to the General Assembly that I haven't thought of Him. And even though He's no longer present with us in the flesh, I'm certain He'll be with us in spirit and I'll continue to think of Him every day."

The remarks of the other five speakers were much along the same line. The Dalai Lama had written a special prayer to honor Jesus. The Buddhist told of Jesus inspiring him and others to not only change themselves, but to work with their Hindu brethren in changing India's caste system. The attractive and articulate woman from Africa said in being elected to head her country, she'd not been sure what she was getting into. But in listening to Jesus, she now realized what she should do. She was more confident than ever she and her nation would succeed in helping to make God's Kingdom On Earth a reality.

There were several times during the service I came close to spontaneously applauding. I could sense that was probably true for many others in the crowd too. I glanced at my watch and saw it was getting close to 4:30pm. A great deal had happened in the past hour and a half, eight speakers, three hymns and two prayers. Martha Seidman was now approaching the microphone. The service was nearing an end.

She said before leading us all in the prayer printed in the program, she had a few comments to make. She explained that in conversations with His followers, Jesus had often said there might come a time when there would be a need to have a new universal prayer that all people could identify with and embrace. She smiled as she said, "Jesus didn't jot down many notes. He didn't use a P.C. much either. His memory was fantastic. His workshop was in His head. However, from the few writings we were able to find and from what we picked up in conversations with Him, we've put together this prayer. We believe it pretty much reflects His message. However, we're open to suggestions as to how it might be improved, something that should be added or possibly even a deletion or two. That said, would you please join me in the prayer.

"Our God, we come in reverence to honor and praise You. Thank You for Your love for us. Help us to share Your love with one another. Guide us in making the right choices in our lives. Give us the strength and courage to act as You would have us act. Empower us to establish Your Kingdom On Earth, a world where all are reconciled and at peace. We ask this of You with our hearts, minds and souls. Amen."

Bob Littleton then came to the microphone again. He told the crowd there still hadn't been a final decision regarding burial arrangements for Jesus. He said one idea being discussed was to have Jesus' body cremated and have His ashes scattered in many locations. As he was talking we noticed that four very large black cartons on rollers were being wheeled out of the tunnel. They were being positioned with one at each corner of the stage.

Bob Littleton was now giving a benediction. As he ended, the cartons were opened. Hundreds of white doves flew into the beautiful blue sky. You could hear the crowd as they ooh'd and ah'd.

"Wow!" Joy exclaimed. "What a service and what an ending. Awesome!"

Chapter LXXII

Exiting the Stadium today was taking much longer than following a football game. The fact everyone was departing at the same time was one reason. Another was the size of the crowd. People were saying it had topped one hundred and twenty thousand. Joy and Beth joined Jerry and me for the walk to the car. We hadn't originally planned to have dinner again tonight with the Hansons, but by the time we reached the car it was already past 6:00pm and Joy and Beth decided we should.

We all agreed the downtown spots would probably be packed. Joy proposed the Campus Inn, saying that even when all its rooms were filled, its dining room never seemed to be overly crowded. "Besides, we might run into some of the celebrities who showed up today," Joy said. "And they have good food, Jerry and I have never been disappointed when we've gone there, even though it hasn't been often."

"Good idea, Joy," I said. "Do you think we'd better call first to make sure we can get in though?" Joy shook her head and said. "Why don't we just go there. We can have a cocktail in the lobby bar and people watch if we have to wait."

"That's fine with me," I replied. Turning to Beth I told her she might get an opportunity to chat with Martha Seidman about the prayer she'd led us in today. "I think she'll appreciate your suggestions and I think all of Jesus' followers are staying there."

The Campus Inn was alive with action when we arrived, dozens of people were milling around the lobby. We saw that only one seating arrangement was available in the bar area. Joy and Beth and I immediately seated ourselves there while Jerry went to check on the availability of a table in the dining room. He came back in a few minutes to report a table would be available in about an hour. We ordered drinks from a very delightful young waitress. She was attending UofM, majoring in political science. She asked if we'd had the opportunity to attend Jesus' memorial service. We told her we had and described some of the highlights, ending with the launching of the doves. She expressed her disappointment over not having been able to be there and thanked us for telling her what she'd missed.

As we were waiting for our cocktails, I told Beth I was going to go up to the front desk and check to see if Martha Seidman was available to perhaps join us for a few minutes. Beth blushed, "You're really serious aren't you, Mike? I'm sure she has higher priorities than meeting with us. She's probably involved in meetings with Jesus' other followers, mapping out where they go to from here. Don't bother her now."

I was not to be dissuaded though, suggesting Martha could always say no. "We have an hour before we'll have a table," I said. "I think our timing might be perfect."

The desk clerk was occupied as I approached the front desk. I could overhear her explaining to a couple that no rooms were available; they were completely full. She told them that a number of rooms had become available following the cancellation of yesterday's football game, but they'd quickly been snatched up.

As I was waiting, I saw a few copies of the latest issue of the

Ann Arbor Observer stacked at the end of the counter. We hadn't received ours in the mail yet. The *Observer* is famous for its covers, artists' sketches of familiar Ann Arbor scenes. This cover didn't disappoint. The scene depicted Jesus standing in an aisle at the Farmers' Market, surrounded by a diverse group of people reflecting all ages and all races. The cover had no doubt been in the works long before Jesus' death. There was probably an article about Jesus, which I was looking forward to reading. If true to form, there'd probably be some new details and information not found in other media coverage.

    The clerk was now free and asked how she could help me. I explained I was trying to contact Martha Seidman, one of Jesus' followers. She said she believed all of His followers were now gathered together in a private dining room having dinner, but that if I wanted to use one of the house phones she'd be happy to ring Mrs. Seidman's room for me.

    There was no answer, but I was switched over to her voice mail. I left a lengthy message, explaining who I was and the purpose of my call. I said the four of us would be in the bar for the next hour and then in the dining room until probably close to 10:00pm. I told her we'd love to have her come join us in either spot, even if it was only for a few minutes.

    I explained what I'd done after returning to the others. I told them the young lady at the main desk thought Jesus' followers were now having dinner together in one of the private dining rooms. I also told them about the *Ann Arbor Observer* cover. Beth suggested it must have brought back memories of when I'd first seen Jesus and I assured her it had.

Beth and Joy filled me in on the number of celebrities they'd seen. In some cases the names meant nothing to me and they had to explain to me who they were. But for most of those they'd mentioned, I immediately knew who they were and was duly impressed. We'd made a good choice in coming to the Campus Inn. We each had a second drink as we were waiting. I was a little disappointed but not surprised Martha Seidman hadn't come to join us.

It was a few minutes past 8:00pm when the maitre'd arrived to inform us our table was ready. The dining room was packed. We were fortunate to be seated at a table in the exact center of the room, right next to a table of eight who appeared to be from the Middle East. I immediately recognized the Iranian who spoke at today's service. He was seated next to a man who appeared to be a Jewish Rabbi. The two were engaged in a friendly conversation.

Our food was excellent. We'd all chosen different entrees and all of us had raved about them. The service was rather slow, however, which was understandable given the large crowd. As our plates were being cleared, there appeared to be some news circulating through the room. The noise level raised as everyone began to engage in animated excited conversation. I asked our waiter what was up and if he knew what was prompting all the excitement. He was wide-eyed as he explained he didn't know for sure, but that there was a rumor Jesus was alive. That He'd appeared in the private dining room where His followers had been having dinner.

"Where are they meeting?" I excitedly asked, hoping we could go and see Him. The waiter replied the room was up on the mezzanine floor, but that Jesus was no longer there. "I heard He was only with them for a few minutes. The media was invited in to see

Him, too. I heard they took some photos of Him. Then I guess He sort of vaporized, disappearing as suddenly as He'd appeared. If I get anymore details, I'll pass them on to you."

We sat for a few seconds staring at one another, stunned by this news. Was it really true? Was Jesus actually alive? Had He returned from death a second time? Was this why He'd died? To show death was not an end, that there is life after death? For Him? For us all? The questions were flooding through our minds. We were excited as we discussed our thoughts with one another.

The waiter approached us again saying he didn't have anything more to report. We ordered coffee and a dessert for all of us to share. As we were waiting to be served I spotted Martha Seidman standing next to the maitre'd stand. Had she come to meet with us? I pointed her out to the others and immediately rose from my chair, navigating through the room to where she was standing. I introduced myself, explaining I was the one who'd left the voice message for her. She smiled, saying she'd just heard it. "If it's not too late, I would love to join you. So your wife has a few suggestions for me?" I smiled and nodded, asking her if it was true Jesus was alive and had come to meet with her and His other followers. She replied yes, that was true. I pointed out where we were sitting as I led her towards our table. "As you can imagine we're anxious to hear all the details," I said as we crossed the room.

I introduced the Hansons and Beth to her and then asked if she'd have coffee with us, or possibly dessert. Jerry had found another chair and was standing behind it, holding it out for her to sit down. She said she'd just have a decaf as she seated herself. "I don't know why I said decaf," she said with a smile. "I'm sure I'm not going to get much sleep tonight in light of everything that's happened. I'm also sure before we get into your suggestions, Beth, all of you want to hear just what has taken place. I'm actually delighted to share the details with you. I think it could be a help to me too, help to clarify my thoughts. Of course we were all hoping Jesus might appear, but none of us were really prepared for it to happen. Let's see, where should I begin?"

Chapter LXXIII

The four of us were enthralled as Martha Seidman explained what had taken place in the private dining room where Jesus' followers were having dinner. She said they'd been tired and exhausted following the events of the past few days. Several had traveled thousands of miles to return to Ann Arbor following Jesus' death.

"His death had left us confused and depressed, even though we all agreed the memorial service had been an uplifting and inspirational time. We were discussing what changes would be necessary in the absence of Jesus. Ernie Smith has become a natural leader of the group during the short time we've been together and several of us were suggesting we should formally be electing him to lead us. Although he was eager and enthused over continuing on with Jesus' mission, he was suggesting there were several others, including some of the women, who were far more able and better qualified to lead us. However, most of us were continuing to attempt to convince Ernie he should be the one to take over the reins of leadership. A couple members had teased Ernie by saying if he was to lead us it meant he'd have to change his name, suggesting Ernie was not an appropriate name for someone assuming such a prestigious position." Martha smiled as she continued. "Ginny Roberts asked him if he liked the name Peter. I said what about Ernest. Then a familiar voice from the corner of the room had asked, "Can I interrupt for a few minutes?" It was Jesus' voice. We turned to see Him standing in His white robe, smiling at us.

"My first thought was that we all must be hallucinating. In so much wanting Him to still be with us, our imaginations must have taken over and caused Him to appear. But I quickly realized that wasn't true. Ginny Roberts had immediately risen from her seat and raced over to embrace Him. It was readily apparent she wasn't clutching an apparition. Jesus was real. He hugged her in return.

"He eventually moved her off to the side and spoke to us. He told us His death had been as much a surprise to Him as it had been for us. He said although He'd now be rejoining His Father in Heaven, He'd continue to always be with us in spirit. As we stared at Him in awe, I could sense all of us were convinced what He said was true. He'll continue to be with us. To guide us, to support us, to comfort us. And yes, to forgive us as we sometimes err in seeking to do God's will on earth. His words were very assuring as He pointed out the many challenges now facing us, the work that remained if God's Kingdom On Earth was to become a reality. As He spoke He circulated around the room, taking a moment to embrace each of us. His words were not just inspiring, they included many practical suggestions, steps we should now be taking. He'd smiled as He said He believed Ernest would be a good choice to lead us. He suggested we should also choose another two of us to assist him in this leadership. When we pressed Him, asking Him who He thought the two should be, He said He was certain we'd make wise choices. We also had many more questions for Him, and He addressed them all. However, His primary message was the ball was being passed on to us. He said we were the ones, along with the many other followers He expects us to recruit, who will have to follow through with His mission. He made it clear God and He would be present to help and guide us. He then took a handful of small rubber balls from the pocket of His robe and proceeded to bounce one to each of us. He told us that whenever we felt discouraged, we should take the ball and squeeze it in our hand. He said it would remind us that God held us in the palm of His hand and was with us."

Martha removed a small rubber ball from her pocket and showed it to us. It was the size children play jacks with. It had a map of the world on it. This ball had the mid-east colored in yellow. Martha pointed out that each ball had a shaded area of the world where the follower who'd received it has been assigned. She has been assigned to preach Jesus' message in the Middle East.

"It was becoming apparent Jesus was soon to be leaving us," Martha continued. "Several of us told Him people would find it hard to believe He'd come to speak to us. They said people would say we'd imagined it or were making the story up, that He hadn't been resurrected. Jesus suggested we bring some of the media people up to the room. They'd be able to see and hear Him, even be able to photograph Him. We knew that a few media people were waiting downstairs for any announcement we might be making following our meeting. There were only a handful of them still around, however. With the heavy coverage of the events over the past few days, most had elected to take a break and had left town. We did invite the few who still remained up to the room. Jesus spent a few minutes with them and several photos were taken and videos filmed. Then in their presence and ours, Jesus began to fade away, offering us God's blessing as He gradually disappeared from view."

We sat there speechless. Martha continued to sit with us silently. Joy suggested it must have been an awesome experience for her and she agreed it definitely had been. I asked Martha if Jesus had mentioned anything about today's memorial service or made any suggestions in regard to the prayer she'd led people in. She'd smiled and said, "Jesus had joked a little about the service, telling us He'd been flattered by the many compliments He'd been paid. And yes, He did have a few suggestions for us in regards to the prayer. But I'm still anxious to hear your comments too, Beth."

The dining room had cleared out as we'd been talking and continued to talk. Martha was very receptive to what Beth had to say. It was nearly 11:00pm and only one other table was occupied as we stood to leave. Finally, we thanked her for sharing the details of Jesus' appearance and she left us. Her flight was scheduled to depart at 9:00am tomorrow morning.

During the drive home we had a very somber conversation, finding it hard to believe everything we'd seen and heard during this very memorable day. We all agreed Martha was a very impressive young woman, very talented, very gracious. I mentioned I was sorry we hadn't had more time to ask her how Jesus fit into her Jewish faith. Beth agreed and said it was wonderful Martha was among Jesus' followers, that she certainly was an asset to the group. Jerry asked what we thought about Ernest as a leader of the group? Though all of us appeared comfortable with the choice of him, we were still finding it hard to believe with our vivid memories of the Ernie of old.

Chapter LXXIV

Beth and I spent Monday morning reading the *Free Press* and *USA Today* and watching several of the television channels. All the news concerned Jesus, from the highlights of Sunday's memorial service in the UofM Stadium to His miraculous resurrection and meeting with His followers. Both newspapers contained about six pages of coverage. The *Free Press* front page featured a photo picturing Jesus' open empty casket beneath a banner headline that proclaimed "Jesus Christ Has Risen Again." The accompanying article reported the *Free Press* had been able to reach the general manager of the Muehlig Funeral Home in Ann Arbor late last night. He'd opened the building to enable one of its reporters and a photographer to examine Jesus' casket. The article said the printing of the paper had been delayed by several hours so that the photo showing the empty casket could be run.

Both newspapers featured many color photos from Sunday's memorial service and abbreviated text from the remarks of those who'd spoken during the service. I thought the color photograph showing the doves soaring into the clear blue sky was sure to become a collector's item. For that matter, I believe the two newspapers and probably this afternoon's *Ann Arbor News* wll also be treasured for years to come. Both papers contained a large photograph of Jesus standing amidst His followers, a photo which they said which had been taken the previous evening in the private dining room where Jesus had appeared.

Ernest Smith had been busy this morning making the rounds of the television shows. Excerpts from their interviews with him are appearing on nearly every channel. His description of Jesus' appearance and what He'd told them dovetailed with what Martha Seidman had told us. Ernest had been asked if Jesus had told them if He'd be visiting them again or maybe from time to time in the future. He'd replied Jesus hadn't indicated either way, just telling them in a convincing fashion He'd always be with them in spirit. Ernest also responded to several questions about what the group of followers would now be doing. He said all of Jesus' followers were currently on planes or would soon be embarking on flights that would be taking them all over the world. He also told the interviewers about the small rubber balls Jesus had given to each of them, while holding his up to the camera so viewers could see the map of the world on it with North America shaded.

During the course of the day all of our children had contacted us. They are thrilled to hear how involved we've been with all the recent happenings in Ann Arbor. They were particularly interested in hearing about the meeting we had with Martha Seidman. They're thrilled to hear Beth and I truly believed Jesus has been resurrected and had returned to meet with His followers. They indicated there were rumors all of this was a huge hoax orchestrated by people in Ann Arbor. We assured them that wasn't the case.

The *Ann Arbor Observer* arrived along with our afternoon mail. Its article on Jesus is an excellent one. It chronicles the many things that had happened since Jesus' arrival in Ann Arbor. Though I was familiar with most, there were several I wasn't. One of these was a talk He'd given to the staff at the Life Science Institute. Another is His chat with the players and coaches of the UofM football team. I smiled, hoping He'd inspired them to have a great season.

As I'd anticipated, the *Ann Arbor News* did a remarkable job of reporting everything that had occurred yesterday. In my opinion, its extensive coverage surpassed that of the *Free Press* and the *USA Today*. For one thing, The *News* featured an abundance of trivia details. For example, I now know exactly how many doves there'd been and where they'd come from. Some of the photos also provided a look at some of the things going on behind the scenes yesterday. There was a photo of a number of observers watching Jesus' casket being closed, for example. The *News* had also been able to arrange interviews with a number of the people who'd spoken at the memorial service. There is even a close up photo of one of the rubber balls Jesus gave to His followers along with an article describing how He'd passed them out by bouncing one to each of them.

Beth and I were exhausted after all our reading and watching television. We had a quiet dinner. Beth lit candles. We joined hands as she offered a short prayer, thanking God for sending Jesus, thanking God for Jesus' resurrection and asking God to bless and guide Jesus' followers.

We had a phone call from friends at church later in the evening telling us that five groups would be going into Detroit this coming weekend. This time we were being assigned to a team that would be working in a river front area. Spotty showers were called for in the early forecast and our friends reminded us to bring rain gear just in case. They also suggested some things we should bring with us;

tools and materials. Our previous trip had been so rewarding, we are confident this one will be too.

Epilogue

Just a few months have past since I first saw Jesus in the Farmer's Market. As Beth and I sit in our living room in front of the fire, we discuss all that had happened since. We've been changed by everything that has taken place. Our friends have changed, Ann Arbor has changed. Members from our church have made nearly one hundred mission trips into Detroit. Beth and I have participated in seven of them. It was slow in coming, but a miracle is occurring there. Residents are now optimistic about their future; about their city's future. The state and the nation are viewing Detroit in a far different way. Its economy is beginning to boom with investment dollars pouring in. There is hope it will become a tourist destination once again.

Contributions through Washtenaw United Way this past fall have been twenty percent higher than ever before. Partnering with many other community organizations, United Way is initiating two new projects this coming year. One is in the area of health care, the other in the area of adult education. There is also a surge in contributions to the Ann Arbor Area Community Foundation which enabled it to make a record number of grants during the past year. Volunteers continue to sign up with the non-profit community in record numbers as well. Ann Arbor's reputation as a generous, caring community is continuing to build.

The ranks of Jesus' followers have swelled to over one hundred men and women of all races, nationalities and religious faiths.

A hundred diverse individuals have joined together to deliver Jesus' message of peace and reconciliation to every corner of the world. Newlyweds, Whitney and Lance Parish, were the first of several couples to be recruited. The two are currently at work in Central and South America. Ernest Smith has been questioned about how he is obtaining the small rubber balls to equip the many new recruits. His response has simply been to say God works in mysterious ways.

Though still a long way from bringing about God's Kingdom here on Earth, Jesus' followers are definitely making an impact throughout the world. In many instances, groups who've had a long history of conflict with bitterness are now working together with God's guidance. There are now far fewer trouble spots in the world. There has been a sharp decline in terrorist incidents.

People are turning to God in record numbers. Places of worship in Ann Arbor are now full. The Congregationalist Church is one of several that has added an extra service to its program. With the enthusiastic leadership of the Pope, the Roman Catholic Church is moving forward with changes. Fellow Christians are now being warmly welcomed to participate in their services of worship and partake in the ritual of Communion. Catholics are now being allowed to fulfill their religious vows and obligations in churches of other denominations. An ecumenical spirit is at work in bringing people together in their worship of God, embracing their common goals and beliefs rather than emphasizing their differences. This is not just true among Christians, in many communities new churches with a mixed congregation of Muslims, Christians, and Jews are being established.

This new found spirit of togetherness is also having an

influence on the secular world. Nowhere is this more evident than in the political arena. The November elections were devoid of much of the bitter divisiveness present in past campaigns. The vast majority of voters did not cast their ballots on the basis of a single issue. They appeared to be thoughtfully considering which man or woman could best lead their communities, states, and the nation in finding solutions to the pressing problems they were facing. There have been a record number of split ballots cast. This is not to say everyone is on the same page, far from it. However, there now seems to be an atmosphere where people are more understanding and respectful of one another's views. The rabble-rousers who dominated the airwaves in the past are now losing their audiences. People are turning to the open debate forums in increasing numbers, anxious to hear opposing views discussed in a somewhat congenial fashion. The idea people with vastly different opinions can come together and constructively work together in a positive way is catching on. Some have been worried that without the religious right to motivate the electorate, either as a villain or as a righteous cause, grass roots financial support for candidates would drop appreciably. More than ever candidates would then be beholden to major givers, large corporate contributors and the unions. But this has not been the case. More people than ever before are reaching into their pockets to support the candidates of their choice.

There are other trends taking shape, too. The crime rate is dropping. Some alleged it is due to the improving economy with a lesser percentage of the population living under the poverty line. Beth and I believe other factors are in play as well. The number of hate crimes is declining far more rapidly than the general crime rate. For the first time in many years people are predicting the prison population will soon be trending down. There are exciting innovations taking place in education. More and more communities are launching preschool programs. Social workers throughout the country are becoming more involved in teaching parenting skills. Maybe all the little things taking place aren't earth shattering, but in combination they are indicating the world is moving in the right direction. Beth and I believe God would be pleased.

Beth and I know we've been blessed to have had the opportunity to have seen and heard Jesus. He is still very much alive for us. We recalled when He recruited His initial group of followers, He asked them to commit themselves for the remainder of the year. Does this mean that something major will be occurring soon or by the first of the year? In our minds we believe something major has already taken place and is continuing to occur. We feel closer to God than ever before. We know we are not alone. We believe others, perhaps even numbering in the millions, now also feel closer to God. Will we be alive to see God's Kingdom here on Earth? Though praying it might be so, we realize it is in God's hands. We've been present to witness Jesus' arrival and to hear His message of love. We've been privileged. Now we have the opportunity to help bring about "God's Kingdom here on Earth."

We're thrilled with the changes we're witnessng. In Ann Arbor and throughout the world changes are taking place for the better.

Our church has initiated a new ending to its worship services. The congregation joins the choir in the singing of *"Let there be peace on earth."*

Beth and I find ourselves emotionally involved as we sing:

Let there be peace on earth, and let it begin with me.

Let there be peace on earth, the peace that was meant to be,

With God as our Father, children all are we;

Let us walk with each other in perfect harmony.

Let peace begin with me, let this be the moment now,

With every step I take let this be my solemn vow.

To take each moment and live each moment in peace, eternally,

Let there be peace on earth, and let it begin with me.

"Let There Be Peace On Earth"
By Jill Jackson and Sy Miller
Copyright 1955, Renewed 1983, by Jan-Lee Music (ASCAP)
International Copyright Secured. All Rights Reserved.